Philip Womack is the author of six critically acclaimed books for children, including *The Broken King* and *The Double Axe*. He was born in Chichester and was educated at Lancing and Oriel College, Oxford, where he read Classics and English. He contributes to many newspapers and magazines, including the *Times Literary Supplement*, *Literary Review*, the *Financial Times* and *Tatler*.

This book is dedicated to my godchildren:
Max Christie, Artemis Elliot and Fergus Hollingshead

The
Arrow of Apollo

Philip Womack

unbound

First published in 2020

Unbound

6th Floor Mutual House, 70 Conduit Street, London W1S 2GF

www.unbound.com

The right of Philip Womack to be identified as the author
of th[...]77
of the[...]this
publicati[...]ystem,
or tra[...]rior
permissi[...]y form
of b[...]ed

A CIP record for this book is available from the British Library

ISBN 978-1-78352-867-7 (trade pbk)
ISBN 978-1-78352-869-1 (ebook)
ISBN 978-1-78352-868-4 (limited edition)

Printed and bound in Great Britain by Clays Ltd, Elcograf S.p.A.

1 3 5 7 9 8 6 4 2

Author's Note

This novel takes place in the long aftermath of the Trojan War, a great conflict in which the ancient royal city of Troy was defeated and burned to the ground by a coalition of Achaeans, led by the high king Agamemnon and his brother Menelaus. Aeneas, a Trojan prince, with a small band of followers, was one of the few to escape the city.

The fall of Troy echoes throughout literature and throughout history. Much has been written about the voyages and returns of the heroes. Aeneas, after many adventures in the Middle Sea, arrived in Italia and there built a new city, which would in time give rise to Rome.

Agamemnon was not so lucky. When he came back to his kingdom of Mykenai with a Trojan concubine, Cassandra, he was murdered by his wife Clytemnestra. His son Orestes later avenged his death.

Very little has been written about the next generation. They lived in a time when myth began to shade into history; when the gods were leaving the earth.

The Arrow of Apollo is set when the heroes of Troy have grown old. Their children must face new troubles, both from the ancient past and from the living present.

Contents

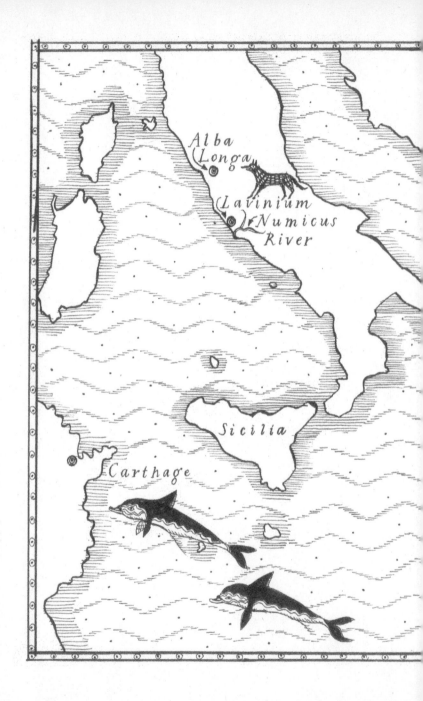

Alba
Longa

Lavinium
Numicus
River

Sicilia

Carthage

Domus Libris

Edwardus Filius Aestatuli

Mathilda Andreius

Albertus Augustinus

Ariadne Caroussis de Chione

Erietta Caroussis de Chione

Theadora de Barenton-Fonte

Electra de Flumine

Elisabetta de Hereforda

Hugo de Laci

Artorius de Palude

Zelda Emilia De Prato Brunis
   Cippis

Elissa Equiso

Alexis Princeps Giedrus

Matilda Filia Gulielmi

Georgius Imprudens Sponsor

Ada Rae Filia Johannes

Dylanus Filius Maris
   Johannes

Inigo Filius Johannes

Mafalda Magna

Lucas Magnus

Tomassus Magnus

Lucia Nobililla

Susanna Nobililla

Isabella Pistor

Otto Rotator

Lyra Rufula Artifex

Hector Saxum Horridum

Lorcanus Ferocillus Saxum
   Horridum

Merlinus Saxum Horridum

Ophelia Saxum Horridum

Emmelina Scaevola

Henricus Superbus-
   Dispensator

Agnes Filia Tommasi

Hugo Xandrus

House of the Wolf

AENEAS leader of the defeated Trojans in the city of Lavinium, in Italia. Father of Silvius and Iulus.

LAVINIA wife of Aeneas, mother to Silvius and Brutus. A native Italian.

IULUS Aeneas's eldest son, by his Trojan wife Creusa. Leads the colony town of Alba Longa.

SILVIUS second son of Aeneas, by Lavinia.

BRUTUS youngest son of Aeneas, by Lavinia.

ELISSA orphaned daughter of Anna Perenna, a princess who was sister to Dido, Queen of Carthage.

Kinghouse of the Lion

ORESTES King of Mykenai, son of Agamemnon and Clytemnestra.

HERMIONE first wife of Orestes, now deceased.

ERIGONE second wife of Orestes. Daughter of Aegisthos.

TISAMENOS son of Orestes, by Hermione.

PENTHILOS son of Orestes, by Erigone.

HERO half-sister of Orestes. Daughter of the Trojan prophetess Cassandra and Orestes's father Agamemnon.

ELECTRA sister of Orestes.

AGATHA nurse to Penthilos.

The House of the Wolf

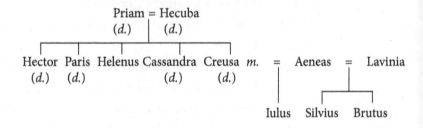

Priam = Hecuba
(d.)   (d.)

Hector Paris Helenus Cassandra Creusa m. = Aeneas = Lavinia
(d.)   (d.)   (d.)   (d.)

Iulus Silvius Brutus

Kinghouse of the Lion

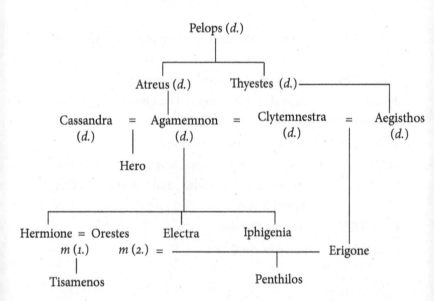

Pelops (d.)

Atreus (d.)   Thyestes (d.)

Cassandra = Agamemnon = Clytemnestra = Aegisthos
(d.)   (d.)   (d.)   (d.)

Hero

Hermione = Orestes   Electra   Iphigenia
m (1.)   m (2.) =   Erigone

Tisamenos   Penthilos

One

The Starlight Visitor

LAVINIUM, ITALIA: HOUSE OF THE WOLF

An eagle cast its shadow over Silvius's eyes as he gazed at the sun sinking behind the hills. The raptor hung, poised, on a thermal, before swooping down onto its prey, out of sight.

Silvius turned his attention back to the dusty, stony road spooling out eastwards in front of him, past the marshes and into the wooded grey-green hills. He adjusted the leather straps of his helmet, which was beginning to weigh down on his black curls, and paced the length of his wall patrol once more. High wooden palisades, taller than he was, rose on either side of a narrow path.

He'd been on duty since the early afternoon, whilst the citizens of Lavinium went about their business below him, safe within the wooden city walls, bartering, selling, sharing jokes, starting fights, solving them. The sound of saws cutting through wood was constant, of timber being hauled and stone being hammered. The smell of sawdust carried to him on the breeze.

There had only been a few traders, trickling in from the other small settlements scattered near Lavinium, bringing deer skins, bear pelts, wines, olive oils, clay jars and bronze weapons. Silvius's older brother Iulus had arrived with a party of riders from his nearby colony of Alba Longa, strutting in on a fine dark stallion. Silvius had watched him, unnoticed, from above.

Silvius longed for something more. Maybe a raiding party, bronze spears glittering like stars. Or better still, if he could see one of the creatures that his father Aeneas talked about with wonder. After a boar hunt earlier that year, Aeneas said that he'd seen, disappearing into the woods, shy, awkward and beautiful, a human head and torso shading into the shaggy legs of a goat, one of the last fauns.

But Silvius hadn't yet been allowed to fight, even in a skirmish, though it was his thirteenth birthday soon, and he was going to be given his first sword.

It wasn't fair. Iulus had been leading the army by the time he was fourteen, when the Trojans had first come to Italian soil, fifteen years ago now, after their long journey over the seas when their city had been burnt to the ground by the Achaeans.

Silvius lifted his spear, sighting along its length as if about to hurl it at an imaginary opponent; he shouted, 'Yah!' and then let it drop to his side.

Almost twilight, and time for his watch to end. The stars were beginning to glimmer, and Silvius stood for a second watching them. His favourite was Orion, the hunter, and he looked for the three stars that made up his belt, before feeling for the studded leather one that held his own tunic together.

He was looking forward to going home, where a bowl of warm venison stew would be waiting for him. Then he would go to the small wooden room he shared with his younger brother Brutus, and his hard, straw-covered bed.

Turning to go, his eye was caught by movement in the distance.

At first, he thought it might be another merchant, rushing late towards the city, eager to get into the walls before the gates were barred. It was no good to be out after dark.

He looked again. The rider was moving fast, faster than any he'd ever seen before, even at the games they held for funerals. Was he running from something?

The horse's hooves were kicking up a huge cloud of dust, pounding the dirt road, and in the dying light it was hard to make anything out. Silvius squinted.

The rider's chest was bare, which was odd.

There was also something strange about the horse's gait. It was maddened, clearly, but also totally in control, the rider seeming a part of it, to flow with it in a way that showed mastery.

Horse and rider came to the end of the straight section of paving that led to the city gates. The sun's last rays gleamed off the horse's chestnut flank.

A horn sounded nearby. Drusus, the boy on duty on the other side from Silvius, was making the alarm. A shout went down to the guards below. 'Close the gates! Bar them! Stranger approaching!'

Silvius heard the hinges beginning to creak shut.

'Let me in!' came the rider's voice, loud, foreign and deep. 'Let me in!'

As the bright moon's shining beams were beginning to spread over the landscape, Silvius realised that coming up the road at full gallop was a centaur.

How could it be? The centaurs were all meant to have gone, cantering away into the stars with the gods. Yet this was a fully grown male centaur. Fascinated, he watched the beast's rippling movements.

'Let me in!' the centaur called again.

Sticking out of his flesh, in his right side, was an arrow.

Silvius gripped the top of the wooden palisade.

He was not meant to desert his post. That would mean a telling-off from Aeneas, or maybe even a whipping. After a momentary pang of indecision, he clattered down the stairs to the gates.

The two guards were already drawing them shut.

'What are you doing? Let him in!' Silvius hung over the banister.

'Orders of Aeneas!' barked one of the guards, a skinny, cold-looking man, face smeared with smuts and dust. 'No strangers after twilight. And that is definitely a stranger.'

4

Silvius couldn't let that happen. He had to see this centaur, talk to him, find out what he wanted. So he leapt down the final two steps to the ground and pushed his way in front of the guards.

The other one, thickset and dark, muscles bulging as he heaved the bolt across, turned to swat him away.

And that gave Silvius enough time to dodge him, set his shoulder to the bolt, push it upwards and kick the left-hand gate open as hard as he could.

'What are you doing?' shouted the thickset guard, roughly. 'I'll have you up before Aeneas! You're deserting your post!'

But before the guard could say anything more, the centaur was through the gap and into the city, scattering the dispersing citizens. The guards rushed, too late, to close the gate behind him.

Silvius caught a glimpse of a long tawny mane, a sweating, hairy torso and a steaming chestnut flank, bloodied and foaming.

The magnificent being swayed, and then, his front forelegs crumpling, he fell to the ground, sending dust flying upwards, his noble head crashing into the dirt. The centaur's eyelids fluttered, a long lock obscuring his forehead.

A circle of onlookers formed around the fallen creature. 'It's not possible!' Blaeso the blacksmith ran the back of his hand across his cheeks, still sweating from the forge. 'A centaur!'

'Kill it!' shouted the thin guard. 'Monster!' There was a scrape of metal against leather as he pulled out his sword.

'Don't do it!' Silvius tried to make his voice heard above the throng, pushing his way through until he was near enough to the centaur to smell his pungent musk. Without really thinking, Silvius blocked the sword's path with his body.

The centaur groaned, his eyes rolled into the back of his head, he shuddered through his entire frame, and went limp.

Silvius dropped to his knees and took the centaur's head into his hands, brushing away the lock of hair. The crowd was silent for a moment, until someone, whistling, went back to his task, picking up his cart of apples from where he'd left it. 'He's dead . . .' said another.

'Could make something out of that hide.' The blacksmith spat onto the ground.

Silvius couldn't bear it. 'Please!' he whispered. 'Please . . .' He wept, and his hot tears dropped onto the centaur's eyes, and he cradled the head, heavy in his hands. 'I thought you'd all gone . . .'

He stayed like that for a moment, and then, wishing to honour him, sat back on his heels and addressed the crowd. 'We should bury him. Bury him like a prince.'

An arm, heavy, on his shoulder. It was a guard, the thickset one. 'Time to go, Silvius. You've got to answer to Aeneas.'

At that name, the centaur's body jerked. His chest rose and fell. Suddenly he took a great, deep horsey breath, and clutched at a casket that hung on a golden chain around his neck. Silvius had not noticed it before, but now his eye was drawn

6

to it; it was about the size of a man's fist, the surface black yet shining and polished.

With a roar, the centaur bellowed, 'Danger. Danger in the hills. Take me to the Wolf. Take me to Aeneas. Now!'

Two

The Swallow

MYKENAI, ACHAEA: KINGHOUSE OF THE LION

A thousand miles away from Lavinium, beyond harsh mountains and across storm-wracked seas, the ancient royal city of Mykenai rose high, brooding between two hills overlooking the wide plains of Argos. The vast stone blocks of the wall, so big they were said to have been made by giants, encircled the whole, and a pair of enormous stone lions stood guard, set into the lintel over the way into the citadel.

Right in the centre of the citadel was the kinghouse, built in a time beyond living memory.

Here, in a corner of the entrance hall, obscured in shadows, the boy Tisamenos lurked.

His father Orestes was leading his new bride across the threshold. Leaning against the damp, crumbling stone wall, Tisamenos clenched his fist, though he was careful to stay out of the torchlight spilling from the many brackets lining the walls.

Orestes was already stumbling a little, his garland askew on his greying blond hair, cheeks flushed, whilst his slender young wife Erigone moved slowly, beaming, her hands proudly clasped on her heavily pregnant belly, fingers glinting with jewelled rings.

Finely dressed guests were thronging the bridal pair, throwing nuts and flowers at them, quaffing from golden goblets of wine, singing and belching. Somebody slipped on a grape and almost went sprawling, but was righted by a giggling flute player.

A lyre player, strolling about, sang of the wedding of a mortal to a sea goddess. Kinghouse servants flitted everywhere, carrying silver plates of dates and finely worked jugs brimming with the sweetest wine from the well-stocked cellars. The spits had been working overtime, and the delicious scent of roasting cattle drifted through the corridors.

Tisamenos bit his fingernail and tugged on a length of his blond hair, which fell down to his shoulders, until he felt a sharp pain on his scalp.

The bride was tall, with bony limbs and long brown hair. She must have sensed Tisamenos's gaze, as, looking over her shoulder, whilst keeping Orestes in a tight grip, she addressed him.

'Why do you skulk, my son? I can call you that now, can't I?' She spoke politely, and smiled, the thin, insipid smile that

9

Tisamenos hated so much. He turned away, and Erigone made a little moue of disappointment.

'Now now, we'll have no more of that, my boy,' shouted Orestes, raising his goblet. He limped towards his son, wincing at an old injury. The King of Mykenai's chiselled features were beginning to soften into flabbiness. 'Come now, and rejoice with your new mother!'

Tisamenos couldn't help himself. Rage was fiercely burning within him, and he let it blaze out. 'No. I won't rejoice with her, or you, or anyone.' His voice, unnaturally loud, cut above the joyous bustle, and the procession of guests, laughing, halted to observe what was happening.

'Isn't that Orestes's pup?' scoffed someone, causing a roar of anticipation to billow through the crowd.

The flame of rebellion coursed deeper inside Tisamenos. 'I won't!' He stepped into the centre of the pillared hall, facing up to Orestes, ignoring the guests. He pointed at Erigone. 'She is not my mother.'

'Tisamenos, please . . .' said Orestes, quietly.

'My mother was Hermione, daughter of Helen of Sparta, the most beautiful woman in the world.'

'Your mother is dead, my dear,' said Erigone, gently. 'She has been dead for a year, and it is time for your father to find a new wife.' It was exactly the wrong thing to say.

'A year! She was barely in her tomb when you jumped into his bed!'

Erigone covered her mouth with her hands, exaggerating her shock. 'Have him beaten!' she said, sharply. 'And this happens on my wedding day!' She began to weep, a hand pressed to her belly, and her attendants fussed around her.

Two servants moved tentatively towards Tisamenos, but he eluded them, and blindly ran at Orestes. He tussled with his father for a moment or two, then beat his fists against the soft wedding robe. Orestes simply gazed at him, while Tisamenos pounded as hard as he could. His father did not react, and, almost sobbing, Tisamenos let his arms drop uselessly.

'Go now,' said Orestes, in an undertone. Tisamenos could see a tiny flame of anger in his father's eyes. It spurred him on. 'We'll talk in the morning.'

'Don't think you can just get rid of me! It's not finished!' He would not be forgotten. Tisamenos was shouting through tears.

'I tell you – go.' The little flame was now a fire. Orestes spoke more urgently.

But Tisamenos was not in the mood for tact. It was time, time for everybody to know what he knew. Time for this whole empty business to be torn apart. Ignoring his father, he addressed the whole lot of them, holding his arms up as he had seen the rhetors do when they were trying to prove a defendant's guilt. 'Hermione was murdered. I know it! And I'll prove it!'

A confusion of rumours and excitement rippled through the crowd. Flushed with success, Tisamenos heard the word 'murder' being passed along from drunken mouth to drunken mouth. That had shown them.

Someone gripped Tisamenos firmly by the elbow, and dragged him away from Orestes, who remained silent, though slightly slumped, his expression unreadable.

Erigone still had one hand over her mouth and the other on her belly. She was gasping a little. Orestes tenderly stroked her cheek and whispered in her ear; she was then led away to her chambers.

Orestes approached his son, placed two fingers under his chin and forced him to look upwards. Tisamenos glared back, unrepentant.

'If you have caused your mother any harm by this,' he said coldly, 'you will answer for it.' Tisamenos looked for that flame. But now in his father's eyes he could only see sadness.

Orestes swept away to the feast, without once looking back. The guests were flowing on already, their attention caught by something else, moving to the prancing tunes of the flute and lyre players.

Tisamenos sank back into a dark corner and wept, letting the sobs convulse his whole body, as he had not done since the day his mother had died.

As he slowed down, he heard someone calling his name. He took a deep pull of air right into his lungs. It calmed him a little.

'Tisamenos . . . my pretty Tisamenos . . . I have something for you.'

He looked up and saw, emerging from the shadows, Hero, the half-Trojan. As usual she had refused to wear the robes of the Achaean women, instead preferring a short brown tunic and a simple leather kilt, with long purple hunting boots.

She showed her crooked teeth. Her dark skin was deeply flushed, as if she had been drinking wine. Though she was a little younger than Erigone, she looked older, as if she had seen and known things that nobody could hint at.

'My pretty Tisamenos,' she said. 'With your beautiful blond hair and your lovely blue eyes.' He flinched. 'I heard what you were saying, dear one.' She reached out and stroked his hair, whispering to him. 'Your mother was torn from you too . . . I never knew mine. Cassandra.'

The prophetess. Tisamenos knew of her memory.

'My mother saw the future. And much good it did her, murdered inside the walls of this kinghouse. Do you think she walks the halls still? Look up there. Look up – what do you see?' She pointed into the shadowy recesses of the great entrance hall. 'Can't you see them? Your grandfather, Aga-memnon, your grandmother, Clytemnestra, their hands drip-ping with blood?'

'I have to go now,' said Tisamenos, standing up. He was on a level with her face. Her eyes glinted.

'Sometimes I hear things about you,' she said, coming further into the light.

'Who from?' He wiped his nose with the back of his hand. His cheeks were wet.

Hero continued, walking forwards with a little shimmering movement. 'Things come to me, as they did to my mother.

From the shadows, from the light.' She shook her long, dark hair, and it fell in shining waves over her brown shoulders. 'I can't always make sense of them. Fragments, dreams. But sometimes I hear things about you.'

'What do you mean?' Tisamenos stepped back from her, warily.

'Long white teeth. Three beasts.' Hero yawned then, and gulped down an olive. 'And something else. Something I do not understand. Something made from stone that yet lives.'

She closed her hands together. When she opened them, nestled in the hollow of her palms was a swallow, a little dark thing, all feather and energy.

'What is this?' Tisamenos craned forwards. 'Street magic?'

The swallow tilted its head to the side, hopped around, then took wing and swooped away. Hero shivered her hips like a dancer, and, laughing, skipped off to the women's quarters. 'They'll say don't listen to me,' she called over her shoulder. Her voice echoed. 'Listen to me . . .'

The swallow was flying round the hall in circles.

Tisamenos watched its graceful arcs for a long time, until the noise of the guests from the dining hall rose into a confused tumult.

It was time for him to return to his chamber, to his nurse, his soft linen and a warm drink. To his astonishment, the swallow swooped down and perched lightly on his shoulder. The feeling of the little claws was ticklish. A voice appeared in his ear, clear and strange.

14

Tisamenos couldn't believe it. The voice was coming from the swallow itself. He looked around, but there was only a white-robed courtier kissing one of the maids.

'Did you say something?' Tisamenos felt foolish.

'Listen to me,' said the swallow. 'Find the swallows to-morrow. You will learn something about your mother.'

'What will I learn?'

'Who killed her,' answered the swallow; and then it was gone, and though Tisamenos ran after it, he could not find it anywhere.

Three

The Vision of Apollo

LAVINIUM, ITALIA: HOUSE OF THE WOLF

'See, I told you I could do it!' A chunk of wood fell with a satisfying thud, and Elissa looked proudly at the thick length of oak timber she'd sawn through. It had taken her a good part of an hour, and now twilight was approaching, but she was pleased with it. 'And it's only a tiny bit jagged!' It would become a part of the city. She called it home, after all. Now there would be something she'd made inside it, and maybe that would make her feel that it really was home. Her black, silky hair had come loose from its hairband, and she pushed it back underneath.

They were working in one of the streets of Lavinium, just by the blacksmith's, where his boy was busily at the bellows, face grimy with soot. People bustled in and out of the long, low wooden houses on one errand or another.

The two young men who'd been in charge of that day's supplies for the fortifications paused in their work and wiped their hands on their tunic hems. 'It'll do,' said one. 'But can't you find something to do in the palace with the women?' He spoke indulgently, and Elissa smiled winningly back at him. She was about to make a suggestion telling him exactly what she thought of sitting around weaving all day with the women, when she heard the voice of her friend, Silvius, calling through the gathering darkness.

She winked at the carpenters, stopping to take the last glistening, juicy olive from a bowl that lay on a bench, and ran to see what was happening. Above her, a comet blazed through the sky, and she watched it disappear over the city walls.

Perhaps it will land somewhere, she thought. Perhaps it had flown over her mother's home, Carthage, far across the Middle Sea.

She sent her wishes with the comet: that she might meet one of her own people soon, that she might discover more about her mother's life.

There was a commotion ahead of her, and she heard Silvius's voice calling out to all. 'Be well! We're going to Aeneas. Be well!' There was something, a note of alarm, in his voice that surprised her. She'd heard the horn earlier, and wondered if it might have something to do with that. Soldiers were looking on with suspicious expressions.

She came upon the procession. It was a strange sight; a

straggle of people, faces indistinguishable, the moon's light partly obscured by clouds.

But nothing was stranger than the beast that was walking next to Silvius. A flutter of excitement raced through her. Could it be? A few nights ago, the girl she shared her room with had woken her up from a dream Elissa hadn't been able to make sense of. The flash of chestnut flanks. The fletch of an arrow. And a man, joined somehow to the horse.

It was her dream, coming towards her.

Dwarfing Silvius, the centaur's torso rose higher than the tallest man Elissa had ever seen. Letting out a whoop, she ran skipping towards them, one sandal loose, and, ignoring a warning glance from Silvius, approached the beast as near as she dared.

The centaur paused, and behind him all the large crowd of followers they had attracted.

Elissa gazed into the centaur's eyes, deep and old. His expression was stern, but it spoke to her. His right hand, huge, was clutching something that hung around his neck on a golden chain. A jolt of power passed between them, and she found herself drawn to the black casket. She fiddled with the dolphin pendant that lay on her breast. It was the only thing she had from her mother.

'Elissa – what are you doing?' Silvius was impatient. 'We've got to get on!'

But she felt something different in this meeting. There was a welcome there, in the centaur's eyes, and yet also a challenge.

She gently stroked his flank. He smiled at her, and she entwined her fingers into the curls of his long mane.

Silvius was glowering slightly, tapping his foot. She had taken his moment away, she knew.

'What's happening?' she whispered behind her hand.

'I'll tell you later.' Silvius, she could tell, was barely suppressing his astonishment. 'We need to get to Aeneas.' And he was also, she reflected, keeping the news back from her. Well, she would find out soon. In step with the gentle clip-clop of the centaur, she moved on.

Awed by the presence of the wild creature, the citizens mostly kept quiet until they reached the forum where Aeneas and the chiefs conducted the city's business during the day. Then they broke out into a chatter, like rooks.

Aeneas's large hut stood at the south-eastern edge, surrounded by buildings, including the new marble temple to Jupiter the Skyfather which, richly painted with reds and golds, glowed in the moonlight.

Elissa was now in front, and she led the centaur quickly up the wooden steps to where Aeneas lived.

The leader of the city of Lavinium was already waiting for them in the atrium, now brightly lit with many smoky torches. Aeneas, his reddish hair greying, was seated on a high carved wooden chair, a wolf skin around his shoulders, the eyes glazed and open, the teeth sharp. He had slain it in the early days of Lavinium, and it had lent him his nickname, the Wolf.

It still awed Elissa, though once, when she was small, she had sat on it when he'd left it behind on a bench.

His wife Lavinia was standing behind him. Unlike most of the Latins, her hair was the bright colour of a buttercup, and it still shone. Elissa smiled boldly at Lavinia, who frowned back, slightly in disapproval.

The centaur had to stoop to get into the room. Aeneas stood immediately, and bowed. Lavinia beckoned to Silvius, but he instead went to join his tall brother Iulus, who was lurking to the side, looking on coolly. Elissa remained with the centaur, enjoying his warmth.

'I am Stargazer, from the centaurs of the hills.' The centaur spoke in a deep horsey voice that was almost a neigh.

'Be well, my lord.' Aeneas made another obeisance. 'You honour us, and Lavinium, with your presence. If there is anything . . .'

Stargazer snorted, and trembled, stamping his front left hoof on the wooden floor.

'His wound,' said Elissa, sensing his pain. 'Lavinia – please could you help him?'

Lavinia approached the centaur gently, and reached out a hand to his flank. He skittered away.

'Elissa. You help me.' Lavinia's face, hardened by the long trials of war, softened into a look of deep concentration.

The centaur tensed, then relaxed as Elissa began to stroke his chestnut withers, where the man part of his torso became horse. Lavinia meanwhile inspected the arrow, and called for vinegar and boiling water. 'Lord,' she said, addressing him directly, head proudly raised. 'If it is permitted . . .'

The centaur inclined his head, and Elissa whispered gently to him, the kinds of things she whispered to the horses to keep them quiet during a storm. She told him about the swallows that were nesting under the eaves of the hut, and then about the dream she'd had of him, and his eyes locked onto hers.

Lavinia gave him a draught full of crushed poppy seeds to drink; he gulped it down, and once he'd done so, she quickly took a knife from the boiling water and searched the wound. 'It's not lodged in bone.' Then, with a sudden, hard movement, she pulled it out. Stargazer did not wince.

Once the wound had been cleaned with the vinegar and bandaged, the centaur thanked Lavinia. She said, 'My father Latinus knew you, in the old times.'

'Thank you, daughter of Latinus,' said the centaur. 'I have not forgotten the old king, and the honour we centaurs owed him.'

When Lavinia had returned to her position, Aeneas, sounding weary, began again.

'We, Aeneas, son of Anchises, greet you, Lord . . .'

'I do not need your formalities,' interrupted Stargazer. 'There is danger. Something stirs in the mountains.' He wiped his mouth with the back of his powerful hand, and Elissa again noticed the casket hanging against his chest. She wanted to touch it, but guessed that Stargazer might brush her away if she tried.

'Something old, and dark.' His words pressed deep into Elissa. She dreaded to think what might frighten this noble creature.

'Why come here?' said Iulus, loudly. 'We know nothing of your mountains, as long as they give us boars.' His small group of friends guffawed.

'Quiet,' barked Aeneas; then, turning to Stargazer, 'I apologise for my son Iulus. He is still young, and has a lot to learn.' Iulus smirked, and popped a nut into his mouth, crunching it loudly.

Stargazer flared his nostrils and continued, dismissing Iulus with a flick of his long black tail. 'Something stirs, and it does things we have not seen before. The arrow – none of your kind would have dared shoot us without provocation.'

'Who did hurt you?' said Aeneas.

'I must start at the beginning.' The centaur cleared his throat, and took a long gulp of water. 'Not long ago the great Skyfather called us together. He had found a place for us, on a different world. There, he said, we would be safe from men, and from what men would do to us soon enough. He opened a way for us into the heavens. I watched all my brothers and sisters, one by one, mount the wide road of light. Beyond it I saw the great grassy plain where we could be for evermore. I saw the shade of great trees, and I saw lakes and freshwater streams. I watched my kind all go. My youngest sister was the last. She held out her arms to me. But I could not follow her.'

'Why not?' asked Aeneas, gently.

'I had sworn an oath, a long time ago. It was in penance for a terrible deed. I killed one of your kind, in madness. When I was well again, I swore to keep watch over you, for as long as I was able. And I was entrusted with a task.' He took another gulp, the droplets running down his chin. The torches crackled in their brackets. 'At first, I sensed a presence in the mountains. A great dark mind, reaching out, trying to break into mine, into others'. I fought its tendrils as hard as I could. One morning, as I wandered the woods, I came upon one of yours. A girl, not much older than this one.' He indicated Elissa. 'I approached her, to warn her away. She simply smirked, and then I saw. Her eyes were lit from inside with red fire. She drew an arrow, notched it, shot – and I ran.'

Iulus snorted, mockingly. 'You ran from a girl?'

The centaur, his voice still calm, said, 'I ran from the most powerful enemy this world has ever known.' The musty smell of his body filled the room, and he shifted on his hooves.

Lavinia offered him some rabbit and fennel stew, which he sniffed delicately before tipping it into his mouth and chewing, surprisingly daintily. The centaur did not speak for a moment. Then he sighed, and said, 'I feared to find out what this creature was. But yet I looked into the stars for knowledge. And I saw there signs, unmistakeable signs. The oldest one. The beast, the snake, born from night itself. He had been laid low by Apollo, thousands of years ago, so that man could live. But now Python rises once more.' The name shivered through

Elissa. One of the dark, old beings of the world that had their domain before the new gods defeated them.

'Hah!' The laughter was abrupt. Iulus stepped forwards, a disbelieving expression quivering on his face. 'Python is a story nurses use to scare infants and babes in arms. There is no such thing. Why should we believe you? Is this a fantastical tale, like one of my father's?'

'Iulus, silence!' commanded Aeneas. 'You've seen miracles. You saw the harpies, and our ships turning into nymphs.'

'I was young. I don't remember. They were just stories you told us to make us feel better about ourselves. Like we had a destiny! To come to this place – this wooden rubbish dump – when we used to live in the greatest city in the world!'

He rounded on the centaur. 'And you, monster, slayer of men. There is no room for you here in Lavinium, nor in my city of Alba Longa. We follow the new rules there. There is no darkness, and there are no gods. Father – dear, pious Father – I'm going back to my people. Let me know when you're out of your dotage. Be strong,' he finished, sarcastically, striding out of the room, and his guard of companions followed him, curling their lips with distaste.

'My lord,' said Aeneas, apologising. Elissa could not help noticing the look on his face. It was as if he'd lost something infinitely precious.

The centaur cut over him with a stamp of his foreleg. Then he carefully removed the chain from around his neck.

Elissa, looking at the casket that hung from it, felt that she might be drawn into it, shrunk, absorbed wholly into its shining walls. She began to feel dizzy. Its surface was rippling with extraordinary colours, iridescent, shimmering. There were three animals engraved upon it. A lion, little more than a cub, was crouched in the right-hand corner. Facing across from it was the form of a young wolf, lips bared. And in between them, splashing upwards as if leaping out of water, was a dolphin.

As she watched, the dolphin glimmered, enticing her inwards.

She barely heard the centaur saying, 'Aeneas. I do not know how we can defeat this thing. But know this.' The tremor in his voice brought Elissa back. 'When the world was young, the god Apollo laid low the great Python with an arrow forged by the smith-god himself, and took the Oracle of Delphi from him. Such a terrible weapon could not be left intact, and nor could it fall into the hands of the enemy. The arrow was split in two. Apollo placed the Arrowhead into this casket, and entrusted it to us, the centaurs of Italia.'

'So where is the other half?' Elissa asked, still gazing at the box, her eyes quick and bright. Silvius was at her elbow, peering over her shoulder. She could feel his hot breath on her neck.

The centaur twitched his nostrils. 'That is only known in Achaea. Someone must find it out, and find how Python can be destroyed.'

'Achaea?' Silvius stepped back towards his father.

A clamour of voices arose from the Trojans. 'Filthy

Achaeans! They killed our king and queen! They burned our city!'

Aeneas quelled them with a raised palm. 'The foul King Agamemnon and his murderous brood are not our friends. What do you ask of us?'

'You must travel to Achaea, as quickly as possible. Put aside your human quarrels. This is greater than anything else. Python enters minds, gives people powers they should not have. Already he gathers an army. If we do not stop it . . .'

'What then?' The room was getting warmer. Elissa could smell the horsey tang of the centaur even more strongly now, tinged with the piny scent of the woods at night.

'He wants to reign over the world. He wants chaos. Night, and chaos.'

Again voices erupted. Elissa noticed that Silvius was standing quietly, listening. Aeneas tried to maintain order, standing up to calm them. People surged around the centaur, buzzing angrily. He was growing agitated, his back legs skittering. Elissa instinctively put out a hand to soothe him. "They mean no harm,' she whispered. 'They are confused. It is a lot to ask of them.'

'But they must do it.'

'Get back,' she called. 'Give him room!'

'Who will go?' Stargazer cried. 'The gods have all but fled. They will not help us! Who will go to Achaea to save the world?'

'Never!' cried someone. 'I would slit an Achaean's throat as soon as see one!'

Elissa saw Silvius hesitating by his father's side. His brother had marched out, leaving Aeneas looking old and alone. Silvius had no quarrel with the Achaeans, she knew. He had not been born when the city of Troy fell.

She recognised the look in his eyes. It was the same look he had when his brother won a wrestling match.

A sudden thought struck her. He would take it on himself. He would think it was down to him, to prove himself.

Before she could do anything to prevent him, he had already moved. She saw Lavinia's pleading glance, but it was too late.

'I will.' He stood upright, hands clenched by his sides.

Few heard him. Lavinia reached out. 'Silvius! No!'

Silvius climbed onto Aeneas's chair, took a deep breath and shouted, his slight frame shaking with the effort. 'I will! I swear to unite the Arrowhead and the Shaft, and discover how to destroy Python! I swear it by all the great gods!'

Silence rippled through the room. Somebody coughed. Lavinia begged, 'No, you can't!' She turned to Stargazer. 'My son . . . he's young, he's barely been out of the city.'

'I have hunted on my own,' said Silvius. 'I lived in the woods with you most of my life. Do you forget the woodcraft you taught me? I have trapped wolves, and I found the stag with the white star on its forehead!'

There was a glint of respect in Aeneas's eye, Elissa saw. 'You deserted your post,' he said, evenly. 'I should punish you. Why should we entrust such a mission to you?'

'I can do it,' said Silvius. 'I'm ready. I will prove myself.' But Elissa saw him playing with the loop of his belt, fingers tightening and then relaxing. She knew what that meant. Half of him didn't know what he was saying. The other half was white hot.

'What do you say, centaur?' Aeneas's tone was heavy.

Stargazer beckoned to Silvius. 'There will be one, but there must be more. Does anyone else present themselves?' Elissa felt a prickle on her neck, and saw Stargazer staring at her with his beautiful wild eyes. Once more she felt that tug of understanding. And Silvius looked so slender, so frail by the side of the centaur.

She knew what the centaur was suggesting. He would need help. And also, that she had some part to play. The image of the dolphin played in her mind, dancing off the shore of some distant coast.

An older soldier, named Achates, stepped forwards. 'I present myself.' He was a broad man, but he was beginning to stoop.

'Very well,' said Aeneas, a challenge in his voice. 'My second son and my oldest companion. Is there no one else among my Trojans? Among my wife's people?'

'Not among the Trojans.' Elissa hardly knew what she was saying. 'I don't quite know what I am, but I'll try.' The pitchy smoke made her cough. She slid her way to standing beside Silvius, greeting him with red torchlight flickering across her mischievous features. He looked at her with something like pain, but she saw also a flicker of gratefulness. She took his hand and squeezed it. He released it quickly.

'Elissa! No, I don't think—' said Aeneas.

'She has presented herself,' cut in Stargazer. 'She will take the test.' There was no arguing against the centaur. Power vibrated in every word.

Elissa nodded. She had expected that answer. Yet she could also see that Aeneas, used to being obeyed, was finding it hard not to disagree.

After a moment, in which he scrutinised both Elissa and Silvius, making her feel distinctly uncomfortable, Aeneas relaxed, and said, 'If the gods will it, it will be so.'

'Then we shall begin the test. You must hold onto the casket for as long as you can.'

Stargazer ordered Achates to go first. The old soldier, smirking a little, looked around, as if expecting some kind of trick. One of the wags in the crowd shouted, 'Come on, Achates! Easier than conquering the Rutulians!'

He grasped it tightly for a second, and then began to gasp, shrieking in pain. Blowing on his fingers, he hissed, 'It's as hot as fire!' He backed away, seeking for water to pour onto his burnt skin. A shocked silence met him.

'Will you take it still?' Stargazer spoke softly to Silvius. Achates had plunged his hands into an amphora of wine.

Elissa watched.

Silvius nodded. He clenched his teeth together, standing firmly on the ground.

At first, he grunted with effort, and Elissa saw veins appearing on his forehead. Little rivulets of sweat were flowing down from his temples, and his cheeks were reddening with heat.

Then suddenly he went limp, his legs crumpling beneath him. There was a terrible stillness in the hall, and Lavinia started forwards. Aeneas held her back.

Stargazer was implacable, eyes unfathomable in the torch-light. This was a wild creature, after all, thought Elissa. They had taken him on trust. But how did they know that he meant what he said? And a spasm of fear shook through her.

Silvius gasped, a huge intake of air, and opened his eyes with shock, seeming to take the room in as if he'd woken from a dream.

'Release your grasp. What did you see?' Stargazer was calm.

Silvius looked up, puzzled, 'I saw . . . Python.' Even the name made Elissa shudder.

'Yes,' answered the centaur. 'Is that all you saw?'

There was a moment's hesitation. 'And then I saw Apollo.' There was uproar from the watchers. 'Only for a moment. His light . . . And he said it was for me!' Lavinia choked back a sob. 'But . . .' And he looked at Elissa, and there was something in his expression, more than envy. He retreated, his look settling into a challenge.

'Elissa must take the test too. Please, Elissa, stand forward.' Stargazer touched her gently on the cheek.

'I really don't think . . .' Aeneas said. 'We can't put her through that trial . . .'

But Stargazer lifted his hand, and Aeneas bent his head in acknowledgement. Elissa finally realised that her sandal was undone, and she quickly did it up. Ready now, she faced the casket, and grazed it with her fingertips, feeling Stargazer's eyes on her.

At first, it burned through her fingers, hotter than a warming pan when it's come straight off the fire. Her entire body was telling her to let go.

She looked up, and into Stargazer's eyes. He nodded, very slightly, and it sent a surge of resolve through her. But as she concentrated through the pain, a different sensation began to take over.

The shadowy, smoky wooden hall slipped away from her vision, and instead she was in a brightly lit grove by a rushing stream. She was no longer holding the casket, and there was no pain.

Standing by the stream was a tall, dark-haired youth, handsome and lit from all around, garlanded with laurel leaves. A glossy-feathered raven was perched on a branch above him, and it cawed. In its eye Elissa could see herself reflected.

Elissa knew the youth was the god Apollo. He smiled, and strummed his lyre. A golden globe spun in the air around him, slowly, dancing. The most beautiful singing she'd ever heard came from somewhere far distant. There was a road leading from the tree, but she couldn't see where the road led, only that there was a great brightness at the end of it.

She moved forwards slowly. 'Do not come near,' said the

god. The force of his voice made Elissa bow her head. The god spoke again. 'I slew the Python once. But he is immortal, like us, and cannot truly die. My father, the Lord of the Gods, whom you call Jupiter, has turned away. My uncle Neptune, the Lord of the Sea, has found a new world made of oceans where he sports all day with his dolphins. Even Pluto, the Lord of the Underworld, they say, has gone elsewhere. I am tempted too to find places made from light, from sound. The other gods forget you. But I remember still. I, and Mercury. You will learn his other name. Hermes.'

Elissa heard a joyous laugh, and turned to see a tall, curly-haired young man hovering a few inches above the ground, wearing winged sandals, a golden winged helmet on his head. Hermes swooped towards Elissa, plucking her on the shoulder, then dashed away as if he were a butterfly darting from flower to flower. 'We will help you,' he called, his voice infectious with brightness. 'I like you mortals still.'

'What should I do?' asked Elissa.

'Go to the land of the Achaeans,' said Apollo. 'Go with Silvius. There is much for you to do. But first, you must stop at Sicilia. There you will be told more.' In front of her, a golden mass was floating in the air, and it formed into the shape of a bow, and suddenly she was holding it, and for one brief second it was as if she was the bow, and the power of Apollo was flowing through it.

Then it was gone, and it was as if the sun had vanished behind dark clouds.

Elissa blinked. She was back in Lavinium. She steadied herself. Lavinia was weeping, and Aeneas was talking to Silvius. She heard him say, 'My son. Rest now. You will be punished for leaving your post in the morning. Then we will talk.'

But there was nobody to take Elissa's arm, and, unnoticed by anyone except the centaur, she slipped away to the tiny room she shared with three Latin serving girls, and soon, whilst they snored, she was lying awake, shifting uncomfortably, playing with her little dolphin pendant.

Four

The Tumbler

MYKENAI, ACHAEA: KINGHOUSE OF THE LION

Erigone's screams sluiced through the stone corridors of Mykenai's kinghouse. It was the morning after Tisamenos had seen the swallow in the entrance hall, and dawn was spearing through the light wells, showing up the cracks in the walls and the frayed ends of the tapestries. A couple of hounds were sniffing at something; they glanced balefully at Tisamenos as he went by, aiming for the women's quarters, in search of Hero.

'. . . up at this time of day, at my age . . .' A voice came from behind him. It was his old nurse, Agatha, stomping past him bearing a gold-rimmed jug of hot water, a pile of the softest fragrant linen towels stuffed under her arm. The scent of sweet herbs wafted from the jug.

He grabbed her by her rather thick elbow. 'What's going on?'

'*She's* giving birth,' panted Agatha, her weak eyes blinking, face blowsy and red. 'She'll have the whole kinghouse down with that wailing. Sounds like a Fury!' For a moment her ancient, creased face seemed to lighten.

'Agatha,' said Tisamenos. 'What do you think about Hero?'

'Hero? That flighty creature? Dancing about in the woods, spouting nonsense? Don't listen to her . . .' Her face settled into its customary tightness, the mouth a thin line and the eyes hooded with suspicion, and she was off again, making the sign against evil, disappearing into the gloom ahead of him, spilling water as she went.

Tisamenos continued in her wake. That's what Hero had said. 'Don't listen to me, they'll say.' If Agatha thought Hero wasn't worth listening to, then maybe Agatha was wrong.

Sometimes a servant would rush past him, carrying wood or a pail of water. A man bearing the staff of Asclepios, the god of healing, with its carved coiled serpent, was hurried along the corridors by the steward. Tisamenos, keeping to the shadows, made sure he was not noticed.

When he reached the women's quarters, down a few hundred paces of dank stone passages, he found the ancient wooden doors firmly closed. A guard was set in front, his bronze spear upright. Tisamenos went to push past him, but the spear came down in front of him, barring his way.

'Not even the son of Orestes is allowed in the women's quarters.' The guard, a thickset, beetle-browed oaf, was unsmiling.

'I used to come to see my mother,' said Tisamenos.

'When you were a whelp. You're too old now. Clear off.' The guard made a shooing motion with his hand, which riled Tisamenos.

'Take a message through,' he said, puffing up his chest. 'I am the king's son!'

'I said, clear off!'

It occurred to Tisamenos as he made his way, deflated, back to his own quarters, that he knew very little about his half-aunt Hero, or where she might be found. He remembered the swallow. Had that been real magic, or a trick of the streets? He had seen people casting voices before, in the agora. Was that what Hero had been doing? Had she simply caught a swallow and, by some clever sleight of hand, made it appear in her grasp?

But the voice had been inside his head. It couldn't have been Hero speaking. The thought made him uneasy.

The wedding guests were now all stirring, and some were thronging the feasting hall, calling for their breakfast, shouting, eating the spitted meat of a boar recently killed in a hunt, quaffing from drinking horns. There were going to be games that day, wrestling, chariot races, foot races. Somebody threw him a challenge as he went by – a young handsome prince from Athens, a grandson of the famous Theseus – and Tisamenos batted it away without thinking.

The hall was decorated with flaking murals showing his ancestors and, by order of Orestes, they were depicted in all their crimes as a constant reminder. There was Tantalos, the bunch of grapes always out of his reach. There was the kinslayer Atreos, whose terrible acts made Tisamenos's stomach turn, even thinking about them. He turned away from the sight.

Instead, he looked about for Hero, in case he had missed her in the throng.

Seeing the huge, crumbling stone throne that Orestes ruled from caused a pang of memory. His mother Hermione would take her place there by his father's side, her long blonde hair piled up in some fantastic arrangement, and she would feed Tisamenos sweetmeats and honey from her golden plate as the kinghouse inhabitants laughed and drank and feasted around them. 'My little lion cub,' she would say. Only Hermione called him that. Her tender fingers stroking his cheek. 'This world is full of evils. Know things, and know the names of them, and you will have them in your power.'

A shout from nearby brought him back to the present. One of the guests, calling to another about some argument they'd been having the previous day.

He turned his mind back to the swallow. It was a message. But of what kind? What could Hero want from him? And could he trust her? He chewed on a piece of crackling, and watched a tussle between two men of Mykenai, squaring up to each other over which of them might win a foot race.

Orestes entered the room as the quarrel began to get serious, and there was a ragged cheer. The two men stopped and shook hands. Orestes limped to his stone throne and took a golden goblet, finely decorated with a stag hunt. He lifted it high and said, over the cheers, 'I drink to Hera, the Goddess of Childbirth!'

Somebody thumped the table, and others took up the action.

'She has given me a child! A son – a fine son!'

A round of hurrahs exploded through the hall. The tables shook, goblets and plates clattering, hounds barking to the ceilings.

'The games will be in honour not only of our marriage – but of Penthilos, our new son!'

Tisamenos stood up suddenly, knocking a silver goblet to the floor, and left the feasting hall. Nobody noticed him go, and he was glad for that.

He headed towards the entrance hall of the kinghouse. For a moment he hung on the threshold, the cool darkness of the building to his right, the dusty, hot street to his left. The noise of the feasting was rising. A group of beautiful ladies wandered through, their light clothes floating about them, their jewels shining on their forearms and on their elaborately dressed hair.

He turned towards them. One of the younger ones let fall a floating piece of cloth, and as she bent to pick it up she glanced at him coquettishly.

Tisamenos did not return the glance.

Instead, he went out, down the steps, into the street below.

As his eyesight adjusted, Tisamenos blinked in the now bright morning. Above him the sky was cloudless, and around him already were cheese sellers and a fuller's boy carrying a pail of something that smelled so rank he almost turned back into the kinghouse. But he didn't.

Swallows. Where did they live? Under the eaves of houses. He looked up, but could see no nests hanging under the kinghouse. A donkey brayed nearby, and a farmer with a goat over his shoulders wandered past, whistling. The goat bleated.

Would he have to look under the eaves of every building in the citadel, from swineherd's hut to kinghouse? The kinghouse alone had dozens of roofs.

This was a test, he knew it. A test he had to pass. She'd said something about his mother. The knowledge that Hero was offering him was just out of his reach.

He wandered through the market in the agora, which was bustling with stallholders. Huge piles of dates, apples, pears and olives glistened on trestle tables. 'Get your finest wild boar from here! Killed it with me own two hands!' yelled a scrawny man who looked as if he'd never been on a hunt in his life.

The city was going about its business, as it had done for hundreds of years, even before the House of Atreos had come to rule, and as it would continue to do until his family were nothing but a memory.

One of the cheese sellers was an old man. Tisamenos watched him, his slow movements as he packed up the cheeses in leaves and straw and parcelled them out to the buyers. It didn't matter to that man who was in the kinghouse. It only mattered that he made his cheese, and sold it, and kept his house safe.

The old man's little grandson was playing underneath the stall, and Tisamenos caught his quick, bright smile as he went by.

The sun was drawing back the shadows, and the market was filling up with cries.

A girl was tumbling in the streets, her brightly coloured clothes falling around her in waves. She was mesmerising, graceful, yet powerful. Her skin was a rich dark brown, tanned by the sun, and her gleaming black hair was loose, flowing with her garments.

A large man with a short sword at his fat waist was also watching the tumbler. He had a hog-like face and small eyes, and a peculiar grin.

She tumbled as if she were on her own, thrilling to the movement of her own body. When she finished, she simply dropped to the ground before righting herself, but she walked away with a rippling, liquid gait. The large man grinned. He grabbed her by the arm and spun her round with a rough heave. Her expression was stony.

'You're coming with me, my pretty,' said the man. The girl scowled, and the man forced her forwards a few steps.

And suddenly Tisamenos was rushing towards him, knocking him on the head with the flat of his own sword. The man yelped, letting go of the girl, and turned to face Tisamenos.

'What fly is this? Buzz off, little fly!' He spat at Tisamenos, hitting his tunic.

Tisamenos, enraged, hurled himself forwards and began to beat him, with all the skill of the wrestling grounds, and all the hatred that had been building up inside him. His mother's death, his father's hasty new marriage, the son born so soon afterwards. He smashed the man on his nose, and a satisfying stream of scarlet blood came out, spotting the man's hands and the street.

His opponent stood still for a second, appraising him, and then punched Tisamenos with as much force as he could muster. It came suddenly, right in his stomach, and, winded, he was knocked over into the dust. The man gripped the scruff of his neck and pushed his head down.

'You're not worth it, little fly.' He pressed Tisamenos's face down into the dirt, before releasing him with a dismissive grunt.

Tisamenos's head was spinning. He managed to pull himself upwards, but the man had already gone. Then he blushed, as he noticed that the girl was watching him steadily.

'I didn't need you,' said the girl, flatly, reaching out her arm.

She was close to Tisamenos now. Her chest was heaving. He ignored her offer of help, and stood up by himself.

'I – I wanted to help you.'

'I don't need a child's help.' She spat. Tisamenos found it shocking. 'Especially a soft, useless one like you.' He was more insulted by her calling him a child. She was hardly older than him, he guessed, though her eyes had the hard wisdom of the streets in them.

'I . . . I'm not a . . .'

She turned to leave, and her tunic rode down her neck. Tisamenos saw, tattooed there, the tiny outline of a swallow.

'Wait!' he called.

She ignored him, and he rushed after her, grabbing her wrist. Irritably, she shook him off.

'Hero. Where is she?'

'I don't know what you mean.'

She ran away to the edge of the agora, where a street led between some low houses. She looked over her shoulder at him, and the look was unmistakeable. It said: follow, if you dare.

Then she was off, darting away like a butterfly.

That was enough for Tisamenos.

He dashed after her.

Five

A Breach of the Walls

The whip lashed down onto Silvius's upper back for the eleventh time. The pain was becoming almost unbearable, burning fiercely. It wasn't close, he reminded himself, to what the casket had felt like. Somehow that helped him.

Yet beads of perspiration were running down his forehead and hitting the ground beneath him. They made dark patterns in the dust.

He heard the noise of the soldier pacing backwards, and steeled himself for the twelfth, and final, stroke.

It was the pauses that were the worst. At least if the strokes were regular, then he could anticipate the next. But his punisher was biding his time.

He watched the shadow of the man on the ground. He relaxed, and then the whip snapped with greater force than any of the previous strokes. Silvius was determined not to show any sign of pain.

But it was hard, and his mind filled with a hot brightness that threatened to spill out into a cry.

In the end, he couldn't keep it in, his voice echoing around the courtyard.

'Finished,' said the soldier, and gave him a hand to pull him up. Silvius wobbled up from his knees, and let out a prayer of thanks to the household gods. He wiped away a tear with a knuckle. The soldier shoved his helmet back onto his cropped head, and sauntered out without another word.

Afterwards Silvius let his mother bathe his wounds in his small room, whilst his little brother Brutus fidgeted about on his bed.

'Why were you whipped?' asked Brutus, twisting his fingers in the thick blanket. Brutus's hair was curly and brown, and he looked much more like Lavinia than Silvius did. He stuck his thumb in his mouth, and gazed directly at Silvius.

'Because I did something wrong,' answered Silvius. 'I deserted my post. And I directly disobeyed Aeneas.'

'I don't think people should get whipped at all, ever,' said Brutus, thoughtfully, pulling his thumb out of his mouth with a pop. 'I'll tell Father what I think!'

'Hush, Brutus. You're only a little child who's not lost his first milk tooth yet.'

Brutus pouted, and then started pretending to be a wolf,

howling with such a tiny noise that Silvius could not help but laugh.

Lavinia shushed his little brother, then carefully put a clean tunic on over Silvius's thin white torso and gave him a wooden beaker of refreshing water from the well to drink, which she'd drawn herself.

She waited till he had finished, then said, 'Well, you have borne your punishment with courage. But go now. Your father wants to speak to you.'

Aeneas was in the inner chamber of the house, a window-less room with only a small fire in the hearth to give light. There, in a recess, were the little carved wooden statues of the ancestors and the household gods that Aeneas had saved from his palace in Troy and brought over the seas to Italia.

He was kneeling before them. He didn't hear Silvius approaching.

'. . . for my sons, for my people, for their safety and their honour.'

Silvius only caught the last part, and then stood in silence. It was only when Silvius had been there for some time, and shifted his weight, that Aeneas looked up, his brow furrowed, his greying gingery hair seeming sparse, his cheeks hollow and wrinkling.

'I wonder . . .' said Aeneas, quietly; he seemed about to say something, and then he changed his mind. 'Do you know why I brought you in here?'

Silvius looked around. He could see only the statues of the gods. There was nothing else there.

'To remind me of my duty to my family,' said Silvius, humbly.

Aeneas nodded, slowly. He shifted himself upright, still strong.

'Always remember, Silvius.' He caught his son's arm, and Silvius saw the depths of sadness in his father's eyes. 'Always remember what the Achaeans did to us. They tore us from our lands, ruined our city, made us homeless. Troy was ancient and powerful. And yet they took everything from us, and now we are here, in this strange, barbarian land ...' He faltered. 'Troy ...' he whispered, and let Silvius go, and, without looking back, he strode away.

Silvius went out into the town. He saw Elissa running around the forum, playing with a wolf cub. She beckoned to him, her dark face dancing with glee.

He did not want to talk to her now. His father's words were echoing around his mind. Elissa did not know what it meant to have that burden. She would not understand. He shook his head, and trudged on, leaving her looking puzzled, stroking the top of the cub's head.

All around him were the sounds of building work. He wasn't paying attention to where he was going, but found himself in front of the blacksmith's. The door was ajar, and he stood watching intently from the threshold.

Even though it was day, inside it was dark. Light came from the forge, and from torches on the walls. The blacksmith was making a sword. His boy was at the bellows, pumping the flames white hot. Blaeso was a thin man, with cropped black hair, bristles showing on his pointed chin; and when he grasped the molten bronze in its container with his tongs, his strong arm muscles showed. Blaeso hissed approvingly through his teeth.

It was hot inside the smithy, and Silvius, though half outside, still had to wipe the sweat off his brow. The movement caused the blacksmith to look up.

'You again?' he said, not unkindly, pouring the molten bronze into its stone mould. 'You'd better get off home. Aeneas will be wanting you, surely?'

'I just wanted to see my sword being made,' said Silvius. The cuts on his back still burned. 'I will need it in Achaea.' He said it with a note of importance, hoping the blacksmith would pick up on it. But Blaeso simply continued his work.

'You'll see it when it's ready,' the blacksmith grinned. 'Now, off.' He made a shooing gesture with his big, blackened hands, and Silvius shuffled back into the street.

He spent the rest of the morning just wandering about the streets, knowing that he wasn't meant to, that he should be engaged in something useful. And people did give him curious glances as he went by. But somehow he felt that he was allowed these few moments of peace. He would know what was required of him soon enough.

As the sun began to slide down from its zenith, Silvius returned home and into the cool first courtyard with its fig trees and their juicy fruits. The centaur was standing solemnly by himself in its shade, the Arrowhead in its casket around his neck on the golden chain.

Silvius thought, with a shudder, of the strange, dark coils of Python he'd seen when he'd touched it. The huge form of the beast, seeming to take up the space of an entire plain, almost as high as a mountain, with eyes red and pitiless. And the voice that insinuated its way into his mind.

He didn't want to experience that again. The light of Apollo had come as a relief, like rain after a drought. He longed for more.

Aeneas was there already. Iulus, conspicuously, was not, but one of his companions, a dark-eyed, slim young man, watched silently. Elissa was in the far corner, playing dice with Brutus. She brightened when Silvius entered, and hurried towards him.

'I saw the centaur eating this morning – he swallowed down two whole sacks of oats!'

Silvius raised his eyebrows. He'd been whipped, whilst Elissa had been playing with the centaur. And, though he hadn't quite understood it, she had been in his vision of Apollo too, surrounded with a great light. The welts on his back stung. 'You didn't!'

'I did.' She folded her arms, challengingly. 'And a whole suckling pig. You should have seen the look on that old chinwag Chickpea's face! Anyway, they're going to decide what to do now,' she whispered, her whole dark face alive with excitement.

Silvius felt annoyed. She had a freedom he could never have, and now she seemed to know more about this mission than he did.

Elissa tied up her hair surprisingly neatly. 'Ready!' she sang out, and scampered to the centaur's side.

'We begin,' said Stargazer, simply. 'Come near so that you can see. I will open the casket. Do not touch it.'

They gathered round him at arm's length. Silvius pressed in front of Elissa. Their arms touched briefly. Stargazer held the box in the palm of his left hand, and with a swift movement, pressed a catch and lifted the shimmering lid.

Inside was an arrowhead. At first, it looked just like any other old arrowhead, hewn roughly out of flint, coming to the point of a triangle.

As they gazed at it, though, a blackness shadowed it from the edges, and it began to pulse faintly. Soon it was entirely jet black.

A change came over the atmosphere in the courtyard. Even the sun seemed to darken, and Silvius found himself wanting to reach out and touch the Arrowhead. His mind filled with images of that giant, tightly sprung, snake-like beast, which then, appallingly, folded itself into the form of a man.

He was tall, and moved smoothly, and his skin was covered in scales. Silvius felt his gaze searing through him. There was a dark power there.

The Arrowhead called to him, for its other half, for violence and destruction. All he had to do was take it.

The centaur snapped the lid shut.

The vision went. Silvius was still stretching out towards the casket. There was a hunger in Elissa's eyes, but she stood with her arms hanging limp by her sides. Aeneas's hands were gripped tightly together, and when the box closed, he released them. He was shaking a little.

'You see?' Stargazer spoke quietly. 'The Arrowhead is a weapon in itself. It took on some of the attributes of Python when it brought him down. You must not use it. The casket must be kept closed at all times.'

'This is a hard task,' said Aeneas, carefully. 'Silvius, I think you are too young for it. And Elissa, you too.' He considered for a moment longer, then made up his mind. 'There is no way that you can undertake this mission. It needs someone more experienced . . .' A babble of worried chatter began.

'I have to go! I saw Apollo! He . . . he showed me the way!' It was true, up to a point. He'd seen the god's light, as if at the end of a long tunnel. Silvius tried to catch Aeneas's attention.

'Are you sure it was a true vision?' said Aeneas. 'The gods have been silent to me in the past few months . . . It might have been a lie, or a trick. Sometimes, to win us, the things of darkness deceive us.'

'It was him! I swear it! And . . .' He remembered the flutter of wings, the curve of an unexpected smile. 'I saw Hermes, too. The messenger.' He turned towards Elissa, seeking her approval.

She stepped in. 'It's true,' she added softly. She glanced closely at Silvius, as if to confirm something, and nodded. 'Apollo told me too. We both have to go.'

'You can't.' Lavinia's hands were crossed against her shoulders. Her forehead furrowed with anxiety.

'I can!' Silvius was determined. 'Iulus was in charge of the whole Trojan army when he was my age! He travelled with Aeneas, he saw everything . . .'

'That was different,' said Lavinia. 'They had no choice. And see what has become of him.'

The tension was building inside Silvius. His mother was ready to plead with him.

'I have no choice either! I told you! I saw Apollo. I saw him and he told me . . .' He faltered. He glanced at Elissa. And then in a quieter voice, he said, 'He told me I needed to go, and Elissa had to go with me. Look, you've always told me to obey the gods. Now we have a direct order from Apollo himself! It's my duty, isn't it?'

A glimmer of resignation passed over Aeneas's eyes. He seemed about to say something. Silvius had never before seen his father lost for words like this.

They were interrupted by a shout, and the sound of feet pounding the ground. A soldier, lean and tall, sprinted into the courtyard.

He hurried to Aeneas, and spoke breathlessly, panic in his eyes.

'Aeneas! We're under attack – come quickly!' He caught his breath.

Immediately, Aeneas's body straightened, and he narrowed his eyes. 'Stay here, Silvius, and you too, Elissa.' Aeneas spoke commandingly. 'It will be some raiders from the north – we'll deal with it easily. Etruscans, probably.'

Stargazer's nostrils twitched, and he shook his tail from side to side. 'Something is wrong . . .' he said. 'These are no ordinary raiders . . .'

As soon as Aeneas had gone, Silvius, ignoring his mother, dashed after him. 'Don't!' Elissa grabbed his elbow. He gently prised her fingers away.

There was confusion in the streets. The men, who had been mostly working, were scrambling for their weapons.

'What's happening?' Silvius asked a soldier rushing by, jamming his helmet on as he went.

'An attack! They're inside the gates!'

Running past the blacksmith's shop, Silvius saw that it was empty. Blaeso must already be fighting. Even the boy wasn't there. Waiting on a side table was his new sword, with its beautiful decoration of stags and boars. Without hesitating, he lifted it up.

It felt good in his hands.

He sprinted towards the sound of the fray as fast as he could.

At first he could not believe what he saw.

Aeneas and his soldiers were clashing with a small band of armed men, women, and even about a dozen children.

But there was something very different about them.

Something very wrong.

Spilling out from their eyes was a crimson glow, as if they were lit from inside. And they were strong, too. A young boy was battling hand to hand with a man three times his size, and getting the better of him.

'What in the name of the Underworld are we fighting?' shouted someone.

'Demons!' The answer tore through the air.

Aeneas was right in the thickest place of the action, in combat with a tall, leering woman who seemed to have the strength of ten. Silvius hovered at the edge. Aeneas caught sight of him. 'Back! Get back, now!'

And then someone was on Silvius. A man, middle-aged, heavy, one whole eye glowing red, the other just a socket, crimson light pouring out of it, his mouth full of yellowing, half-blackened teeth.

He hurled himself at Silvius, who ducked only just in time, with enough presence of mind to jab with his sword sideways, slicing at the back of his opponent's legs.

Most men would topple.

This one didn't.

Silvius had never fought like this, not with people he knew being cut down all around him. The groans of the injured, the stabbed and the dying filled the air. There was a hissing noise, as if a thousand snakes' tongues were flickering.

The red glow of his enemy pressed in on him. His new

sword was heavy in his sweating hands and, attempting to ready himself, he accidentally dropped it.

The one-eyed man was about to slice Silvius through but he gurgled, choked, grabbing at his neck, and fell forwards, an arrow sticking out of his back. Powerful arms lifted Silvius off the ground, and suddenly he was astride Stargazer's back.

The centaur hurled him up onto a flat roof where Elissa was sitting with two bows, and quivers full of arrows. She gave him a bow, and, breathing heavily, he collected himself and began to shoot. His first arrow hit home.

'Who are they?' gasped Silvius.

'The Enemy,' answered Elissa. 'They are Python's people. It's what Stargazer was warning about.'

Stargazer stormed through the melee with a sword, slashing about him at the Enemy, running people down with his hooves. His eyes were rolling into the back of his head; the madness of battle was on him. Silvius was glad that Stargazer was on their side.

As if they knew that he was carrying the Arrowhead, one of the Enemy turned their glowing eyes towards Stargazer, and made their way near him, circling him, surrounding him.

Silvius picked off a couple, unable to notch arrows fast enough. He was worried too about hitting the centaur. Aeneas's men regrouped and began to charge, but the centaur shouted, 'No! Stay back!' Some halted, confused; others continued.

One of the Enemy rushed at Stargazer from behind, and the centaur kicked out, knocking him backwards.

'What is he doing?' Silvius was already putting his bow down and scrambling to the edge. 'We should help him!'

'No,' Elissa restrained him with her hand. 'Look!'

Stargazer was opening the casket containing the Arrowhead. He uttered a short command. It sounded like 'Destroy!' The hissing from the circling attackers grew louder. At first, Silvius could not quite understand what was happening.

Tendrils of black smoke curled out of the casket, as if it were a lit brazier. After a moment's pause, in which the Enemy edged closer, the smoke burst outwards, forming a circle. Stargazer's eyes were bright and maddened.

Then a black cloud obscured him and all around him.

It had an extraordinary effect. One by one, all the Enemy staggered and collapsed.

Their bodies fell limp to the ground, and the red light left them, vanishing into the darkness.

With a final effort, Stargazer closed the casket. The soldiers of Lavinium were standing open-mouthed. Many had fallen, and their companions began to help them up.

'Now you see,' Stargazer said, panting with effort. 'It can destroy, if you will it. But it has killed me too. I did what I could. I watched over you. It was not enough. Take it to the Achaeans, find the Shaft. And then – slay Python.'

Stargazer collapsed onto his side, and lay there limp, his eyes dulled.

Only the casket, hanging around his neck, still darkly gleamed.

Six

A Test for Tisamenos

There was a wooden door in the stone wall running alongside the street, so discreet it was almost hidden. It couldn't be seen unless a passer-by was paying particular attention. The dancing girl, without looking over her shoulder, opened it and slipped through.

Tisamenos, feeling clumsy, did the same a moment later.

In the gloom of the interior, he could see nothing. He blinked, his eyes adjusting.

He called out tentatively.

A cloth was thrust over him and tied round his head. Strong hands gripped him as he struggled, and they spun him around and around until he was dizzy. He was marched along, but he could not tell whether it was to the left or the right.

Eventually, he came to a stop, and the blindfold over his eyes was removed. Blinking, he found himself in a large, dimly lit chamber, full of strangers. He couldn't see the dancing girl among them.

He wondered if he'd been led into a trap. He was the king's son, after all. A tall man with heavy muscles was looking at him with a hostile expression, and suddenly the muscleman's hand was at his throat, a knife edge pushing aside his costly tunic and grazing his belly.

'Who's this?' said the thug. He was hard and lean, and he had a cold glint in his eye.

Tisamenos looked around wildly for the girl, but she had vanished. There was no sign either of Hero.

'I followed someone in here,' said Tisamenos, before realising that was an obvious thing to say. 'I mean, I followed the swallow.'

The flat of the knife pressed further into his stomach. He stood rigid, aware of movement, talking, whispering. He thought that if he died here, it would be a while before anyone noticed. Would Orestes even do anything? Maybe not whilst he had his new son to think about.

'Don't know what you're talking about,' said the thug, gripping his shoulder. 'I'll have to take you to the chief.'

Tisamenos was led through a low archway into an inner room. Light slanted through from a light well up above, and he could make out the edges of the chamber. There was no furniture, but a dozen or so people were standing there, features indistinguishable in the shadows. His whole body was trembling, and he did not want it to show.

He was pushed into the centre, and encircled by the group. The thug was joined by a wizened old lady, all shrunken and creased, and a small man with amber-coloured skin and long, drooping black moustaches. A monkey sat on his shoulder, chattering.

The stench of smoke and sweat was unbearable. He had no sweet herbs to put to his nose now. He felt ashamed of his fine clothes, and of the smallness of the room, and the people's poor, torn, dirty rags.

A figure wearing a bird mask approached him, and knocked him hard on the shoulder so that he fell to his knees.

'Who comes to the Temple of the Swallow?'

'Tisamenos,' he replied, looking up. The figure kicked him in the guts, and he grunted.

'Who comes to the Temple of the Swallow?'

'Tisamenos, son of Orestes, King of Mykenai; grandson of Agamemnon, High King of all the Achaeans, of the ancient and royal House of Atreos.' He clenched his teeth, and tried to stand up. A ripple of mocking laughter shimmered round the room, and he was shoved back into the dirt.

'I asked you before, and I will not ask you again. Think very carefully before you answer. If you answer wrongly once more, your tongue will be cut out, so that you will never be able to talk of what you have seen.'

These people knew who'd killed his mother, Tisamenos reminded himself. He thought furiously. He didn't doubt that they would cut his tongue out and think no more of it than of wringing a goose's neck. The monkey chattered, and leapt onto his shoulder. Startled, he brushed it off, and it jumped away, cackling.

What could he say? He heard someone whisper, 'He's soft. Born in softness. Let him die in hardness.'

He knew that about himself. He knew his house, his family, were ancient, rotting. His father, half-asleep on the throne, clinging to the past. And his mother, dead, out of reach. He saw Hermione in his mind, turning to him, holding out her hand. 'Know things and know the names of them . . .' she whispered. He felt the strength of the lion course through him.

He knew what to say.

'I am Tisamenos.' The hand pushed him back down, but he pressed against it. 'I am Tisamenos.' He stood up and looked right at the figure in the bird mask. 'I am Tisamenos, unworthy son of Hermione. And I have come to lay her ghost to rest.' A murmur ran around the room, and Tisamenos was not sure whether it was approving or not.

The figure called, 'Silence!' Then it removed its bird mask, and there, stern, her dark eyes flashing, was Hero.

'Good. Now you will learn. Are the watchers in place?'

Somebody called assent from the back.

'Good. Repeat. By the Mother of the Gods we swear. I will

not repeat what I hear. If I do, may I be struck down, my tongue cut out, my hands cut off, my nose slit.'

Tisamenos repeated the words, the rest of the group's voices resounding around him.

'So will you tell me?' he said, when he'd finished. 'Will you tell me who killed my mother?'

'He must show his loyalty first,' said the thug.

Hero paused, and looked thoughtful. 'It is true,' she said. 'All here have sworn to the band of Swallows.'

'But he cannot,' said the amber-skinned man. 'He is one of them. One of the soft ones.'

'What should I do?' said Tisamenos. 'I will do anything.'

'Bring us the head of the Last Gorgon,' said the thug, suddenly, his deep voice full of mockery. 'And then you will know.' There were calls of derision and approval from the crowd.

'You must do it,' said Hero. 'We have all done such things. I brought the teeth of a Hydra.' She went to a box, plain and wooden, and opened it. Inside were two pointed canines, as long as a grown man's arm. 'Slick with poison,' she said, and then held out her arm. Along it was a long, vivid scar. 'And this is what even the corpse of a monster can do to you.'

Staring at the teeth, Tisamenos said, 'But – but that's impossible. The Last Gorgon is a story, a legend – she's not real!'

'She is dead. But her head is still on her body, and her head is a powerful weapon. Bring it to us.'

'What do you need weapons for?' said Tisamenos.

'We can't tell you that,' said Hero, curling her lip a little.

This was dangerous. Tisamenos was in a nest of rebels. They wanted power, but for what exactly? How could he do what they wanted? Did they mean harm to Orestes?

And yet they would help him. He thought again of Orestes, and of Erigone. He had to do it. He had to find out who killed his mother. 'I – I don't know where to find her . . .'

'Then look.'

Someone blindfolded him, and a stinking hand was put over his mouth; he was spun round and round, and, his mind ringing, he was led in a zigzag way for what seemed like an age. Finally, he was shoved against a wall, and a voice said, 'Wait till you hear the hoot of an owl, then take it off. Do it before then and we will kill you.'

He waited until he was sure he heard the sound, and then slowly removed the blindfold.

The chitter of a squirrel eating a nut. It scampered away from him. Some garments, fluttering from a window, left out to dry. A pool of dark water into which someone had thrown something that smelt revolting. His guts turned. He was in an unremarkable alley, somewhere near the far walls. A magpie was pecking about in the dirt.

He made his way slowly back to the kinghouse.

The Last Gorgon. It was a shadow, a legend.

And how could he bring back a shadow?

Seven

Elissa Makes a Plan

The casket containing the Arrowhead drew all eyes as it sat on a trestle table in the middle of the forum. Everyone who could be spared had gathered there, Elissa noted. She saw fear in their eyes; fear in the faces of people she had known all her life. Little children clung to their mothers, sensing something was wrong. Older ones hung on hands, tugging to get away.

Though the forum was full, there was a ring of space around the Arrowhead. Nobody dared to go near it.

It was the day after the attack. Aeneas had doubled the guards on the walls, and work on the fortifications was continuing ever faster, the sounds of hammering and sawing rising into the air all around.

The night before, the people of Lavinium had built a funeral pyre and placed Stargazer's body on it, and all the dozen others who had fallen. Watching the fire burn, Elissa saw the ashes rising into the clear night sky.

Now she was thoughtfully scratching the wolf cub's belly, whilst watching Aeneas pace up and down, talking with Iulus and his advisors, playing with the handle of the short sword at his waist.

Silvius was upright and staring straight ahead. He looked so slender, so lonely, and Elissa felt a surge of sympathy for him. She could not get the horror of the Enemy, their glowing red eyes and their relentless power, out of her mind, and she could see it in his eyes too, in his trembling hands.

The light of Apollo would destroy Python. And she had seen it. There was no question about it. He would need her.

She scrambled up and jogged to join Silvius, the wolf cub scampering at her heels. He grasped her hand gratefully.

'Aeneas!' she interrupted the leader, tugging on his sleeve. 'You've got to let us go.'

Silvius looked shocked at her boldness, but she pressed on. 'Please!'

All at once, Aeneas broke away from his conversation, and said, powerfully, 'You can't. It's too dangerous. You are too young, and know nothing of what lurks in the wilds. You have never even been on a ship. The Arrowhead may have sent you both visions, but we don't know if we can trust it.'

Silvius took a long breath. 'You let a vision build this city,' he said. 'When you came here, you followed a white sow and her piglets, and built your foundations where she settled.'

'That was different,' said Aeneas, slowly. 'It was a true prophecy, from one of our own – my cousin, Helenus.'

'He has a point,' Iulus cut in suddenly. 'Why not believe this one?' Elissa saw a coolness in Iulus's gaze. He was trying to get at Aeneas, she knew. She saw the grateful look that Silvius shot him, and how downcast he was when Iulus didn't return it.

Aeneas replied, 'These are difficult times. Silvius represents the union of the Trojans and the Latins. We cannot lose him. I cannot lose my son.' He picked up the casket, hung it around his own neck and stalked away.

And what do I represent? thought Elissa. Her Carthaginian mother, long dead. Her father, who joined her in the Underworld soon afterwards. The Trojans did not care for the Carthaginians.

She was clearly not as important.

The meeting in the forum broke up. Elissa had no duties, so she went with Silvius, on his way to his guard duty on the wall. They walked in silence for a while. A litter of piglets ran squealing in front of them, followed by their ungainly mother.

Then they reached the blacksmith's, and Silvius, face a little flushed, stopped. 'I just need to go in here,' he said to Elissa. 'Come with me if you like.'

She nodded, and followed him into the heat of the forge. 'I'm sorry I took the sword,' he was saying, holding it out to Blaeso.

The blacksmith merely smiled. 'Keep it,' he said. 'You'll need it, whatever comes. Now go, and be strong.'

'Be strong,' replied Silvius, and returned to walking, Elissa and the wolf cub skipping along beside him. She knew he was building up to ask her something, and let him take his time.

'What did you see in your vision?' asked Silvius, when they were in a more deserted area. 'When you touched the casket?'

Elissa paused, and the wolf cub flopped down at her feet. She couldn't tell all of it to him. It was too private, too pure. But she could give him something. 'When I saw the centaur, I knew he was here for me. I'd dreamed of him. And now, since he's died, I think I owe it to him. You know there isn't much for me here. What can I hope for? I want to go away from here. Maybe I'll even get to Carthage!' Silvius's lips tightened. 'How about you? What did Apollo say?'

But Silvius did not answer, and Elissa saw the pain and conflict in his eyes flickering there for a second.

'You know I think of him – all the time.' She spoke gently, placing a hand on his arm.

Silvius squeezed her fingers gratefully. 'Me too – and Python.'

'Don't.' Elissa shivered. A group of women went by, carrying baskets of clothes to be washed, some balancing them on their heads, others on poles that they had over their shoulders. Silvius and Elissa sprang apart.

'Elissa, come on there, lend a hand, will you?' shouted one cheerfully, a blowsy woman with a red face.

'All right, coming!' And then, quietly to Silvius, 'I'll see you at noon.'

Unusually, there was an armed guard with the women, and there was a sense of tension in the air.

All the morning, as she went about the tedious work of scrubbing linen, her hands getting red and sore, Elissa felt the call of Apollo, his soft light, his gentle music, urging her onwards to act.

The women didn't talk to her much, and she mostly got in the way, but as soon as the shadows shortened, she slipped off to see Silvius.

She passed the stables of Lavinium at the western gate. The stalls were mostly full of sturdy horses used to pull carts and loads, but there were a few fine, fiery beasts that Aeneas rode in battle. Perhaps they might be able to take one.

Silvius was waiting for her at the corner of the street. His hair was plastered onto his forehead from where his helmet sat. She pulled him into the shade, and they shared some dry bread and cured pork.

'Delicious, this stuff,' said Elissa as she licked her lips. Silvius hadn't spoken, just eaten. She could see how tense he was, how he kept fiddling with his dagger, his buckles, how he kept scanning the faces of passers-by, as if each one might have a message for him.

'Elissa – we need to think about how to get out.'

'We'll have to sneak out. It's the only way.' It would be easier for her to do than for Silvius. His rooms were in the most closely guarded quarters, whilst hers were nearer the latrines.

Silvius nodded slowly. 'If I get up at midnight, I can take

the casket from Aeneas's room whilst he's asleep. It will be stealing . . .'

'But you have to do it. Think of it not as stealing, but borrowing.'

'Yes,' he answered, nodding seriously now. 'You're right.'

'Then we both go to the stables. We take a couple of Aeneas's horses, and ride to the port. It's not far.'

'There'll be traders there. Someone who can guide us.' A sunbeam played across his outstretched hand. The touch of Apollo, perhaps, thought Elissa.

'We'll need coins,' said Elissa. 'You know I don't have any of those.'

Silvius scratched his nose. 'I've got some. And some things we could sell.'

'We could even find a Carthaginian!' continued Elissa. 'There'll be more of them than Achaeans. Or even,' and here her voice grew more excited, 'a Phoenician!'

Her family, before they had gone to Carthage, had come from Tyre, a city on the coast of Phoenicia, and Elissa had always wanted to go to that city, and was eager for news of it.

'You must promise not to tell anyone this, not even the slightest breath of it.' Worry showed in Silvius's drawn brows.

Elissa's eyes glowed. She put her fingers to her lips.

'I promise.'

Their planning was broken off by a call from Lavinia, who was glancing anxiously across at them. The women had

67

returned from washing, and they were singing a mournful lay about two parted lovers.

'What are you two plotting?' Lavinia approached. She was smiling. But there was a tension in her poise, basket at her hip.

'Just telling Elissa about the . . . bird's nest I found, near the guard's hut – there are some lovely blue eggs. I thought she might like one.'

'Your patrol's over. Come home with us. Your father needs you.'

Elissa said goodbye. Again, she felt a stab of jealousy. Nobody wanted her, or needed her. She watched as Silvius left, marching straight but small by the side of his mother.

He would need all the help he could get.

And she would do her best to give it to him.

Eight

Into the Cave

The bridal party had now become a celebration of the birth of Penthilos, and it was still in full riot as Tisamenos returned to the kinghouse. Avoiding the men lolling drunkenly, and stepping over the prone bodies of a few revellers who'd over-indulged, he sneaked back to his chambers, and settled on the soft silk-covered couch in his anteroom. The kinghouse servants were, as ever, busy about him.

His old nurse, Agatha, was chattering in the background. She was a large, bear-like presence, her eyes, though weak, still sharp in her fleshy face. He looked at her wrinkles, lined with all the troubles of the House of Atreos.

She had been near middle age when Agamemnon had apparently sacrificed his daughter Iphigenia to the goddess Artemis; she had seen Agamemnon slain in turn by his wife

Clytemnestra after the Trojan War; and she had seen Orestes and Electra kill their mother in revenge, and all the torments that followed.

Yet she'd remained within the palace walls. She had suffered, but she had survived.

'The Furies never rest,' Agatha was saying. 'They'll keep on wanting their revenge. I don't like that Erigone. She is the daughter of Aegisthos, after all.'

Tisamenos accepted a goblet from her.

'Drink this, you look awful.' She began dabbing at his face, and instead of batting her away, he let her continue. She combed his long blond hair, muttering as she did.

'. . . and your poor aunt Electra, all mad, though I shouldn't say it, and nobody ever going to visit her, though I do sometimes, if only to give the poor thing a kind word or two, and at least your aunt Iphigenia came out all right in the end, thank the Hunt Goddess.' He'd heard all this before, many times, but rather than stopping her, he wanted her to continue. He understood how much she might know. She made a move as if to tie a bow round his hair, and he batted her away playfully.

'Nurse,' he said, when the heavy wooden door had closed behind the last servant, and Agatha was plumping the finely worked cushions on his bed. 'Have you ever heard of the Last Gorgon?'

She stood up sharply and fixed him with her gaze. 'Where did you hear about that?'

'I heard someone on the street near the agora. I'd never heard of the Last Gorgon before. I know about Perseus and Medusa . . .'

'You don't want to go getting mixed up with anything like that,' Agatha said, blinking furiously.

'I don't know what you mean. It's just a story. Isn't it?'

'There are stories and then there are stories, my boy. Don't you forget I've known you since you were a little puling infant crawling about on the tiles. The Last Gorgon is one of the ancient terrors of the earth. She is Medusa's sister, who crawled back here after Medusa was slain, to hide herself. Last I heard of her was when your father Orestes was clearing out the countryside of such beasts. She was killed, like all of the others.'

Then bringing her head would not be that troublesome for Tisamenos. It was just a matter of finding her old lair and then the skull of the Gorgon – it must be a skull by now, surely? Then all he would need would be a sword, and maybe a dagger, in case of bears or wolves. A couple of torches, too, to light the cave.

And was it true that the Gorgons turned people into stone? Surely that was just a legend. But just in case he would need a shield, so that he could look into it. And a sack. He shuddered inwardly at the thought of the sack. To put her head in.

'Where was her lair?' he said, offhandedly.

Agatha regarded him unblinkingly for a long time. Then she made the sign to ward off evil, and said, 'They used to say in the foothills of the mountains. But – oh I see your grandfather Agamemnon in you!'

A burst of pride filled Tisamenos's chest. But it faded as Agatha continued. 'Be careful, my sweeting. You are not made for this terrible world.'

Orestes that afternoon was engaged in watching the first races. The athletes were preparing as Tisamenos went by the palaestra, oiling themselves and flexing their muscles. He kept to the shadows, a cloak wrapped around his head. He felt a pang of anger when he saw Erigone by Orestes's side, a young nurse carrying the new baby. Orestes, who loved the games, was clearly enjoying himself. He wouldn't notice if Tisamenos was missing.

Tisamenos stalked through the streets, wondering at every turn where the headquarters of the Swallows were. Soon he went past the last few poor huts where goatherds and swine-herds lived. A pig grunted, then he was out through the Lion Gate, and hurrying down the winding road to the plain below, and the forests.

He had been into the forests before, out hunting, but usually with a large retinue. His father on the finest horse, surrounded by the boasting huntsmen. His own mount, smaller but some-times quicker. But he'd never been on his own.

As soon as he passed beneath the trees, he felt a chill. Every branch seemed to point itself into a finger, warning him. Every rustle, every creak, made him look over his shoulder.

Steadily, though, he made his way northwards, keeping to the rough deer track that the hunters used.

Eventually he came to the foothills. There was only one cave that he could see, and he decided to investigate. There were no goats, or any other signs of life. The mouth of the cave was low to the ground, under a lip of rock, and he examined it for a long while. It was only when a swallow swooped across the space in front of him that he steeled himself. He lit one torch, and went inside.

Immediately the cold sought out his bones. This was a dank, dark place, one that nobody had been into for years. Surprisingly, this made him feel better. There were no robbers or brigands to deal with. He wedged the torch in a cleft near the entrance, and the flames spread their light across the walls. The dampness seemed to get in everywhere, into his mouth and down into his lungs. The stench of a rotting dead animal hit his nostrils. He faltered for a moment, stumbling, and almost fell to the rocky ground. Then he righted himself, and lit the second torch, which he placed in a narrow fissure. He could now see that the cave was quite large, and that it seemed to lead into a tunnel that went further into the mountain's roots.

A slight sense of panic began to grip him. He wasn't prepared to go that far. But there was no sign of a Gorgon's head, or of anything else, on the cave floor around him. He began to curse his foolishness. Even so, he gripped his shield hard and unsheathed his sword; biting his lip, he went further in.

A rustling sound made him halt. Instinctively he turned so

that he wasn't looking directly at it. In the shield's mirrored surface he saw a form, its outline that of a woman. He almost sighed with relief. It must be one of the Swallows, come to tell him that he'd passed. Maybe that was the test – simply to come to this awful place.

The woman remained still, and for a moment he observed her in the shield. In the glow of torchlight she was beautiful. Long golden tresses hung around a smiling face. She beckoned to him. He didn't recognise her from the meeting, but he said, 'Did I pass?'

He would have put down the shield there and then. But the woman's tresses were moving strangely, as if stirred by a breeze. His skin began to prickle. There was a hissing, and the long, thick locks of hair became a mass of seething, spitting snakes.

It was her. She hadn't died, after all. Confusion rushed through him. The Swallows had sent him to his death.

It was the Last Gorgon.

What could he do? He could turn and run now, and return with a mob of townspeople. He looked at the woman's reflection, her face now sharpening, lengthening, teeth bared and eyes glowing. His shield arm shook. Remember Perseus, he thought. Look in the mirror. Perseus defeated the Gorgon by looking in the mirror.

He saw the snaky head in his shield's surface. All he needed to do was feint to the left, then come in from behind her and he would be able to get her in the neck. He readied himself, the snakes hissing all the time.

Then he realised that something strange was happening to him. He was holding the shield but he could not move his middle finger.

He managed to wrench his gaze away from her eyes and focus on his hand.

The Last Gorgon laughed, and her voice filled the cave. 'They did not tell you that, did they? The Last Gorgon is the most powerful of all. A mirror does not stop me. My gaze pierces all.'

There was a tickling sensation in his finger.

He gasped with horror. He was in a damp cave with only one exit, the Last Gorgon approaching him, and his middle finger was turning to stone.

Nine

Night Mission

LAVINIUM, ITALIA: HOUSE OF THE WOLF

Brutus was snuffling in his sleep, tangled up in a coarse woollen blanket. Silvius's little brother was lying on his front, as if he'd fallen asleep as soon as he hit the bed, arms spread-eagled, one leg poking over the edge. Moonlight shone brightly through the window, and every outline in the room was sharply sketched out.

As Silvius reached the door, he stopped. Brutus did not move.

It was a huge thing, to leave this place, this new city built by his father. This symbol of new hope for his father's people.

He knew what he symbolised for Aeneas. He was the living embodiment of the alliance between the Trojans and the Latins, the promise of the future.

If he disobeyed Aeneas and left the city, what would await him when he returned? He knew that it would be worse than a whipping.

But he had to do it. And as he reminded himself, he was half-Latin, and knew only the woods and the rivers and hills of Italia.

Troy was just a story, something that grew fainter and fainter with every retelling. He didn't have to hate the Achaeans. If his father had built something new, and Iulus was making his city in Alba Longa, then why couldn't Silvius strike out on his own?

What had Aeneas said? *Remember. Remember what they did to us.*

Silvius, growing up in the forest with Lavinia, had not really understood what the old Trojans were talking about. Lavinia was a local Italian princess, and she simply taught him all the things that she knew about the ways of the wood.

Troy seemed a distant place, somewhere that people sang songs about.

Deep in his heart he felt no hatred towards the Achaeans. In fact, he even felt a curiosity about them. Who were these blood-thirsty barbarians? Why had they torn down a city over a woman? All these things he might be able to see, to understand.

He checked his small leather pack. Dagger. New bronze sword, rolled up in cloth. Water pouch. Some hard bread he'd taken from the stores. The wooden box on a thin chain which he was going to use as a dummy. He thought for a second about waking Brutus up. Be strong, he would say to him. Be strong and obey your parents. He knew that wasn't what he was doing. But it would be better for Brutus to stay safe.

Aeneas's room was further along the corridor from Silvius's own. The family's sleeping quarters all faced onto a wide earthen-floored courtyard. Lavinia's rooms were the largest and most comfortable. She had furnished them with soft things from her home city, fine materials from the tribes further north. Her Latin maidservants slept in the ante-chamber. Silvius crept past her door, aware that a candle was lit within, aware of every creak of a plank and hoot of a bird.

But nothing stirred, and he arrived unchallenged at his father's door. He paused at the threshold to put down his pack, removing the decoy box. Taking a deep breath, he entered. The wooden hinges creaked slightly, like the timbers of a ship, and Silvius was momentarily startled by something brushing across his face; but he held his breath, and stifled the shriek of fear that was trying to escape his lips. It was a moth, whirring away.

He stood with his back pressed against the door.

The room was doused in moonlight. It seemed spectral, unreal almost.

His father was lying on his back, hands by his sides, without a cover, wearing a day tunic, his polished armour laid out ready on the floor next to the bed. A sword, unsheathed, was within reach.

The rest was almost completely bare. For the first time, it struck Silvius that his father really had lost everything at Troy. There was a small chest under the window, which Silvius assumed held linen, and a statue of the goddess Venus, big-thighed and squat. The only other thing that broke up the wooden walls was a tapestry that hung opposite Aeneas's bed. Silvius had seen it many times before, and even now he could pick out the scene: the towers of Troy, burning to the ground, the Achaean soldiers looting, slaughtering and causing chaos. It gave him pause. Was he doing the right thing, plunging into the land of their enemies? In the top left-hand corner, a small group of Trojans, led by Aeneas, was escaping, ready to make their desperate way somewhere else. His father had made a difficult journey. Why shouldn't he?

Gulping, he stepped carefully towards the bed across the clean wooden boards. The golden chain was hanging around Aeneas's neck, the casket holding the Arrowhead a dark lump upon his chest. Silvius tiptoed closer. He could hear his father breathing deeply and evenly.

Now he was near the bed, a mere hand's breadth away from his father's sleeping body. He reached out as gently as possible, and put his thumb and forefinger on the lid.

Immediately he felt a freezing, tight sensation, as if something were coiling round his neck.

He had to ignore it. Now was the time. As delicately as he might have held Brutus when he was a baby, he raised it from Aeneas's neck. His father shifted, and the chain snagged on his ear. A surge of terror ran through Silvius, and he stood as still as a frightened rabbit; then, after scratching his nose and moaning something, Aeneas settled.

As steadily as he could, Silvius lifted the chain and put it carefully around his own neck, then placed the decoy around Aeneas's neck. He had to move his father's head a little way to do so, and pulled back quickly. Aeneas, deep in sleep, must have realised something was happening. He mumbled, and put his hand to his chest, as if seeking the casket; his fingers closed around the replacement, and he was at rest once more.

Silvius, mouth dry, tiptoed to the door, then came out, picked up his pack and made his way as quickly as possible to the eastern side of the House of the Wolf where the main latrines were. He paused for a second when he smelt the familiar tang of waste, and half-elated, half-terrified, held the casket. It was heavy in his hands, and he let it drop back against his chest, cool and dangerous.

A shadow detached itself from the greater darkness as he arrived. He said, 'Be well, friend. The stars are bright tonight.'

'And the moon looks down upon us kindly.'

Silvius relaxed. That was the phrase he'd agreed on with Elissa. 'Quickly,' he urged, as Elissa's features became more distinct. He showed her the golden chain. She nodded, and made a small bow.

'You did it,' she said softly, touching his hand for a moment. 'It's the right thing. Apollo told me. Now let's go.' She shifted the small bag she'd brought around her neck.

First, Silvius climbed up the fence, using the corner of the latrine to steady himself. Without thinking too much about it, when he reached the top he turned around and let himself drop the ten feet or so, falling into a crouch. Ignoring the stink, he stood up and held out his arms for Elissa. But she dropped down beside him.

They kept to the city wall, out of the sight line of any guard who might be looking out across the plain for attackers. Soon they smelled horseflesh and manure, and knew they had reached the stables.

Now came the part of the plan that Silvius liked least. There was a guard set on the stables, and they would have to knock him out, and maybe even the stable boys too, if they were there. A large wicker gate was set into the city wall, wide enough for two horses to pass through, and through it could be seen the light of an oil lamp, and a man singing to himself.

Silvius peered through the crack, and saw a young man sitting on a stool with his back to them, carving a piece of wood to pass the time. He'd taken his armour off, and was singing an old song about wood spirits. Silvius's heart sank. He knew this young man. He was the son of a Trojan warrior and a Latin woman, like he was himself, and not much older.

He looked back over his shoulder at Elissa, and beckoned to her, pushed open the wicker gate and stepped inside, Elissa just behind him. The smell of fresh hay and the comforting rawness of horse sweat engulfed them. A chestnut mare in the stall right next to the door noticed his presence, and swished her tail in greeting. Foolishly, he put his finger to his lips, before recalling why he was there. The guard stopped singing, and placed his carving down upon the floor, looking from side to side as if he had forgotten what he was about to do, then put both hands on his thighs, about to stand up.

The guard looked absurdly unprotected from behind. A metallic taste came into Silvius's mouth, and without stopping to think any more about it, he picked up an empty sack from the floor, crept up behind the guard and stuffed it over his head. The guard cried out, but Silvius kicked him over, drew his sword and pressed it to the man's exposed belly.

'Make a sound,' said Silvius, 'and you'll feel it.' Then, a sick taste in his throat, he knocked hard into the guard's head, sending him sideways, prone in the straw.

Elissa was watching him, shocked.

Silvius checked the guard, removing the sack. He was out, clean, his eyes closed, lids fluttering. Then, feeling suddenly disgusted with himself, Silvius looked about for Aeneas's horse, Blaze.

The huge, glossy stallion was stabled by himself. He snorted and stamped his foot. As Silvius went up to him, he was awed. Aeneas's pride stood high, over sixteen hands. Silvius reached out and tried to catch the horse's head, but it shied away.

'Not like that.' Elissa was beside him.

Whispering a few gentle words, Elissa stroked the stallion's nose, feeding him some roots that were in a bag tied to the stall. Then, as if it were nothing, she took a bridle and gently placed it on the horse, with the reins attached to it, and opened the stall, leading him out.

She gave the bridle to Silvius, and jumped onto the horse's back, holding onto its mane.

Blaze stamped his foreleg once.

Silvius waited to mount, ashamed that he had not been able to quiet his father's steed. 'I can ride better than you. I'll take the reins.' Elissa shuffled backwards, being very careful with her pack, settling it in her lap. 'Are you ready?'

He was on, and her arms were around his waist, her breath hot on his neck.

'What have you got in there?' He peered over his shoulder.

'Nothing,' she said, avoiding his eye.

The guard on the floor groaned, reminding Silvius that there was no time to spare. This was it. They had to leave. If he went home now, he would have to face punishment for stealing and disobedience. It would be a lot worse than the lashes. And so he clicked his tongue softly, and they left the stables.

The wicker gate stood wide open to the cool night, the stars spotting the dark sky. Orion the hunter was above the horizon.

But still they could not run. A wall guard might see them, and then they would be chased, and caught, and all would be over. They would walk to the woods, and only then would they gallop.

'Gently now,' whispered Silvius, and, nostrils flaring, the stallion stepped out.

Ten

The Last Gorgon

In horror, Tisamenos swung away from the Last Gorgon as she slid over the wet cave floor towards him.

He was now facing the dimly outlined entrance to the cave. A hissing, murmuring laughter made him shiver with terror.

'Nobody has ever escaped me,' she called, and he heard her slithering over the sodden ground. 'Your father Orestes came rampaging here with many men before you were born. Clearing the countryside of monsters, he said. He dared to call me a monster – I, the most beautiful of all!' Tisamenos felt a stinging sensation on his bare arm, and jumped with shock. 'We struck a deal, he and I. I did not kill him, and he let me stay here, undisturbed.'

The thought that his father had bargained with this creature made Tisamenos shudder even more. He took a step nearer to the cave entrance. He could still escape, with the shield stuck to his arm until he could smash it off.

Escape, and be nothing.

But what else could he do? His sword was the only weapon he had. That and the two torches. He could only tell where the Last Gorgon was by the sound of the snakes hissing. He guessed she was about twenty paces away from him, in the gloom of the cave, near the second torch. The echoes made it difficult to judge exactly where she was.

That was his only hope. To get to the torch and fling it at her, so that her robes might catch fire.

The first thing he had to do was release his grip. Bending slightly, with his right hand he scrabbled around for a rock. The snakes' hissing increased in volume, but the Last Gorgon seemed to be toying with him, slithering back and forth across the same cold patch of rock.

He found a flint, and holding it tightly, he smashed it repeatedly onto his new stone knuckle. Panting with exertion, with a final loud grunt he shattered the joint, and the stone finger fell to the cave floor, releasing his hand. He dropped the shield, and it clattered hollowly.

Where his finger had been was now a hard stump. He felt it gingerly. Necessity compelled him.

He had to go on.

The first torch was guttering right next to him. He tore it from the cleft. With his back still to the Last Gorgon, he listened hard for her movements. Her snakes were hissing nearby, but she seemed to have come to a standstill.

He spun round on his heels with his eyes clamped shut, and flung the torch at where he thought the Last Gorgon was.

It clattered to the cave floor, and the Last Gorgon laughed again, her light human voice shading into the unsettling hiss of the snakes.

He'd missed, and now there was only his sword and the second torch, further into the cave, nearer the Last Gorgon. He scrabbled for his sword, and at the same time, his skin prickled again with something like fire, and he felt something sticky when he put his hand to it, before quickly bringing it away.

Venom. The snakes were spitting venom at him.

Wildly grasping, he recognised the shape of the sword hilt and lifted it, at the same time finding the shield and settling it onto his arm with difficulty, covering his head.

Tisamenos had never fought anyone before, not properly. The sword had never been used. He thought of the Swallows, all those hardened, weathered, cold-eyed people. He thought of his bed, so soft and huge, and the downy pillows, and the golden goblets in his rooms. He thought of his father, drunk, on his crumbling stone throne, a dancing girl sitting on one knee, a cupbearer on the other. His stepmother, Erigone, watching everything, and the new life she'd brought into the world.

The echoes in the cave intensified, pounding round his skull. A rustle made him jump sideways, and a huge slug of venom stung his unprotected hand. This time it burned his skin, leaving a large welt.

The other torch. If only he could get to the other torch.

But how? He remembered the touch of his mother. *My little lion cub.* He needed that fierceness now he was more than a cub. What she'd said to him had worked in the Swallows' meeting place. He remembered it now. *Know things, and know the names of them, and you will have them in your power.*

He needed to keep the Last Gorgon talking. If he could find out her name, distract her, he might have a chance. She had bargained with his father, after all.

He tried to remember what he knew about the Gorgons. They had been beautiful once, favoured by the gods; then turned into monsters.

His upper lip was tingling with sweat. The pain in his hand was intensifying.

'Don't you want to see me, Tisamenos?' The Last Gorgon's human voice was enticing.

'I do, I do. You are so beautiful.' Tisamenos edged forwards, eyes squeezed shut, feeling his way first with one foot, then the other. His toes were wet, though he couldn't remember having stepped in a puddle.

'I am beautiful,' answered the Last Gorgon, sighing. 'I was more beautiful than Medusa. And I have outlived her, and my other sister. So, boy, look at me, look at me, look on the beauty of the world.' The echoes in the cave took up her call, and the snakes seemed to repeat it too.

Yesssss, yessss, looook at herrrr.

Tisamenos turned his head away, and half-opened one eye. The second torch was crackling where he'd left it, and he sensed that the Last Gorgon was about the same distance away from him on the right.

'I will look at you,' he said, closing his eyes once more and sidling blindly towards the torch. 'But first, please, I must know what your name is.'

The Last Gorgon hissed with pleasure. 'I am Euryale.'

'Euryale,' repeated Tisamenos, his heart thudding as he felt for the torch. 'A pretty name.' He recalled how earlier he'd felt the tingling sensation as soon as he'd looked at Euryale's reflection. He'd been able to tear himself away just in time. A moment later, and he knew he would have been entirely turned to stone. Could he risk it now?

In order for his plan to work, he would have to open his eyes and let Euryale see him. It was dangerous.

He could feel the torch's heat, and remembered Hero in the room of the Swallows.

'I am sure,' he said, locating where the torch was stuck into the rock, and aiming for its shaft, 'that you are the most beautiful woman the world has ever seen.'

'More beautiful than my sisters?'

Mooore beautiful than my sissstersss, echoed the snakes, rebounding around the cave.

'Oh, more, much more.' His voice was false, high. He hoped that she would not be able to tell how absolutely terrified he was.

Tisamenos found the torch's shaft. In doing so he felt another sting of venom. His skin was burning where the poison fell. He couldn't carry both sword and torch, so he placed his sword down, knowing he would be able to reach it again if he needed it.

'Well then, Euryale,' he said. 'Let me see your beauty, and know you.' The hissing stopped, and Tisamenos opened his eyes.

The woman he'd seen before was in the reflection of his shield. Her tresses were now red, tinged with gold, falling around her face like flame. She smiled at him, a smile that encompassed the universe. No wonder gods had loved her, he thought. Long white robes swept the ground.

The tingling began this time in his ear, stronger now.

At that moment, her fiery locks transformed into snapping red snakes.

It was now or never.

Tisamenos protected his eyes with his shield, and prepared to throw the torch.

The snakes let out a terrible noise, like steam from a boiling cauldron. The Last Gorgon shrieked. He didn't dare to look.

It took a moment for Tisamenos to realise that she was shrieking in pleasure at her reflection.

'See! See! I am so beautiful!' she hissed, and her voice was now indistinct from the snakes. Tisamenos heard her swishing towards him, her tattered robes flowing.

The torch was ready in his hand. 'Oh, see! See my golden tresses, and my lips so red. How beautiful!'

Euryale glided nearer, and Tisamenos gasped as her taloned hands gripped either side of his shield. Her nails were long and filthy, her skin pallid. He could not move from fear.

This was it. If he wasn't turned to stone, the snakes were going to poison him to death, or he would be torn apart by her claws till he was unrecognisable.

He tensed himself, ready to go down fighting, ready to thrust the torch into her.

But nothing happened. She was muttering to herself, gazing at the mirrored surface of the shield.

And then he realised.

Clasping the shield, and looking at herself, she had entirely forgotten him.

She crooned, enchanted by her own image as the hissing of the snakes reverberated around them. Gently, slowly, Tisamenos released the handle of the shield so that she was holding it by herself. She did not notice the movement, whispering quietly, her red snakes dancing about her head in glee.

Warily, Tisamenos slipped round her until he was to her left, with the cave entrance behind him, and picked up his sword. The guttering torch he placed back where it had been. Then he gathered his strength, rocked back on his heels and sliced. The snakes spat venom, spattering his face.

The Last Gorgon didn't scream, but fell, still holding the mirror. As the snakes began to droop, she still whispered to herself, 'You are so beautiful . . .'

He saw his own face in the shield's surface, distorted but triumphant. Three beasts, Hero had said. This could be the first. He shuddered to think what would come next.

Tisamenos's sword was reeking with gore. His long blond hair was stuck to the sides of his head, his skin stinging with acid venom. With his mutilated hand hanging by his side, he waited in the stuttering torchlight for the Last Gorgon to die.

Eleven

At the Port

LAVINIUM, ITALIA: HOUSE OF THE WOLF

Silvius and Elissa were lucky. Perhaps, even in the sharp moonlight, it was hard to see the black stallion and the two cloaked figures seated upon it; or perhaps the guard on that section of the wall of Lavinium had dozed off. Either way, they managed to cross the narrow plain towards the woods without any sign that they had been noticed.

Once they were under cover, Silvius pressed his ankles gently up into the stallion's hot flanks, and they began to trot down the goat path that led into the forest. They would go the long way round, to confuse anyone who might be following them, and to avoid the marshes to the south as well.

Blaze went well, finding his way without mishap, snorting occasionally and flicking his ears back but generally keeping in good temper.

The forest had a spectral quality to it as the moon silvered the branches of the trees and the undergrowth. Silvius found that he liked the quiet, and that his ears were becoming attuned to the sounds around him. It was cool, and he loved feeling the rush of the breeze through his hair and over his face.

Elissa had one arm tightly grasping Silvius; with the other she was carefully keeping her pack to her breast.

'This is the first time I've been in the woods!' she whispered, as if awed by the darkness. 'Keep him steady. I don't want to drop my pack.'

'What have you got in there?' Silvius asked again.

'Oh, just some useful things,' she said airily. 'Keep going!'

Soon they came to the end of the goat path through the forest and were at the edge of the road, which stretched out to Lavinium's small port along the coastline from the south. It was a new, paved road that Aeneas had built, and it ran straight.

'Now remember, we're just travellers now,' said Silvius, and he uncloaked himself. Elissa did the same, but in doing so she dropped her pack, and there was a sudden confusion as the bag came to life and began to run round in circles. The stallion reared, and Silvius, taken unawares, came off, as did Elissa. Silvius managed to grab the reins; he whispered in the horse's ear as he'd seen Elissa do until he was calm.

Elissa meanwhile had jumped on the pack and seemed to be hiding something.

'What have you done?' asked Silvius, when Blaze was gentle once more.

Giving him a shy glance, Elissa straightened, and from her lap tumbled the wolf cub that she had been playing with over the last few days. 'It's just ... I think his mother's dead, and there's nobody at home to look after him, and he'll be really helpful ...'

The wolf cub pawed joyfully at Silvius. Blaze whinnied, but soon settled. Elissa looked so contrite, and the wolf cub's eyes were glinting so brightly in the moonlight that Silvius was moved. 'Well, all right then. But we have to get going now.'

Elissa put the wolf cub back in her pack with his little head poking out, and Silvius dug his heels into the stallion.

Soon they were galloping, and the thrill of it rushed through Silvius's body.

He would be away from Aeneas, from Lavinia, from Iulus and Brutus. He was going to be without his family for the first time in his life.

Elissa whooped with excitement, her hair rushing backwards in the flow. The stallion's hooves pounded the flagstones so loudly that Silvius began to fear that they would be heard back in Lavinium.

But there was no pursuit, nothing, only the silvery road stretching ahead.

Soon, Silvius reined in Blaze. In the moonlight they could see the port ahead, a small collection of wooden buildings where the river Numicus met the sea. Here the Etruscans from the north traded across to the Achaean colonists in the south of Italia, and here also came ships from all over the Middle Sea. It was not as busy as Ostium, further north, but they were still likely to find passage quickly.

They dismounted, and Silvius led Blaze to a nearby rivulet which fed into the Numicus, where the horse gulped deep draughts of water, snorting through his whiskery muzzle. Elissa released the wolf cub, and he also slurped thirstily from the edge of the bank. When they'd finished, Silvius took Blaze, turned him in the direction of Lavinium, patted him sharply on the right flank, and the horse galloped off homewards.

Silvius gazed at Elissa for a moment, the stars glittering above them, the waves of the sea tugging at the shoreline nearby. In his friend's dark eyes, Silvius saw his own excitement reflected back.

Had he made the right choice, bringing Elissa with him? He remembered his vision. The power of the snakes, and the terrible pull of Python; then Apollo's soft voice intruding, and that tantalising glimpse of light he'd had, and longed for again. It was right. They had both seen the god.

Elissa enticed the wolf cub to her hands, and hefted him up into her arms. Now they had to find a boat. First, Silvius opened his pouch to show Elissa the things he'd brought to trade: a silver amulet and a few silver pieces.

Elissa laughed, the sound piercing the wash of the tide. 'Do you want to get caught?'

'What do you mean?' Not for the first time, Silvius blushed fiercely. The amulet was the most precious thing he owned. It had been given to him by Lavinia's father Latinus to mark his tenth year.

'Imagine – Aeneas sends men after you. They hear of a young boy who's been trading costly silver pieces and an amulet made by Latin craftsmen.'

'Well, what have *you* got?' He pushed the silver back amongst his other belongings.

Elissa tipped out some corals, tin, and other cheap things.

Silvius was suddenly aware of the Arrowhead around his neck, and he concealed it beneath his tunic, feeling its surprising weight hang against his skin. Also heavy at his side was his new sword.

'Look. This is our story.' Elissa spoke softly. 'We need passage to Achaea to visit our cousins. We're the children of simple traders. We have things to trade for our passage.'

It was a good plan. 'We can offer help too,' Silvius suggested. 'I'm sure they'd be pleased to have extra hands.'

'You've never been on a boat before,' Elissa sniffed.

'Neither have you!'

'I have,' said Elissa, jutting her chin out in defiance. 'I'm always hanging about the boats on the lake.'

'That – that's different.'

'Well, I've done more than you.'

'Look, just hide the wolf cub, all right?'

'His name is Ruffler,' she said. 'Because of his ruff.' She tickled his neck and nestled him back in the pack, leaving it open a little so that he could breathe, where he remained, uncomplaining, bright eyes blinking slowly.

Nobody was about on the streets. There were really only two: a wide road that led down to the harbour, and one running across it, with a shrine at the crossing point, along which were a few settlements. No lights burned in any of the windows, and no sounds came from anywhere.

They arrived at the harbour itself. The waves were licking the shoreline gently. And here, Silvius began to get worried.

Because the whole curved bay was empty.

Not a single ship lay at anchor. His plan was suddenly in ruins. They'd need to wait till morning, by which time they would almost certainly be found.

'What do we do now?' Silvius tried not to betray his annoyance. He thought how foolish he'd been. They should have joined up with a trade convoy on the road, then they would have been bound to find a ship.

But he couldn't go home now. He was on Apollo's mission, and it had to be carried out. He shuddered at the memory of the Enemy they'd killed in Lavinium.

'We should wait till morning and ask the harbour master then,' said Elissa. 'We can find somewhere to sleep. Ruffler will keep us warm.' She tipped him out of her pack and he stretched himself gladly, his blue eyes winking in the darkness.

'We can't waste time!'

'Well, we need our sleep.'

Silvius glanced around. 'We can find somewhere out of the way.'

They began to look for a spot where they could huddle together. There was a little copse beyond the settlement, and they headed in that direction.

Ruffler suddenly stopped; he turned round and growled, hackles raised all along his back.

'What are you doing there, boy?' Elissa reached out to him.

There then came the sound of galloping hooves. Silvius's heart started to beat faster. Could it be possible? A horseman appeared on the road, coming towards them, and Ruffler set up a furious howling.

'Shut that dog up!' came a voice from a window. But Silvius didn't pay any attention.

Because coming towards them was Aeneas's stallion Blaze. He would have recognised that proud beast anywhere. And astride him, face fully lit in the moonlight, clearer and clearer as he came closer, was his older brother.

Iulus pulled up the stallion in front of them and leapt down, landing squarely on both feet in a way that Silvius couldn't help but admire, even through his anger.

He strode up to Silvius. 'What in the name of the Underworld do you think you're doing?' he spat. 'We received a message from Lavinium – I was out on this side of the woods, resting from the hunt, and a soldier came saying you were missing and so were Elissa and Blaze. When Blaze appeared looking for home, I thought at once that you'd escaped on him. Of course you *would* think to come here, wouldn't you – the obvious choice,' he sneered.

'Iulus! You can't take us back!'

'The rest of my men are approaching behind. We'll take you back to Lavinium as quick as thought. And then, by the Sky-father, you'll pay for it.'

'No! We can't – we've got to go. We must do this. For our new country. For the old. For Apollo!'

Iulus clicked his teeth together and sighed. 'When are you going to realise, little brother, that these gods do not care for us any more?' Silvius winced at his tone. Elissa was glaring at Iulus.

'They fled, long ago, beyond the skies.'

'That's not true! I've seen him! I've seen Apollo!'

'You think you've seen him. We will be able to defeat this new threat ourselves. We are strong, well-trained. And you need to learn how to obey your elders!' He struck Silvius with the back of his hand. The pain stung Silvius, and he threw Iulus off him.

Now they were squaring up to each other. Ruffler was growling deep in the back of his throat.

'Leave him alone!' Elissa called out. Iulus ignored her.

'You can't tell me what to do!' shouted Silvius. 'I have a mission—'

'You and your mission,' snarled Iulus. 'You're making a lot of trouble for us. Apollo! As if, even if he were here, he would ever choose to speak to you. It's probably a delusion.'

'I'm not coming back,' said Silvius, coldly.

'Too late,' said Iulus, and he pointed down the road. There, moving at a steady canter, were a group of about a dozen of Iulus's hunting companions, all mounted on good, strong horses.

Silvius caught Elissa's eye. There was nothing they could do. They had been stymied at the first hurdle.

Suddenly Elissa broke away and ran headlong to the harbour, Ruffler bounding at her heels, with Silvius not far behind.

'What, are you going to *swim* away?' called Iulus after them.

Silvius splashed into the freezing waves. 'There must be a boat here somewhere, a rowboat or something,' he said to Elissa. 'Can you see anything?'

'I'll try over here,' called Elissa.

'Keep looking!'

Iulus laughed, his hands on his hips. 'Give it up now, Silvius. Give it up. I almost admire you, little brother. You must get that from Aeneas, not from your Latin mother.'

The insult burned through Silvius. He knelt in the waves, his mind listing from side to side. 'Apollo,' he whispered. 'Apollo, please help me.'

'Those peasant Latins, living like beasts in their huts. I'm the only true Trojan,' Iulus spoke harshly.

Silvius was trying to pray, trying to see Apollo and feel his light. But he kept noticing the weight of the Arrowhead. Again the strange hissing noise at the edge of his hearing. The casket wanted to be opened. Stargazer had said destroy. And it had worked. His fingers moved towards it. Surely he could not use it against his brother, his brother's people. It burned against his skin.

From somewhere far off he heard Elissa. 'No, don't!' she called. 'You can't do that! You'll kill us, kill us all!'

She was kneeling beside him in the waves now, and her hand was on his arm, and he saw her quick eyes shining in the moonlight. He let his hand drop, and caught hers.

Iulus's men had reached their leader, and a few of them had dismounted to watch.

'Apollo, please . . .' called Silvius now, stronger, trying to drown out the hissing that was swelling around him. Was that a snake in the water, twisting towards them?

Elissa joined in. 'Apollo, please, we pray to you!'

Then they were both calling, 'Apollo! Apollo!' until the name was just a string of sounds, blurring and falling over each other.

'Go on,' Iulus was commanding. 'Go in and get them.'

Apollo wouldn't come. Silvius knew it. The water was boiling now, and he could see sea snakes everywhere, curving and sinuous, circling and getting ready to strike. Elissa gripped his hand tighter. 'Come, Apollo, come!' Her prayer sounded weak.

And then, from all around, a deep voice, answering them.

In amazement Silvius looked up from the roiling waves. A patch of white light was floating on the sea, which grew and expanded until it was splashing against his legs. He jumped backwards until he was on the shoreline once more, Elissa beside him.

From the centre of the light, a woman's form was rising out of the foam. She was entirely naked, and her skin was like the sea, dark and rippling, speckled with starlight. Seaweed was draped around her shoulders like a scarf.

She raised her hand and pointed at Silvius. 'You,' she said, her voice like the surf. 'You are his son. The son of Aeneas, who gave us life.'

'What?' He didn't know what she meant.

'The ships!' called Elissa. 'The ships! It's true! The Trojan ships that turned into sea nymphs!'

Silvius remembered. When the Trojans had reached Italy, their boats had been blessed with divine life, in recognition for their service.

'Apollo calls to me from on high, and I hear him. He still watches you mortals. Many of my sisters have gone now, through a gate into another world.' There was a deep sadness in her voice which touched Silvius. 'Yet for you, I will, for a time, renounce my new form, and return to the shape of a ship.'

She swam back into the sea. There the nymph drew her arms together into a point, and bowed forwards. Her eyes closed, and her body creaked and groaned and grew larger, turning entirely wooden; and then she rose out of the swell. The rush of waves that followed caused Silvius to fall flat onto his back in the surf, and he watched, open-mouthed, as a small, beautiful sailing boat raised itself from the harbour waters.

It gleamed dark grey like a dolphin's skin, the beautiful carved form of a woman as its figurehead. She spoke once more, though her lips did not move. 'Climb on now, and we will go.'

Iulus and his companions were watching in wonder. One of them had brought out a net of the sort used to catch deer, and was preparing to throw it. But Iulus stopped him, gripping his wrist.

'Let him go,' he said, thoughtfully. 'Let him go.' He called across to Silvius, 'Be strong, little brother. Be strong. You will need it.'

Silvius turned, and held up his arm in farewell.

Elissa had already swum out to the ship and was clambering up the rope ladder, the pack and the wolf cub on her back. She turned to look at Silvius, eyes alight. 'Come on!'

Silvius splashed into the waves, and gasping from the cold, swam as powerfully as he could to the bottom of the ladder, and then, panting and soaking wet, he toppled onto the deck next to Elissa. He was filled with a sense of lightness. He steadied himself on the rail that ran around the ship.

Now they were both on board, the ship turned gracefully, and began to sail towards the horizon. Silvius gripped onto the rail, and soon could see nothing; not Iulus and his companions, or the port. There was a single shout, and then they were out in the sea, the moon shining bright above them, the wolf cub tearing in excited circles at their feet.

'We're on a boat! We're out at sea!' Elissa was lit up with delight. 'Like the Phoenicians!'

They'd done it. The first stage of the journey had worked, thanks to a miracle. But Apollo had not listened only to Silvius. He looked shyly at Elissa, at the joy in her eyes. She wasn't leaving anything behind in Lavinium; no mother, no father.

'Thank you – thanks for helping me pray. I don't think I could have done it on my own.' He didn't mention the hissing and the snakes.

The sea was a stretch of blackness all around. As he turned to investigate the rest of the boat, out of the corner of his eye he spotted a red light.

He stood at the stern and watched it, skin prickling with the cold. The Enemy. They had already found a boat and were coming after them.

'What is it?' Elissa asked, frowning. The little wolf cub scampered to his side.

Silvius didn't answer for a moment. The ship creaked.

'Come on,' he said at last. 'Let's see if we can find somewhere to sleep.' They would soon see in the morning.

Twelve

Revelation

Tisamenos set two oil lamps in his window, as Hero had told him to do as a sign that he'd performed his task, and sat on the edge of his silken bed to wait. The Last Gorgon's head, its snakes still clamped to the shield, was in the sack at his feet.

He did not like to be near it, but he did not want it to be far from him either.

He had avoided Agatha, asking one of the maidservants to fill up the copper bath for him. Earlier, as he had sunk into the warm water, he had become increasingly aware of a low, hollow tapping sound. He'd thought it was coming from water dripping onto the stone, but could not locate the source of it.

He had scrubbed away the blood and gore from his body. A stone jug full of small ale stood on a table within reach, and he gulped down a mouthful. Then, after soaking for as long as he could, he stepped out, and looked at himself in a mirror.

His face and body was spotted with livid welts where the venom had got him. The middle finger of his left hand had gone, and the stone stump was heavy and painful. How he would explain all this to his father and his nurse he did not know. Delicately he tapped the place above his right ear. It was hard, harder than bone.

In shock, he examined it in his reflection as carefully as he could. The skin was discoloured, grey even.

A terrible thought came to him: he had been affected by the Last Gorgon. It wasn't only his finger – a small patch of his head had turned to stone.

He'd closed his eyes, steadying himself on the edge of the bath. The tapping sound became louder. Where was it coming from? He stared at the sack. But it wasn't that. Again and again it came, and he accidentally knocked over the table with his elbow as he turned to look. Ale splashed everywhere.

A rage gripped him, and he turned over a chest, kicking the contents all over the place – tunics, sword belts, a fine ivory draughts set – until he sat down in the middle of his room and placed his hands over his ears.

Now the tapping sounded even louder. It rang around inside him, seeming to overwhelm everything else.

Then he realised. It was horrifying, but it was the only explanation.

It was coming from inside his mind.

He looked at himself once more in the mirror. His own eyes glared back at him, lidded, heavy, with a hardness he'd not seen in them before.

Now, calmer and quieter, he sat in his hunting tunic, a dark linen cloak ready beside him, a new pair of sandals on his feet. He did not know in what guise the Swallows' reply would come, but he was ready for anything.

Later, after about two hours had passed, judging by the level of oil in the lamps, his skin was itching, and even though he knew the Last Gorgon was dead, the presence of her severed head so near to him was a real, malevolent thing.

He had to stay awake. But he was so, so tired. His eyes were drooping.

And then he was back in the cave. The rank smell, the dankness. And he had no reflective shield, no sword; he was defenceless, and a beautiful woman was coming towards him, stretching out her arms, eyes so deep he felt himself falling into them, and her hand was grasped around his wrist, and it was turning into a talon . . .

Something tickled his nose. He opened his eyes and saw, drifting to the sheepskin rug at his feet, a swallow's feather.

He stretched out a hand and caught it.

Another one fell, and he caught that one too, automatically, with his left hand.

A third and then a fourth fell at his feet. Suddenly, a torrent of feathers whirled down from the ceiling, swooping around his body, tickling his skin, knocking him off balance. A voice, clear through the rustling, issuing an order. 'Grab the Last Gorgon's head.'

He crawled the few hands' breadth to where the sack was, and took hold of it firmly. He could feel the head beneath the material. It was horribly cold.

The rustling and the wind immediately stopped, and Tisamenos looked up. He was no longer in his room. He was somewhere else, somewhere he didn't recognise. This wasn't where he'd first met the Swallows. Alert, he was aware how defenceless he was. But he was ready now.

The chamber was much larger, cut into stone, perhaps underground. Seated on four stone chairs were figures in masks: a swallow, a lion, a dragon and a bear. There was light coming from somewhere, bright, flickering.

'Who are you?' shouted Tisamenos. 'What is this place?'

'We are the Swallows,' answered a voice, though Tisamenos could not tell where it came from. 'We watch and we wait, until we will act.'

He lifted up the sack so that it was level with his head, the stone ringing in his skull. 'You sent me into danger,' he said, voice thrilling with anger. 'I went into the cave of the Last Gorgon. I faced her, and I defeated her. So much for my softness.' He hurled the bag down at the feet of the watchers. 'I dare you. I dare you to open it.' He held up his mutilated hand so that they could see the stump.

None of the figures moved.

'Cowards,' he snarled. 'Hiding behind tricks and masks!'

A voice came from the lion mask. 'We did not know Euryale was still alive. I am sorry.'

Tisamenos exploded. 'Open it! Open it and see – look on her! Then tell me who killed my mother. I have earned that.'

The figure in the swallow mask stood up and revealed her face. It was Hero, looking with interest at Tisamenos. She made the sign to avert the evil eye, and opened up the sack. Immediately she gasped, closed the bag, then gingerly tipped the head out onto the floor.

The shield and the head clattered onto the stone, locked in eternal admiration.

'The head of the Last Gorgon – think what we could do with that . . .' gasped the figure in the dragon mask.

'Remove your masks,' commanded Hero, sharply. The seated figures did so, some slowly, some fast. Sitting there was the tall thug, who nodded, eyes downcast, at Tisamenos. The one with long moustaches bowed low, and clasped his hands together. The dancing girl simply stared at him.

'You have faced more danger than I imagined,' said the thug. 'Our tasks were not so difficult. You have given us a thing of great power.'

But Tisamenos was too quick. In a second he clamped down on the head, and returned it to the sack, out of reach behind his back.

'Tell me,' he demanded. 'Who killed Hermione? Who killed my mother, the daughter of Helen, the most beautiful woman in the world?'

Hero said, 'What will you do with this knowledge?'

'I will act on it.'

'What will you do? Answer truly.'

Tisamenos's voice was strong. 'I will take my revenge. It is in my blood.'

A half-smile played across Hero's lips.

'Do you swear?'

Tisamenos clenched his hands together, feeling the stump, the pain of the past day, all the past years.

'I swear by the gods above and the gods below, I will take my revenge.'

'Then take your revenge,' said Hero, gently, 'on your new mother. Erigone.'

Thirteen

An Attack

THE TYRRHENIAN SEA

Dawn was touching the edges of the sky when Silvius and Elissa had fully recovered themselves. Ruffler, the wolf cub, was curled up between them as they lay in the small cabin below deck, his head on Elissa's thigh. Silvius, wanting air, clambered up the rope ladder and went out onto the deck, lifting Ruffler up with him.

Above them a white sail spread out, filled with the wind. They were far out to sea, and could not see land anywhere.

But still, on the horizon behind them, the red light was following them.

A sudden panic gripped Silvius. He did not know where they were, or even where they were going. He had never been on the open sea before, and he found the lack of any trees or cover disturbing. The motion was also making him feel distinctly unwell.

After a few seconds he pitched towards the port side of the ship, looking about him with his back to the sea. His stomach heaved suddenly, and he was sick over the railing. Queasily he slumped down.

The ship was quite small, and, as Silvius watched, he was amazed to see that it was sailing itself, making little adjustments to ropes and sails. The helm was moving from side to side, as if an invisible hand were guiding it. He wondered if he could still talk to the ship nymph, and made his way to the bow where the carving was. Ruffler, ears pricking up, followed him, gambolling at his heels. Silvius watched the foam breaking off the keel.

The carved effigy of the nymph was looking out to sea. She had bluish skin that seemed to change as the surface of the water changed, like wine in a bowl, and the hair was white like foam. Silvius did not know how to address a ship nymph, so he said, 'Be well, nymph of Aeneas's fleet. May I ask where we are going?'

Elissa appeared through the hatch, mightily cheerful.

'By the Skyfather, when I woke up I thought I was on a boat! Then I realised we are! We did it then!' She stamped her feet in the circling dance the maidens performed back in Lavinium on feast days. Marvelling at her steadiness, Silvius glugged down some water she held out to him, and managed a weak grin back at her.

A gull swooped down and perched on the rigging, regarding them steadily.

'Good morning, ship nymph!' called Elissa, pouring some water onto the deck as a libation.

'Good morning,' came a voice from all around them. The gull flapped off. Ruffler cowered in a corner, and Elissa rushed to comfort him. It was the ship nymph. 'We sail to Sicilia. I will see you safely there, as this I have sworn to Apollo.'

'I thank you,' said Silvius. And then, in answer to his un-asked question, the gull reappeared, and dropped a flapping fish at their feet.

They had brought tinder and kindling, and soon a fire was crackling and they were roasting the fish in the embers. It was the best fish Silvius had ever tasted, and he and Elissa greedily scoffed it down, letting the juice run over their chins; they ate the burnt, blackened skin with relish, not even minding if they crunched on a bone or two.

When they had finished, Silvius went to look out to sea. The red light was nearer now, and appeared to be coming from a small rowing boat with two hunched figures in it.

'It's still there.' He hugged himself.

Elissa shuddered. 'We need to keep an eye on them,' she said. 'I'll watch first.'

'Thank you.' Silvius sat by the mast. He took the chain off his neck, lifting it over his head, and stared at the shimmering black casket containing the Arrowhead.

It made him dizzy. He wondered if Apollo had a message for him still, and he closed his eyes, pressing both hands onto the lid. His mind went blank.

Apollo, he thought. Apollo, come to me.

But there was nothing; no light, no handsome young man. Only the power of the Arrowhead throbbing darkly. He saw Elissa watching him with a concerned expression.

'Your stomach,' she said.

'It's fine.'

'You don't look well.'

It was true. And it wasn't just the seasickness.

'Why don't you rest for a bit. I'll call you if anything happens,' said Elissa, and Silvius went thankfully down into the cool of the cabin beneath.

The bare wooden space, cramped and uncomfortable, reminded him of something. Guiltily he remembered taking the casket from his sleeping father.

This was how Aeneas had spent so much of his life, Silvius realised. This was why his room was so bare. Perhaps this ship nymph had been the same one that had carried him from Troy. Away from the burning city, away from everything that he had known, into a world of monsters and war. He had seen so much, and now he was trying to build a new home for his people. And Silvius wanted, more than anything, to prove to his father that he could be a hero too.

A Latin lullaby Lavinia used to sing to him drifted through his mind.

> *Lulla lulla*
> *Sleep, my child*
> *Lulla lulla lay . . .*

And he was soon asleep. He slept lightly, though. He dreamed. The rope coiled in the corner of the cabin began to uncurl by itself, and it slithered towards him, turning and turning in ever widening circles, and he realised with a sickening lurch that it was no rope but a great snake, revealing its smooth pointed head, its enormous dripping fangs, and those two glowing red eyes.

'I know what you have . . .' hissed the snake. It was slithering towards him, longer than a man.

'You have felt, it, haven't you . . .'

'I don't want it.'

'You saw what the Arrowhead can do. Think what you could do with it! Imagine, no Iulus – you could rule Lavinium and all of Italia.' The snake was nearing him, the teeth gleaming. 'You can learn how to use it, so that it does not harm you. The centaur was stupid.'

It was true. He could go back now, and with the Arrowhead he would be the most powerful person there; more so than his father, than Iulus, than Latinus . . . The snake's red eyes glowed, and Silvius shook himself.

'I don't want it. I've sworn to destroy you . . .' Suddenly the snake was around him, the grip so tight he felt it was squeezing the life out of him.

A shout woke him. He sat upright in the berth, gripping the Arrowhead. He looked down. He was all tangled up in rope. Terrified, he pushed it off him. There was a red mark on his belly.

Python. He'd come to him in a dream, had somehow caused the rope to wrap itself around him.

'Silvius! Come up! Now!'

A second later he was scrambling up onto the deck. 'What is it?'

Elissa was pointing out to sea. The boat was much nearer.

There were two people in it, rowing steadily, and apparently gaining on them. Now they were close enough to see that these people had the glowing red eyes of those controlled by the Enemy.

A frightening thought flashed through Silvius's head. Had they taken Iulus? Perhaps it was Iulus, himself possessed. If it was, would he have to face up to the thought of killing his own brother? His dream came back to him.

No. Pushing all those things away from him, he grabbed Elissa by the elbow.

'I could try the Arrowhead, divert the force or something.' Guiltily he remembered what Python had said.

'No! You'll kill us both!' Elissa was shocked.

'Is there nothing else on the ship? No other weapon?' They only had their bows; they could not afford to lose too many arrows in the sea.

'Let's look.'

They searched it thoroughly, but there were only ropes and a pair of oars. It was as if they were not in a ship at all. Again Silvius was struck by the strange grey texture of the ship's surface.

The Enemy's boat was now near enough for Silvius and Elissa to be able to see who was rowing it. One was a squat, middle-aged woman; the other was a young man, not much older than Silvius himself. The red glow from their eyes lit up the boat, and as he looked, the two hunched figures seemed to be the coils of a serpent rippling in the water.

Their ship was rocking.

The ship nymph's voice moaned in wild anguish. Silvius and Elissa were thrown from side to side, a flap of wet sail hitting Silvius in the face.

'The Enemy!' he shouted. 'It must be hurting her.'

'What shall we do?' Elissa yelled, as waves crashed over and drenched them.

'Try to shoot them in the head.'

His eyes stinging, Silvius scrambled around for his weapons.

They strung their bows with great difficulty, balancing on the slippery deck, though it was tilting violently.

Silvius managed to notch an arrow and took aim. It was impossible – he was swinging wildly, his targets moving too. At least the Enemy boat was travelling in a straight line. He would have to try his best.

Their ship listed sideways. 'Silvius!' Elissa called, dark eyes alive with fear, and suddenly she was diving across him, landing on Ruffler, only just preventing the wolf cub from being hurled overboard. As their ship heaved, Silvius fell too, dropping his bow and arrows.

The Enemy boat approached, relentless as the tide itself.

Fourteen

Electra

MYKENAI, ACHAEA: KINGHOUSE OF THE LION

The knowledge of his mother's killer smouldered inside Tisamenos like an ember.

Erigone.

Erigone.

Erigone.

The name echoed in his skull. Erigone had killed his mother Hermione, so that she could marry Orestes. She had done it in revenge for the murder of her own father Aegisthos.

And that meant that now his half-brother Penthilos had been born, both Tisamenos and Orestes were in danger. She had a son, a claimant to the throne. She could kill Orestes and exile Tisamenos.

Or kill them both.

The whirl of swallow feathers had deposited him back in his room. Now he sat once more among the silk and the finery of his chamber. He didn't know what time of day or night it was. He couldn't see the sun out of his window, but the shadows in his room were long.

Agatha burst into the room, mid-sentence: '. . . looking after this princeling when there's a new baby to see to . . .' She spotted Tisamenos and immediately he covered up his mutilated hand. Her eyes narrowed. 'And where have you been? Gallivanting about all day . . .'

'All day?'

'Yes, all day, and you know that very well too.'

Her eyesight was none too good, and she didn't appear to notice the marks on his face. He would have to find a way to keep his hand covered permanently. His mind was spinning, and he ignored Agatha as she flounced about the room, plumping up cushions and rootling in chests. Eventually, when she had finished whatever she had come in to do, she left, still mid-flow, and Tisamenos went to the door and stood with his back against it, out of breath.

Who could he turn to? He had sworn to take his revenge.

The Swallows – what were their motives? They'd wanted the head of the Last Gorgon as a weapon, but for what? Were they bent on the destruction of his family, his kinghouse?

He'd kept the Last Gorgon's head. He had not wanted to render it to them, unsure of their plans. Because he held it still, they had not been able to take it from him.

And if he did take his revenge on Erigone, what would then happen? Orestes would have him killed, surely, or exiled.

Maybe that was a better fate. To be exiled, into the lands of Achaea. To be a wanderer among the cities, like the bards; an adventurer, living on his wits alone.

And at what price?

He remembered the stories. How Orestes had been haunted by the Furies when he'd killed Clytemnestra.

But Electra had helped him. And Electra was still alive.

A thought fired through Tisamenos.

Electra. His aunt Electra. He would go and see her now. She had always been rather a distant figure, glimpsed at ceremonies and the larger family events, a dark-clothed, ghostly presence.

She knew about revenge. She knew its cost.

He found his aunt in her quarters, near those of the women of the kinghouse, but spacious and apart.

Arrows of light pierced the gloom in her apartment. She was standing by the window, looking out, as she often did, at nothing, her hands clasped to her bosom. Her attendants were not with her.

There was no loom in the room. Electra did not occupy herself with weaving. The only furnishing was a small table with a chair set by it, and on it an open wax tablet on which Electra had been marking something down.

Before he announced himself, she said his name softly, and then turned round. Her face was cast in shadow, and

Tisamenos thought she looked old. Her skin was wrinkled and sagging, her eyes surrounded by darkened skin. She wore black, as she had done for as long as Tisamenos could remember, like a peasant woman from the outlying villages. Her hands, though, were unblemished by work. Faced with her staring eyes, Tisamenos blushed.

Electra never quite looked anyone in the eye. Even now she stared slightly over his shoulder, as if waiting for someone. Someone who would never come. Tisamenos stuttered a greeting.

'Be . . . be glad, my lady Electra . . .'

'The kinghouse can never rest,' she said, ignoring his politeness and feeling the stone walls with her long, pale fingers. 'I listen to her breathing. She has seen so much. There was never a family that has suffered as ours has. Every day I relive it all . . .' She gasped and coughed, and held a hand to her throat. Tisamenos ran to help her, but she pushed him away, instead gripping onto the window sill for support.

'I wanted to ask you something,' said Tisamenos. 'About . . .' He steeled himself. 'Revenge.'

Electra let out a cry. 'I knew it would happen! I knew it, I knew it!' She spoke with cold fervour. 'You don't understand what it was like, to watch that vile Aegisthos with my mother . . . You don't know how long I had to wait for Orestes to come . . . Always looking for him; every stranger that came into the palace, I wondered if it was him. And then he came! Revenge. They call it revenge. It wasn't revenge, it was natural!'

She went to the table and picked up the wax tablet. 'Here,' she said. 'I set it all down, all of our bloody history. You must learn it, Tisamenos, you must learn it and know that we did the right thing.' She seemed infused with a strange inner light, like a beacon, and she pressed the tablet upon him, her hands forming into claws, the sinews in them straining.

There was a sound at the door, and Electra looked up sharply. 'Orestes? Orestes, is that you?'

The door opened, and a flurry of Electra's women entered. They tutted at Tisamenos and ushered him towards the door. 'Can't you see you've upset her?'

'But I need to know. I need to know! Electra!' He called again. 'Electra! Is it worth it? Is revenge worth it?'

She caught his gaze then, and it was like looking into the eyes of a spirited horse. She smiled, slowly. And then she began to laugh, a hollow, mad laugh.

Tisamenos dropped the tablet and fled. Even the closing of the stone door did not muffle the laughter, and it rang in his mind until he found a quiet corner near the kitchens, where he paused, breathing in the smell of roasting boars.

Who else was there? Nobody in the whole kinghouse, in the whole city of Mykenai, could help him now. *Revenge . . . it's natural!* Electra's words pulsed through his head.

He ran, bewildered, through the corridors, ever pursued by that mocking laugh, which was joining now with the tapping noise in his head, booming louder and louder.

He bumped into a secretary as he rounded a corner; he

knocked a stone jug from a maid's hand, and milk spilled all over the corridor. He ran, until he was outside in the dusty streets among the goats and the pigs and the dirt, and then he continued running, blindly, until he was at the massive stone wall on the edge of the citadel. The Lion Gate loomed above him, vast, the two carved lions facing each other.

Here, under the shadow of the gate, with nobody looking on, he threw himself down into the dust, and wept, until he could weep no more.

Through the confusion of his mind loomed Orestes, stroking Erigone's cheek, holding Penthilos in the crook of his arm, saying, 'I see myself in him.' And Electra, raving, twisted by her single-minded purpose, stretching out those terrible hands, those long white fingers.

Even when the sun went down, he did not notice the cold.

Fifteen

Python

THE TYRRHENIAN SEA

Tilting, the ship was creaking alarmingly. Elissa grabbed Ruffler and managed to squash him, squealing, into a pouch slung around her neck. She steadied herself. What was the matter with Silvius? He wasn't moving. He'd dropped his bow and arrow. Hers were too far away to reach.

'Silvius! Get up!' He seemed distant, glazed.

A wave crashed and drenched him. Spluttering, he gripped the side of the ship and pulled himself up, acknowledging Elissa as if he'd only just realised she was there.

'They're nearly on us!'

The Enemy were now only a few boat lengths away. The red glow from their eyes was tingeing the sea, making it seem like they were forging through a lake of blood. If it wasn't for that, they would have resembled a woman and her son out for a fishing trip.

Trembling, Elissa leaped forwards and grabbed the fallen bow. It was like an eel in her hands. Cursing, she managed to fit the arrow to the string.

She remembered shooting deer and birds in the forest outside Lavinium, and pretended to herself that she was on dry land; that made it easier to stand firm.

She sighted along the arrow. She needed to aim a little nearer to the ship, as the rowing boat was moving so fast.

Should she go for the bulky woman, or the young man? The woman looked stronger, but they were both rowing with equal intensity. The woman had long, curling brown hair. It could have been any of the women in Lavinium. She wondered who was waiting for her, back on land. Whether there was a little girl, feet bare, asking for her mother in some village.

The man was on the side nearer to Elissa. So, biting her tongue, she imagined she was simply shooting a grouse, and twanged the bowstring, letting loose the arrow.

The arrow struck the port side of the boat and skittered into the waves.

Silvius was now beside Elissa. 'I'll hold you steady,' he said, bracing himself, gripping her by the waist. The extra weight was just what she needed.

No longer trembling, she fitted another arrow, sighted, took into account the motion of the rowing boat. A twang of the bowstring. This time the arrow stuck firmly into its keel.

'It's too difficult!'

'Let me try,' said Silvius. They swapped places, Elissa steadying him, but his arrow overshot, making a white splash in the red sea.

'We're losing too many arrows,' she said.

'We'll have to fight them here.' Silvius sounded uncertain.

'They'll have to climb on board first – we'll get them before that.'

'Push them back into the sea.'

It seemed impossible. But it was the only thing they could do.

They found two oars, and stood waiting with their bows as the Enemy's boat beat remorselessly onwards.

These moments were unbearable. Ruffler was whimpering at Elissa's chest. She could hear the relentlessness of the Enemy's oar strokes; the cries of the ship nymph; Silvius, trying to breathe calmly next to her. All was held in tension, waiting for something to snap.

Elissa could now see the young man clearly. He was handsome, with black curly hair and a pale, sensitive face. A sick feeling surged through her. She knew this young man. She'd seen him, one of the traders from the outlying settlements, bringing pottery for sale to Lavinium. He'd shown her how to paint the figure of a god on a stone. She glanced at Silvius, but he showed no glimmer of recognition.

With an expression of blank determination, the trader threw a grappling hook over the ship's side. As if she had been bitten, the ship nymph screamed in response.

Elissa was ready, and rushed to try to prise the hook off, Silvius clawing at it too. But it was biting, hard.

A pebble hit Elissa sharply on the cheek, and she staggered and lost her grip. The woman was throwing them. It was enough time for the young man to hurl another hook and lock the two craft together.

As quickly as a cormorant swooping into the sea, the woman vaulted onto the ship. Elissa shot from close range.

Half a breath later, the arrow pierced the woman's thigh. She took as little notice of it as she might a wasp's sting, and drew a long sword from her belt, advancing on them.

Elissa was terrified. She had never fought like this, could not fight off a woman possessed by Python and armed with a sword, the red light from her eyes glowing demonic. There was no emotion in her face at all.

A movement caught Elissa's attention to her right. She saw with dismay that Silvius was fingering the casket holding the Arrowhead.

'Don't,' she muttered.

'Centaurs are wilder than us. I think I can control it.'

'Don't risk it now!'

As the woman advanced, the curly-haired young man also leapt over the side, and the pair strode forwards in a pincer movement.

'You're still people!' shouted Elissa. 'You have homes, families, friends!'

Implacably the two marched onwards, forcing Elissa and Silvius against the stern.

The bag Elissa was carrying moved, and out shot Ruffler. He landed on the deck, and then skittered straight towards the woman, biting her in the leg. She stumbled.

Instinctively Elissa notched another arrow, this time as quickly and as neatly as if she was on dry land, and it lodged in the woman's neck.

She fell to her knees, clutching at her throat, but she did not utter a sound.

The red light left her eyes, and for a moment she became just a terrified dying woman.

Elissa had killed someone. Someone who had had the terrible misfortune to be taken by Python. She felt suddenly numb.

'Where ... what ... My flower! My little flower!' She sobbed, and then she was gone. Her body slumped onto the deck, and a wave caught it, and rolled it over the side of the ship.

Elissa ran to where the body had disappeared, and watched it dip under the surface, hair floating around the body.

A harsh grip was on her shoulder. The curly-haired man, the one who'd been so patient with the paintbrush, had her in his grasp. She shrieked.

'Give the Arrowhead to me,' her captor hissed. 'Give it to me, or I will kill her.'

'Don't!' squealed Elissa.

Ruffler bit into the Enemy's leg, and worried at it. But he took no notice.

'Python rises,' said the man, eyes glowing crimson. 'He calls us and he rises. He will take back his lands. He will rule Delphi! The gods are leaving. Python will return. You will all worship him. Give it to me, join us and live!'

'Don't!' shouted Elissa once more. The young man kicked Ruffler away, and the wolf cub arched his back, baring his teeth. Elissa watched Silvius, aghast. The golden chain glinted on his neck.

Looking at the Enemy, Silvius nodded, briefly. 'Tell me what to do,' he said. A clammy terror gripped Elissa. Was Silvius giving in? She searched desperately for some sign in his eyes, but he was ignoring her. Had Python got to him already?

'No, Silvius, please!'

Waves crashed over the deck, and the Enemy held out his hand and smiled.

Sixteen

News from Italia

Orestes was drunk again. Lolling on a plush silken cushion on a chair at the head of the great table in the feasting hall, he leaned over too far and fell off, landing on his face.

The hundreds of guests all roared with laughter and banged the table with their goblets. Erigone, seated next to Orestes, joined in, adding her shrill voice to the cacophony. Sheep and oxen were roasting on spits all around the edges; the men were yelling and boasting, as usual, whilst dancing girls fluttered in the alleyways and delicate-featured boy cupbearers kept the strong wine flowing. Smoke billowed through the halls. Everyone was befuddled with drink.

Everyone apart from Tisamenos, who watched from his position nearby. He had fashioned a kind of linen bandage for his hand; he couldn't help feeling it, where the stump was. The echoing in his head had gone, drowned out by his thoughts of revenge, but his fingers kept straying up to the stone section of his skull, as if they could not quite believe it had happened.

He was paying close attention to whatever Erigone did. She was reaching down to help Orestes up, her hand on his goblet. She released her fingers from it as he came back up, seemingly careless of it, and Orestes, with the aid of a couple of other friends, reappeared at the table to a chorus of cheers.

'I'm fine, I'm fine,' Orestes stuttered. His lips were purple from wine.

Erigone caught Tisamenos looking at her, and for a moment a cloud passed over her apparently joyful features. It cleared quickly, though, and she beckoned to him.

'Come and join your parents, Tisamenos,' she smiled.

Tisamenos scraped his chair on the floor, and walked over, slowly, keeping his bandaged hand half-hidden.

'My, you've broken out,' said Erigone, looking him up and down. 'All those pimples. We'll have to get you some poultices. Isn't your nurse looking after you properly? Come and sit by your mother.'

The babyish insinuations didn't hurt him any more. Orestes belched, and called for another goblet of wine. Tisamenos kept his head downcast as if he were a little shy of Erigone. He would let her think that he was warming to her.

'Now now, Tisamenos,' purred Erigone as she arranged a cushion behind his back. 'We've had our differences. But we should be friends, don't you think so?'

Tisamenos watched as she poured him a goblet of wine and added water to it. She pushed the heavy gold goblet towards him. It was carved, he noted, with the image of a lion. She was using his father's emblem as if it were hers. He grasped it by the stem and brought it to his lips, taking as small a sip as he dared so as not to get drunk. Then he set it down again.

'I heard you visited Electra,' she said, quietly. She was smiling, her eyes lit up. But Tisamenos could hear the ice in her voice.

'Yes, of course – I always visit her.' The lie came to him surprisingly easily.

'A fine thing, to be so close to one's relatives.'

Tisamenos realised she must have a spy among Electra's women. He'd been stupid. He should have known. Did that mean she knew that they had been talking about revenge? Did she know what was in his heart? Now he must act the innocent, maybe even pretend to be on her side. He wondered how long it would be before she made her move.

Orestes was slapping his good leg, as a bard had appeared and was singing about the great deeds of his father Agamemnon at Troy.

> *The wide-ruling king, beloved by all*
> *Set sail with a thousand black ships*
> *To rescue fair Helen, the bride of his brother,*
> *Whom weak-hearted Paris had stolen . . .*

'Have you thought about being king?' Erigone was speaking softly, twisting her fingers in her hair.

Tisamenos remained mute. Act dumb. That was the way.

'Things don't always turn out as you'd expect,' said Erigone. 'My father was king here, you know. For a while. Whilst your grandfather sat on his haunches on the shores of Troy.' She was silent, and there was no mistaking the look in her eyes now. It was calculating, cool, the words a veiled threat.

She clearly suspected that he knew about Hermione, and fixed him with her gaze. It was penetrating.

He did his best to appear completely innocent, and looked away first.

Then she clapped her hands.

'Sing the song of Cassandra!'

The bard faltered.

'Bard!'

He began again, singing of how she was dragged from the steps of her altar and taken as a slave by Agamemnon. A frown passed across Orestes's face.

Tisamenos immediately looked about to see if Hero was there – and she was, in the corner, half in shadow, watching. Her own mother, sung about in the halls of her enemy. But Hero made no sign of annoyance, or even of recognition, and simply folded her arms.

Tisamenos knew what she was capable of now, what the Swallows could do, what their magic could do. He wanted to go and talk to her, to find out more, but couldn't let Erigone see him do so.

The great doors to the hall burst open, and a man came running in, straight up to Orestes; shouting over the bard, he said, 'Orestes, King of Mykenai, I bring a message.'

'So urgent?' answered Orestes, removing his hand from a flute-player's bare shoulder and putting down his goblet. The hall went silent, except for the occasional muttering or drunken belch.

'Our friend in Italia says there is trouble there. Certain information is not forthcoming, but an army is massing in the north. And he gave me this to give to you.' He held out a sealed tablet, and bowed.

Orestes suddenly straightened. Erigone pursed her lips as Orestes broke the seal and studied the tablet carefully. Then, without warning, he stood up, pushing back his chair, and strode towards the great doors. As if remembering something, he stopped, and said, 'Tisamenos. Come with me.'

'Orestes?' called Erigone.

'Just Tisamenos,' replied the king.

'But, Orestes, if it's news, shouldn't we discuss it together?'

'I said just Tisamenos.'

Giddily Tisamenos got up and went to his father, leaving Erigone fuming.

'Come,' said his father, looking at him with an expression that Tisamenos could not read. There was worry there, certainly, but also something that Tisamenos had never seen before. Fear. And behind that, a glimpse of the warrior that Orestes had once been.

'You're surprised,' said Orestes.

'I . . . I thought you were drunk.'

'Sometimes it's good to appear softer than you are. Follow.' He grabbed a torch from an attendant.

Tisamenos went at his heels, through the dank corridors of the kinghouse, past the old storeroom that had fallen in, and into a quarter that he'd never seen before. It was dark, forgotten, damp. Moss grew on the walls, and there were no torches lighting the way. The pool of light from his father's flame was small, and he stumbled often.

Looking from side to side, Orestes went to the darkest corner and pushed at something. A stone in the wall slid, groaning, to the right.

The king went through, Tisamenos after him. Orestes pressed the lever that must have opened the door, and then they were in total darkness.

Seventeen

Cai

'I will give the Arrowhead to you,' said Silvius, dangling the casket out to the curly-haired young man who had his arm around Elissa's neck. 'Let her go first.' It was the only thing he could do. He saw Elissa's expression change from horror to determination, and she struggled against her captor's grasp.

'The Arrowhead.' The Enemy was toneless, implacable.

'I will give you the Arrowhead,' Silvius continued, steadily, 'when I have my hand on Elissa.'

'Move forwards,' hissed the Enemy.

Silvius did so. The Enemy's eyes glowed and flared in anticipation. He released Elissa, keeping hold of her shoulder, and at the same time, he reached for the Arrowhead.

'Silvius!' choked Elissa. 'I know this man! He's from the villages . . . Do you recognise him?'

136

The curly hair, the pale cheeks. Yes, Silvius realised, he had seen him, in Lavinium.

'I think his name is Cai!'

There was a flicker in the red glow.

'Cai.' Silvius kept his voice calm, though he was trembling all over. 'Do you remember Elissa?'

'You came to Lavinium,' she took over, 'a few months ago now, when the winter was hard. You had some pottery with you – your father had made it. I asked you how you drew the wood god, and you showed me, with your fine paintbrush.'

Something seemed to shift inside Cai. A glimpse of blue-grey eyes behind the red. 'Elissa . . .'

'Yes.' Silvius swallowed. 'And I'm Silvius.'

Cai's grip loosened.

'Elissa . . . Silvius . . .'

'Yes, that's right . . .'

'Elisssssa . . . Sssilviusss . . .' Their names began to shade into the hissing of a snake. A change came over Cai's face. His features hardened, his mouth set into a harsh line. 'Python is here . . . and Python rises,' roared the Enemy, and he lunged for the casket, as Silvius went for Elissa's right hand, dodging out of the way.

The Enemy grinned, and suddenly his face was no longer the same. He was a man, still, but his skin was scaled, as if some hidden snake part of him was coming to the surface, and his eyes were yellow with a black slit of a pupil. A flickering forked tongue appeared between his sharp white teeth.

'My enemy's weapon,' he hissed. 'Give it to me. The Oracle will be mine again. And I will reclaim my own!' There was exultation in his voice, and now his whole body was stretching into a long, thin snake, curling powerfully, the size of a man, yet with human hands, one still grasping Elissa.

There were two forces tugging at Silvius. Perhaps he should yield. How could they hope, he and Elissa, to destroy this creature? They were so small, and Python's powers were so vast.

Then he caught sight of Elissa's pale face. She was pulling as hard as she could against those unrelenting fingers.

'No!' he shouted. The Enemy hissed, and cast Elissa aside. She fell, sprawling, to the floor.

The casket was glowing brightly, and already giving out heat. A horrible smell filled Silvius's nostrils and he looked down to see the Enemy's fingers blackening. 'You will not keep it from me, boy.'

Silvius, terrified, grasped the chain. Though it was searing into his skin, he dulled the pain with an effort of willpower.

There was no divine vision. Just the eyes of the Enemy, and his burnt fingers clamped around the box, dragging the chain forwards, so that it dug into Silvius's neck. The flesh fell away from the Enemy's hands, which meant that for the smallest of moments he lost his grip, and Silvius jerked away, whilst his adversary lunged back at him, now in the form of a man once more.

Something smacked the Enemy on the side of the head, and he stumbled. It was Elissa, panting, with an oar. Hardly thinking,

Silvius kicked him hard in the stomach, and the Enemy wobbled, keeling over. But all the time he was smiling.

'Ship nymph!' Elissa called. 'Help us!'

'He's too powerful . . .'

'Please!'

'Hold fast . . . I'll try . . .'

Elissa scooped up Ruffler, and both she and Silvius flung themselves at the rigging, grabbing on. The Enemy was crawling towards them, dragging himself forwards, pointed tongue still flickering from his human mouth.

Nothing could stop him.

The world tilted, as the ship nymph rolled herself port-wards, hurling the Enemy off balance. As he scrambled uselessly to find purchase, she shifted herself starboard. The Enemy, taken unawares, was flung over the side of the ship, and landed with a great splash in the sea.

The ship nymph righted herself, and the two companions rushed to look out. A brief flash of red lit up the waters from beneath.

Then there was nothing.

They collapsed, exhausted, onto the deck.

'Thank you, ship nymph,' said Silvius to the figurehead when they had recovered.

She inclined her mast in reply.

'Python's forces reach far . . .' Elissa said. 'Apollo told us to go to Sicilia. Will we find directions there? I don't think that I can face another attack like that.'

'I hope so . . . And I don't think I can either . . .' They lay, side by side, until the terrifying memory of the snake-like man was eclipsed by the gentle sound of the waves.

After a while, Elissa got up and began murmuring quietly to the ship nymph, looking about to see what damage had been done. Where the grappling hook had cut into the side, there was a darker shade, as if the ship had been bruised. She paused there and stroked it gently. Silvius busied himself with tidying up their belongings, cleaning the oar and making sure the bows and arrows were in working order.

Then, when they had finished their tasks, Silvius stood at the helm and let his thoughts wander, whilst Elissa and Ruffler played together.

'What do you know about Python?' Silvius asked the ship nymph.

'He was one of the most powerful gods before the Olympians came,' she replied, her voice seeming to come from all over the ship. 'He used to rule from Delphi, and then Apollo defeated him. And now the Olympians are leaving, he wants to return.' The ship shuddered along her beautiful length.

'So after Sicilia, where should we go?'

'You may find out in Sicilia. It is not given to me to know any more. We nymphs do not have the gift of prophecy. Although some say it is more of a curse.'

The ship nymph, calm now, sailed placidly on. Occasionally a dolphin or two would leap around the bow, and click in its own tongue, exchanging news with her.

As Elissa was gazing out over the stern, she called excitedly, 'Look! Silvius! Quickly!'

Joining her, Silvius's eyes followed the length of her arm, and saw, rising out of the white foam of the sea, the wild, pale faces of the sea nymphs. They pointed and stared, and as the ship approached them – a little haughtily, perhaps – the sea nymphs scattered. The ship nymph, aware of their attention, opened the eyes of her figurehead, and said, 'Poor things. They've never seen such a thing as me before. Peace, sisters, go back to your watery homes.' But Silvius could tell she was proud of being a new, wondrous thing. The sea nymphs, giggling, dove back down into the depths, seaweedy hair trailing behind them.

Soon a dark mass hove into view on the horizon. It was now late in the afternoon, and the sun's heat was mellower, and Silvius and Elissa stood watching as the land mass resolved itself into mountains, woods, harbours and shorelines.

It was a relief to see land again, although Silvius did not know what dangers might await them there. But there was no way they could turn back now.

The ship nymph brought them gracefully into a deep harbour, and anchored herself. 'Sleep now,' she said. 'There is no danger.'

'How do you know?'

'The dolphins tell me all is quiet. I will watch, and for now, you should rest.'

Resolving to make for shore as soon as they woke the next morning, they curled up in the berths. Ruffler snuggled into

Elissa's side. Silvius was very much aware of how near Elissa was to him. The ship nymph sang a song, deep, ancient and sad.

> *Bold lady Dido, queen of the seas,*
> *Led her people to settle new lands.*
> *She burned with love for a Trojan prince . . .*

Silvius could see a smile spread across Elissa's face as she fell asleep, comforted by the song. He lay awake until the ship nymph had finished, and fell asleep to the surge of the sea.

Eighteen

The House Accursed

Orestes and Tisamenos were now in a large chamber under-ground, lit only by a small opening in the wall far above them, through which a shaft of moonlight came, and the dim glow from the torch Orestes was holding. It took a moment or two for Tisamenos to be able to make out his father. Orestes was fumbling with something, half-hunched over, muttering to himself. He straightened up, the crack of his knees ringing loudly, and then, after a few attempts, he lit another torch.

Clean air came from above, and the torch flame flared brightly. Tisamenos felt a cool breeze on his face as his father moved around. At every few steps he paused and lit a torch. Soon there were a dozen or more, all blazing.

Tisamenos could now see clearly the huge black stone structure that occupied the centre. It was carved with all sorts

143

of pictures which, as he drew nearer, he saw were human figures.

'Here they all are,' said Orestes, gruffly.

'All who?' said Tisamenos. Orestes drew closer and traced his hand over the image, as if he were caressing it.

'All of them. All of us. There.' He grabbed his son's wrist, and pulled him to the right-hand side of the cube. 'Tantalos, your ancestor, who out of arrogance served his own son to the gods.'

'That's just a story. Isn't it?' Tisamenos said, nervously.

Orestes laughed, and Tisamenos could smell the wine on his breath. 'Depends on what you mean by just a story.' Tisamenos gulped. 'There is a lot of truth in stories. And here, look, is Atreos, who killed his own brother's children – apart from one, of course. Bit closer to home, that one, isn't it?' Aegisthos had been the one that survived. Aegisthos, Erigone's father. Could Orestes know about Erigone too? Had Electra told him? If he did know, why wasn't he taking his own revenge? Why was his father bringing him down here, into the dark, away from the light? He felt suddenly afraid.

'Father – what do you want me to do?'

'To see, of course. To understand.' He pressed the face of Tantalos, and a small opening appeared in the surface of the cube. Stretching down into the darkness was a flight of stairs.

'Here. Now. Come and see.' Orestes went first. All trace of the uncertainty had left his steps, and Tisamenos was beginning to see something of what Orestes had been like as a young man returning from his forced exile to reclaim his kingdom from his own mother and her lover. Orestes was going briskly down, and Tisamenos wondered how often his father came here.

A scratching noise, like that of claws on stone, unnerved him. It was much colder now, and there were goosebumps on his arms. The noise was outside of him. Was it some kind of beast? The scratching sound became a scrabbling, as if whatever it was that was down there had sensed they were coming.

Halting at the bottom of the stairs, Orestes spoke. In the light of the torch he looked bold and powerful.

'Don't go near her,' he commanded.

They were now deep underground. How large the chamber was Tisamenos couldn't tell. In front of him, larger than a grown man, manacled by a long, thick iron chain, was a dark, hunched-up creature.

Tisamenos gasped, as it flung up its head and opened a pair of large, leathery wings, hissing and showing sharp fangs. It pounced so that it landed on all fours, looking up at them, yanking at the chain, grunting, and Tisamenos was relieved to see that it was firmly fixed to a huge, solid ring.

'What is it?' he whispered. The second beast, he thought. He shivered. Was his father bringing him here to fight it? Was this another test? The thing hissed again, and lashed its long, whip-like tail back and forth.

'The House Accursed,' said Orestes. 'When I ... avenged your grandfather, the gods released the Furies. They tormented me, night and day, until ...'

'Until you went to Athens, and Athena absolved you, and the Furies were chained up under the Temple of Justice,' finished Tisamenos. He knew the story well. Or at least he thought he did.

'You have learned your lessons,' said Orestes. 'So they were. Two of them, at least. But what nobody knows – nobody else, not Electra, not Hermione, not Erigone – is that I was not fully absolved.'

Tisamenos felt dizzied. His father was giving him knowledge that nobody else had.

'My crime was too great. To kill a mother ...' His voice broke a little, and he turned his eyes full onto his son. 'I hardly knew her. She wasn't my mother. I had no memories. She was a symbol. I had to kill her, for myself, and for my father. And for Electra, of course ... she goaded me on. I do not blame her, Tisamenos. I do not blame anyone. It had to happen that way, and no other.'

Erigone was a mother, too. Little Penthilos, wrapped in soft linen. Was it any of his fault? What would revenge cost him?

The beast snarled, and shook its wings.

'I was forced to keep one of the Furies here, in the foundations of this terrible house – a constant reminder of the pollution that I loosed upon the world. I'd hoped you would never know, never see, because the Fury will go when I die. But now ...'

He moved to one side, and the Fury followed him, revealing behind it a long, narrow ledge, on which was a box.

'I swore an oath to Apollo, Lord of Light. I swore to him that I would do everything I could to purify the world, to try to blot out the stain I had made. And he gave me something to guard.'

Orestes reached out, and the Fury, growling, let him pass. Trembling, he took the box, and moving nearer to the stairs, showed it to Tisamenos.

'What is it?' the boy asked, reaching forward to take it. Orestes pushed him out of the way, just in time, as the Fury lashed at him. Springing back, he watched warily as she skittered her claws on the ground.

'Only I may touch it,' said Orestes, 'until I have passed it on to somebody pure in intent. Somebody who can bear the light of Apollo in this filthy world.'

Orestes stroked the box with the tip of his finger, and placed it back on its shelf. The Fury roared, saliva dripping from her teeth, and spread her wings so wide that Tisamenos thought for a moment that the creature would engulf them both. Then she settled in her guardian's position once more, growling softly.

'I do not know what is in there,' Orestes said. 'But I know that soon we will need it. Something is coming, Tisamenos. And we will need all our strengths to fight it.'

Nineteen

The Lion Rider

SICILIA

The bay of the island was wide, sunlight glinting on the waves. The ship nymph glided onto the shore, dragging herself up onto the beach. She was sleepy, still resting after the attack. Elissa was in the bow, gazing out, whilst Silvius busied himself with checking the weapons again and readying barrels for water. This was the first land other than Italia that she'd seen. It was opening up some place in her heart, the sea breeze seeming to tell her things that she'd always wanted to know. That there was a place for her, somewhere, that the waves had seen, that there were cities and landscapes she could know that were far bigger and stranger than the ones around Lavinium.

'It seems clear,' Elissa said over her shoulder. 'It looks beautiful. Ruffler will love it!'

'Come on, lend a hand!' called Silvius, good-naturedly.

Feeling almost light-hearted, Elissa scampered to his side, and joined him in rolling a barrel.

'We'll need plenty of fresh water,' Silvius said, wiping his brow. 'That's what our generals are always telling us!'

'Then we can take the bows and arrows out for game.'

'Good. Bet I get the first deer!'

'Not if I get there before you!' Elissa leapt over the edge, splashing up to her knees, followed by Ruffler, who happily paddled to shore as if he had spent all his life in the water. Elissa grabbed the stern and Silvius landed beside her, and together, laughing with the exertion of it, they dragged the ship nymph onto the scrubby sand beyond the tidemark.

'Let's go on ahead!' Elissa wanted to rush into the woods to see what they could find. 'All we know is we were meant to come here – we should look for clues.'

'No, wait. When I was living in the woods with my mother, we'd always do this when we went somewhere new.' Silvius found an oddly shaped stick, and pushed it into the sand.

'Hurry up!' Hardly waiting for Silvius to follow, Elissa was off into the scrub.

Ruffler scampered along beside her, his ears pricked up and twitching. Silvius was behind her, though he walked more softly than she did; he was used to the ways of the woods.

The vegetation was becoming lusher, and after a short while of walking westwards, Elissa heard the sound of a stream. Between the dappled tree trunks she glimpsed light on water.

And without thinking about it, she ran towards the bank, tearing off her outer tunic, hurling down her bow and arrows and throwing herself into the coolness of the water. It gave her a delightful shock, and she ducked underneath.

When she resurfaced, Silvius was on the bank, stripped down to his undershirt. The chain was still around his neck. He jumped in with a splash, almost knocking her over.

It felt wonderful to Elissa to wash away the stench of fish and salt. It was even better to feel that she was also washing away the touch of the Enemy.

She dipped in and out of the water, swimming naturally, whilst Silvius, a little more ungainly, kept to the shallows.

They drank till they could drink no more, and filled their water skins until they were tight and round.

'I never want to leave here!' she cried.

'For the moment,' answered Silvius, 'neither do I.'

After a while, Silvius scrambled out and, having put his clothes back on, flopped in the shade of an olive tree; he was soon dozing and drying out. Elissa followed him dreamily, and sat on the bank, dangling her toes in the water.

Looking at the stream, she wondered about how it connected to the sea, and how all the rivers fed into the great Middle Sea. Her mother's city was a fearsome power, on the shore of Africa. Could she find the way to Carthage? Could she find out about her mother? All she remembered was her soft touch, and the only thing she had from her was her pendant, shaped like a dolphin.

A sharp howl from Ruffler brought her back to the present. Silvius woke, suddenly alert.

'He's scented something.' Elissa watched the wolf cub's ears pricking, his whole little body pointing like an arrow.

They scrambled up, taking their water skins, and followed Ruffler as he scampered away.

'Do you think it's a stag?' called Elissa as they ran, bows and arrows clattering. 'I've always wanted to be at a stag hunt!' Aeneas had never let her join a hunt, saying she had to be older.

'I hope so!' answered Silvius, and, laughing with the joy of it, they sped onwards.

They came to the edge of a thick wood. As soon as Elissa entered its bounds, a gloom fell over her, and the sun's warmth vanished, filtered away by the leaves and branches. She was aware of the sun's position.

'What direction are we going in?'

'Still westwards,' answered Silvius. 'But . . .' He looked puzzled.

Elissa was feeling confused. The trees all looked the same.

'I forgot to leave a marker,' Silvius spoke uncertainly.

Now it also seemed that they were a lot further into the trees than Elissa had thought, as if the forest had somehow dragged them inwards. Suddenly she longed for the clarity of the stream.

Ruffler, ahead, flattened his ears and growled. Then he turned tail and pattered back to Elissa, hiding behind her legs.

She could see along a clearing towards a path where, in the gloom, she could make out a shape. Hunched over, it appeared to be on four legs. It raised its head, and from the angle she was at, it resembled the silhouette of a centaur.

'Maybe a friend of Stargazer!' said Elissa, relieved, stepping forwards. Silvius grabbed her elbow.

'Careful . . .'

Ruffler was right up against Elissa's legs, his back arched, his hackles raised. The silhouette stepped into a patch of grey light.

It wasn't a centaur at all. It was a beast, tawny and huge, with black, wet eyes and a rough, shaggy mane.

'A lion . . .' breathed Elissa. The sense of power coming from it was immense.

And on the back of the lion was a woman, dressed in a simple brown tunic, with long golden-brown hair. There was something odd about her, and it took Elissa a fleeting moment to work out what it was.

Her eyes were milky white.

'She's blind,' she said under her breath.

'Let's back away,' Silvius replied. 'Quietly.'

They began to inch backwards.

The lion shifted its head lazily, and yawned, a huge pink tongue lolling out. The woman's head turned sharply and she uttered a word of command. The lion started padding, at first slowly, then loping; soon it was charging towards them.

'Run!' Silvius sprinted away, Elissa close after him. There was no sign of Ruffler. Hoping that the wolf cub would find them later, she ran onwards through the undergrowth.

She caught up with Silvius. 'What shall we do?' Elissa panted.

'Find a tree?'

'And wait on a branch till we starve?'

'Let's shoot at her!' Silvius turned to go back.

'No, wait!'

The lion rider appeared over the brow of a ridge, fierce and fast, the blind woman's hair billowing behind her.

There was a tall tree a dozen or so paces ahead. Silvius was right. It was the only thing to do, and Elissa flung herself at it, scrambling up from a thick low branch to a thinner one above. Silvius followed her, sat astride the lower branch and had just enough time to fit an arrow to his bow.

Elissa breathlessly watched the flight of the arrow.

And gasped in horror. It never reached its target. Instead, the woman made a small movement with her hand, and the arrow simply shrivelled into dust in mid-air.

The lion rider laughed.

'You are in my woods now, mortals, and you would do well to follow my commands.'

The lion was now at Silvius's heels, and he scrambled up to a further branch.

'Who are you?' Elissa called.

'Come down, and you will know.'

Elissa stared into the eyes of the lion. There was something in them, a fierceness that she recognised, a wildness that reminded her of Stargazer. The sightless eyes of the woman seemed also to emanate something that she could feel, tugging deep in her heart. Perhaps this was what they were meant to find.

She glanced at Silvius, who stared back, wide-eyed.

'I'm going down.'

'No, don't! Elissa!'

Taking a deep breath, she jumped down, and landed in a crouch.

The next thing she knew, the world had become lion, and all she could see was its sharp white teeth, and all she could smell was the stench of meat from its huge maw.

Elissa uttered a shriek of terror, and the laughter of the lion rider resounded in her ears.

Twenty

Plots and Poisons

MYKENAI, ACHAEA: KINGHOUSE OF THE LION

All the next day, Tisamenos looked at his father with a new respect. He saw, now, behind the sloppy facade, the reddening cheeks, the cheery jokes and the limp, the cold watchfulness of a hawk.

He could not shake away the memory of the Fury. Knowing it was down there, in the depths of the kinghouse, a visible reminder of his father's torments, was itself a torture. Could he invoke those beings by taking his own revenge?

As he was leaving his chambers in the morning, he had felt suddenly dizzy, the stone part of his head weighing him down terribly, and he had stopped to rest his forehead against the stone lintel. It was crumbling in places, and there was even a bit of moss growing at the place where it touched the floor.

He'd rested there for a moment, alone in the dark corridor. It gave him a strange sense of comfort.

Whispering made him look up.

'The blood . . . the shadows . . .'

Nobody was in sight. He'd called Hero's name, and there had been no reply.

Now he was hidden on a ledge, watching Erigone as she sat in the large courtyard of the kinghouse. She was talking to one of her attendants. The others were throwing a ball between themselves, whilst one was teasing a tabby cat under the shade of a tree. A wet nurse was holding Penthilos, a tiny, wrinkly bit of life, wailing in his swaddling clothes. If he killed Erigone, then would Penthilos want to take revenge on him? It wasn't his fault, this little thing, his mouth wetly open.

Tisamenos had vowed to watch Erigone, but he could not be caught doing so. He listened intently.

At some point he must have dozed off, as he woke with a start. 'Gone . . . she's gone . . .' came a whisper in his mind, and sure enough, when he looked down into the courtyard, Erigone and her companions were no longer there.

They must have repaired to the women's quarters, and Tisamenos slid down off the ledge and made his way there.

Most of the guests were at the games, taking place in the large open space in front of the kinghouse, and he could hear their laughter and shouts echoing. The passageways were colder and danker than ever, the hallways silent; even the kitchens and storerooms, with all the servants out watching a wrestling match.

As he neared that part of the kinghouse, he paused, remembering the guard that had sent him away so abruptly last time.

Was there a way past him? The women's quarters were on the ground floor of the kinghouse, accessed by that one great door. But there must be other ways in – windows, archways. Instead of going down the corridor which led to the main entrance, he turned left, and passed through a stone arch that opened to the outside of the kinghouse.

It was warm, and he breathed in the air deeply, feeling the sun on his face. He couldn't see round to the front, but he heard a roar as the wrestling match came to its no doubt ferocious conclusion.

He leaned against the stone of the walls, and closed his eyes.

At once his mind filled with whispers. 'The blood . . . the shadows . . . the knife . . . the poison . . . Find her, see her . . .' He shook his head angrily to clear it, standing abruptly away from the wall. He was going mad. The thought made him horribly afraid.

And yet, he had to find out what was happening to him. Orestes was always telling him to face up to what frightened him. Resolute, Tisamenos placed his head once more on the cool wall. Like the hum of tiny insect wings, the words buzzed around his mind once more. 'Traitor . . . traitor to the house . . .'

The stone. It was the stone. Trembling, he closed his eyes, and instead of resisting, he allowed the whispers to course through him.

'On the steps . . . the blood flowing down . . . under the net . . . she does not forgive . . . she waits, she watches . . . the spiral turns . . . you are us, you are us . . .'

Had everything he'd seen and learned finally sent him insane, or near enough, like his aunt Electra? But no, the sounds in his mind were real. It was the stone, and it was talking to him.

Listening to the whispers, he began to sense that they had different qualities. Some were cool and dank; others were warm, as if they had been baking in the sun. As he listened, he began to see the whole kinghouse in his mind. It was as if he was seeing it from all angles at once, and yet it was not confusing. He saw patterns and beauty in the way it was put together that he'd never seen before. It was timeless, ancient, as if it had been hewn out of the very ground itself.

Within his mind he followed the lines of the building until he came to the women's quarters, and he knew that if he went along the outside of the wall, he would soon come to a place where he could climb up onto a ledge and look down into them through a light well.

He opened his eyes, and the image lingered for a second, and for a moment he had a strange feeling that he was in some way the house itself; then it passed.

He felt elated as he went. The kinghouse was talking to him.

The outside wall was grey and moss-covered, yet to him, now, it was beautiful and alive. He wondered if this was what Electra had meant when she touched the walls. Did she have some other way of seeing into the stones?

Tisamenos found the ledge easily, in a recess just at the north-western corner of the kinghouse. The whole of the building was between him and the games. Opposite, beyond the citadel wall, was a cluster of houses and temples, but he caught no flash of movement. Nobody was watching. He climbed onto the ledge, and soon was on the roof of the women's quarters, looking down through the large light well, exactly as the stones had shown him.

It was Erigone's chamber. He could not see very much, only the small square courtyard of lighter stone, through which women would saunter, bangles glittering or headpieces shining. There was a definite sense of movement below. A sudden flurry sent some women scattering, and Erigone's voice floated up to where Tisamenos lay crouched.

She was sending her attendants away. By the sound of it, as footsteps shuffled out, there were none left – although he couldn't be sure. He inched further forwards, leaning on his elbows, and peered as far in as he dared.

Now he could just make out Erigone. She was seated at a marble dressing table, and a maid was removing the golden headdress from her piled-up hair. A square of mirror hung above the table, and Erigone's locks, falling around her head, curled into coils.

On the table was a scatter of little pots. Erigone fingered a few. Then she said something to the maid, who scuttled away feverishly.

Once she was alone, Erigone removed a key from around her neck and unlocked a drawer in her table, pulling out a garment, silvery and beautiful, which she held up to the light before laying it down flat on the table. She took up a small casket from the same drawer, and with a fine brush, gently pasted the ointment from it onto the garment's inside lining.

When she'd finished, she held it up carefully. As if she needed a better look, she came into the area where the light fell. Tisamenos instantly drew back. He must have made a noise, as when he dared to peer back again Erigone had gone, and the room was empty. There was no sign of the ointment or the silvery garment.

He remembered how Medea was said to have killed the Corinthian princess, before his grandfather's time. She had sent a poisoned dress, and the girl had died a terrible death, clawing the garment from her skin. Could this be a similar device?

He leant forwards once more, and satisfied that there was nobody in the room, he jumped down, landing in a crouch, and headed straight to the dressing table. This could be his chance to expose her. He had to be quick, before she returned.

Twenty-One

The Sibyl's Prophecy

Laughter, drifting into Silvius's ears. Laughter that he recognised, light, rippling, coming in short bursts. A moment ago,
he'd been in the tree, watching Elissa jump down to the lion.
And then . . . had he fainted? He opened his eyes. He was lying
on his back in a grassy glade. Elissa was tickling the belly of a
huge lion, the afternoon sunlight pouring all around them.

Silvius sprang up. 'Elissa – I don't think that's safe . . .'

The lion was lying on his side, yawning with pleasure.
Elissa, looking around, found a stick and began to scratch
his back.

'There you are!' she said. Silvius blushed. 'Don't worry – he's
a pussycat. Aren't you,' she said, nuzzling into its mane. The
lion beat his tail upon the ground, for all the world like
a dog.

He took in his surroundings. They were still in the forest, the trees growing thickly together, but near a pleasant-looking wooden dwelling. A woman appeared from his right, bearing a pail of milk full to the brim.

It was the blind lion rider.

'Elissa, what are we doing here?'

The blind woman set the pail down, and Elissa came bounding over and dipped a wooden beaker in, then brought it to Silvius. He tried to look for concern in Elissa's eyes, but she was smiling.

'She's our friend. She's who we came to see.'

'How do you know?'

'Just drink this.'

He gulped it down gratefully.

'From my best cow, son of Aeneas. She was grumpy, but her milk's good.'

Silvius looked sideways at Elissa, who shrugged, and said, '*I* didn't tell her who you are.'

The lion rider went to a natural hollow between two trees, and sat down, as if on a throne. Her blindness was no impediment to her movement, and she walked gracefully, sure-footedly. She didn't look very old, but her skin was weather-beaten, and her golden-brown hair, he saw now, had streaks of grey. Her entirely white eyes moved around, as if seeing things that could not be seen by normal sight.

'I give thanks to you,' said Silvius. 'But . . .'

'You are wondering who I am?' said the lion rider. 'I often wonder that too. They call me the Sibyl. A blind woman, cursed with prophecy, given power over animals. Sometimes I remember what happened, but most of the time I do not look at the past; it is too full of horror. I look at what will come. I see the shapes of things, I see the way towards them, reaching out into places and things I do not understand . . .' Sleepily, the lion swatted at a fly with its tail. 'Would you believe me if I told you I have seen ships flying through the air? I have seen a world without gods . . .'

Silvius glanced at Elissa, whose brow was furrowed. She was listening, scratching circles in the dirt.

'And you too, daughter of Anna,' said the seer. 'I know what you are both seeking. I saw it, around the neck of the centaur. I saw those people, lit from within with unholy fire. You have it now. I feel it burning through the air. I feel how it longs for the rest of the arrow. I have rarely felt such power.' She clasped her hands together, her long fingers trembling. 'I have seen you both,' she continued, steadying her voice. 'Both of you, and one other. Everything converges.'

One other. That must be Python, Silvius reasoned. Two children against an immortal. It felt pointless. 'You know about him?' he asked. 'You know about Python?'

The Sibyl said, 'Before the Olympians, when the world was young, he ruled in Delphi, over a race of monsters, and Apollo laid him low. But you cannot slay an immortal entirely. His essence remained, and now he has gathered himself once more.'

163

'What does he want?'

'He wants his rule back. He wants the Oracle. He wants to take the place of the gods. He will bring destruction.'

She stood up suddenly and disappeared inside the hut. The lion got to his feet and loped off into the forest.

'The Sibyl!' Silvius turned to Elissa. 'I remember my father talking about the Sibyl – the priestess who took him through the Underworld. I didn't think it was true! This must be her daughter.'

'She'll know where we need to go.' Elissa hugged her knees.

A few moments later, bearing some herbs and a small jug, the seer reappeared. There was a fire prepared in a ring of stones in front of the hut, which she lit with dexterity, sprinkling the herbs over the flames. Silvius did not recognise their scent, pungent and sharp. He watched the Sibyl suspiciously, whilst Elissa closed her eyes, seeming to breathe in the fumes with relish.

As the Sibyl weaved slowly around the stones, she chanted, words which had no meaning for Silvius. She jerked her body from side to side, inhaling deeply. With a sudden movement, she upturned the jug's contents, and a thick, dark liquid caused a flash of bright white.

It did not catch fire in an ordinary way. Silvius watched with mounting horror as it spread across the ground to the hem of the seer's robes. He grabbed the jug of water. Elissa stopped him, frowning.

Now the Sibyl was sheathed in white light.

She spoke in phrases they could barely understand.

Starwolf
lionstone
dolphinlight
three will slay
one will die . . .

She choked, as if preventing herself from saying more. The flames became the light of Apollo and for a fleeting instant Silvius saw the young god's face in hers, and his heart filled with joy.

Then it flickered, and shifted; the eyes grew red, and for one brief, horrifying moment, he saw Python.

It passed, leaving Silvius relieved, and the seer's expression was once more grave, gazing at him with her impenetrable eyes.

'What do the words mean?' asked Silvius, as she gathered up her materials.

'I cannot tell you. It is for you to discover. I will feed you, and then you must go. The tide will be high soon.'

As they were preparing to leave, there was a rustling in a nearby bush, and a small, excited wolf cub came bursting out and threw himself into Elissa's arms.

'Ruffler! Where have you been?' Elissa tickled him joyfully and the wolf cub wriggled away, skipping in circles around her. The lion padded after him.

'I sent Leo to look for him,' said the seer. 'He had not gone far.' Ruffler was indeed now being given a hearty lick by the enormous lion. Running towards him, Elissa threw her arms around his neck, and buried her face into the mane. Silvius looked on, smiling.

'You have a long way to go,' the Sibyl said, quietly. 'I know that we will see each other again.'

'Where are we to go?' asked Silvius.

'Into the heart of your enemies. To Mykenai, home of Agamemnon, where now rules Orestes. Into the heart of the spiral.'

'To Orestes?' Silvius's heart sank. Somehow, he had known that this would be the case. 'His father destroyed our city!'

'All your cities will be destroyed if you do not stop Python. And then what will you do. Argue over the ruins?'

'And what must we do there?'

'You must tell him that Apollo is offended by lies that have been told, and that the lies must be revealed.'

They said their farewells. 'I am sorry that I have nothing to give you,' said Silvius, remembering the laws of guest-friend-ship. He bowed to her, and placed his hand on his heart. A hand that grazed uncomfortably close to the Arrowhead, and he felt the gaze of the Sibyl as if she could penetrate his inmost thoughts. What could she see in the future? What shapes and patterns were ahead?

Lifting a small pouch from her robe, she handed it to Silvius. 'These herbs are for healing. When you reach your boat, you will find a barrel of fresh water on it, and rabbit meat and bread.'

They departed, and following her directions soon reached the shoreline. Elissa ran up to the ship, calling out to the ship nymph, whilst Silvius came more slowly behind.

The ship nymph greeted them warmly. 'You have been a long time,' she said. 'I was beginning to wonder if I shouldn't turn back into a nymph and return home.'

The sun burning his neck, Silvius turned to see on the shoreline the Sibyl and her lion, watching them. Silvius had assumed that she meant them harm. But she had given them knowledge and directions. Knowledge that he could not make out, but it was a hint, a clue into the darkness of the future. Into the heart of the spiral. He didn't like that image, whirling down and down into nothing.

And soon, they were surging onwards through the waves, to the land of the Achaeans.

Twenty-Two

Entrapment

The Games at Mykenai had come to an end. The guests were departing; some in wagons but most on foot or horseback, returning to Argos, Thebes, Corinth, Athens and the other cities of the mainland, some with longer journeys out to the islands in the Middle Sea. All those roaring princes and decrepit heroes, weighed down with gifts from Orestes, wrapping up their silver goblets and finely carved drinking horns like thieves.

Yet Tisamenos was sorry to see them go. The kinghouse already felt emptier. Along with about half the city, he followed them to the Lion Gate, and stood as they processed out, back to their hilltop fortresses and their hard lives, still drinking, still boasting.

The revenge oath he had sworn was still burning in his mind, as if engraved in letters of fire. He'd been unable to unlock the drawers in Erigone's room, and had scuttled out without being seen.

As he went back to the kinghouse, he wondered if the stones might be able to tell him something. But when he placed his palms on the pillar by the entrance and closed his eyes, all he had was a sudden dizzying sensation of anger, and the whispers of the stones echoing in his skull, he took his hands away.

Entering the feasting hall, he caught sight of Hero. Though he was still suspicious of her, she was the only person who might be able to help him. There were a few servants clearing things away in the room, otherwise the place was empty. She was conversing with one of the boy servants; when Tisamenos neared, the boy bowed and scuttled away. Hero looked up haughtily and met his gaze full on.

'I need to talk to you. Somewhere private.' Tisamenos spoke out of the side of his mouth. He wanted to ask her about Erigone, about the three beasts. But then Hero didn't always see things clearly.

'Better here, my princeling. You can explain to anyone why you're here. Better than lurking in some hidden storeroom.'

This was his house, his hall. And she was telling him what to do. 'And you?'

'Making sure the servants are fulfilling their duties, of course. Don't look as if you're saying anything to me other than a friendly enquiry.'

He would play along with her for now. Tisamenos put his

hands on his hips and let out a laugh, as if Hero had just said something funny.

'Good. Now speak, and quickly.'

'There is a tunic. An ointment. Erigone means harm.'

Hero pursed her lips. 'To Orestes?'

Tisamenos nodded. Hero flashed a look of enquiry. 'I did not realise she would act so quickly. I have seen nothing about her in my visions.'

'She's been waiting all her life,' he replied, reaching forwards and gripping her arm. The doors swung open, and a group of maids spilled in and began mopping the floors. One of the men servants, following, called out a joke, and they all laughed.

'It's dangerous. You must move carefully.'

'I will accuse her.' Tisamenos released her arm. A swill of water touched his sandaled foot. 'And I hear Pylades won the wrestling,' he exclaimed, as a bent-over maid determinedly swept from side to side.

'You have to wait. Wait until you can catch her in the act.'

'What if I'm too late?'

'Be on your guard.'

One of Erigone's ladies entered the hall.

'I must go to the palaestra,' Tisamenos said loudly. 'I have some training.' Hero bowed, a slightly mocking light in her eyes. Tisamenos returned it with a curt nod, and made a deeper courtesy to Erigone's lady, who smiled thinly, before proceeding into the corridors.

Returning to his chambers, he felt a sense of prickling unease which did not leave him. The kinghouse steward glared at him as he passed him in the hallway. When he called to his father's Spartan hunting dog, it merely slobbered and turned away. That group of ladies, sorting through linens – why were they giggling as he went by? He thought he heard his name.

He reached his chambers, pausing at the door to listen. His imagination filled his room with agents of Erigone. Perhaps Erigone herself was in there already, searching through his things. He kicked the door open.

Of course, it was empty.

He flung himself onto his silken sheets.

He lay there for some time, as the day drifted onwards, turning over what he might do. He seemed to be at an impasse. If he accused Erigone, he would have to prove it. And he had no proof – only what the Swallows had told him. And he still did not know what they wanted, why they were helping him. But if he waited, then Erigone might act further.

When the sun began to set, Agatha hobbled in, and scolded him roundly for not eating anything. She left him a plate of dates, but he could not touch them. He washed, enjoying the steaming, scented water on his face and hands. He paused when he rubbed them together, feeling the unfamiliar stump. Then he lay down.

Drifting into an uncomfortable sleep, he heard the steady dripping noise of water on stone, leading him back into the horror of the Last Gorgon's cave . . . No, he thought, not now . . . Then the drips became footsteps. Real footsteps, hurrying down the corridor outside. The door to his room creaked open, and a glow of torchlight spilled over the threshold. There was the outline of a breastplate, and a long narrow shadow pointing across the floor.

Now he sat up fully awake. More footsteps approached.

'Search the place,' snapped a voice. Erigone's voice.

'What . . .' Tisamenos half-stumbled out of bed. She marched into the room, past the guard, and with a half-asleep Orestes following her.

Another guard followed, and the two diligently opened presses and chests whilst Erigone looked over them, a cruel expression distorting her features.

'My dear, this really is not necessary,' said Orestes.

'Father, what's going on?'

'A misunderstanding. It will be cleared up in no time at all.'

Tisamenos felt groggy. His throat was parched. Something in his mind, a knocking.

One of the guards was looking through his clothes chest. He paused, and stood up sharply.

'Here, my lady.'

'Careful!' Erigone came to the chest and peered over the guard's shoulder. 'Yes, that's it.' Her expression twisted into one of triumph. She put both hands into the chest and pulled out some silvery cloth.

'P . . . p . . . please, Father, what's happening?'

Erigone gave a sharp command. Another guard entered, leading a pig by a ring in its nose.

'Don't pretend you don't know, Tisamenos,' snapped Erigone. 'We have knowledge. We have a witness. A slave who saw what you were doing, who heard what you said.'

'I'm sure there's some explanation,' said Orestes, looking hard at Tisamenos. 'You can explain this, can't you, my boy?'

'I don't know what it is! I don't know what you're talking about!'

'Come here!' barked Erigone. A slave shuffled in, one of the kitchen slaves. Tisamenos had never seen him before. 'Tell what you saw.'

'I was sweeping up outside the prince's door,' said the slave, looking at the ground. 'And I happened to look through the crack. I saw him with this garment. He was holding it up, and he said, "This will do it."'

'What? I don't know what he's talking about!'

'Tisamenos, is this true?'

'No!' He looked beseechingly at Orestes.

'Tell him what you heard him say!' Erigone said.

The slave, still looking away from Tisamenos, said, 'And then he laughed, and said, "That's it for Orestes."'

'What?'

'What did you do to the garment, Tisamenos?' said Erigone.

A guard was rooting around in another press. He stood up smartly and suddenly. In his hands were a vial and a brush. Tisamenos recognised them from Erigone's room.

'Tisamenos, what is this?' Orestes's voice was seething with anger.

'I don't know! Father, I don't know what that is!' A horrible feeling came over him, as if he were caught in a net.

'You've been blind, Orestes!' shouted Erigone. She flung the silvery garment over the pig. 'This garment is drenched in poison. And he – your son, this viper – was going to give it to you!'

With a sudden white spark, the garment burst into flames, and the pig let out a terrible, almost human shriek. Tisamenos grabbed his water jug and threw the contents over the poor creature, but it was no use.

The creature was silenced by a guard, who stabbed it through with a sword.

Maybe that was it. The third beast. A pig, slaughtered. And it seemed now to him that there was nothing afterwards. This was the sign of his own death.

In all the horror, Tisamenos barely noticed the hands placed squarely on his shoulders. He was pushed out of the room, and as he left he saw Erigone, perfectly calm, consoling Orestes.

'She did it!' he called, gathering his wits, battling against the guards. 'She did it! I saw her!'

'You see, Orestes? Quite mad with hatred against me.' Erigone's voice trembled with anger. Anger that Tisamenos knew was feigned.

'Father, please!'

Orestes faced his son squarely. 'An accusation has been made, Tisamenos. The evidence is . . . here. You will have your chance to defend yourself.' But his voice was shaking, and his hands were curled up into fists.

The guards dragged Tisamenos away through the king-house, down to a corner of it he had never seen before, where there was a large, damp room with a barred gate. One of the guards fumbled with a key, and threw him into it.

Tisamenos, bruised and battered, grabbed the bars. He shouted until his voice caught in his throat. But the guard remained immobile.

Eventually, in almost complete darkness, he slumped against the wall.

Blood, came the whispers in his head.

She has won . . . she has won . . .

Twenty-Three

Towards Mykenai

THE ACHAEAN MAINLAND

Elissa stood at the stern as the ship nymph cleaved across the Ionian Sea, looking out ahead. She loved the salt spray that blew in her face. Far above in the sky, a bright dot flared, a star falling through the ether to the south, where Africa lay, and Elissa wondered what it might mean, before it vanished. She remembered the meteorite she'd seen in Lavinium, the night Stargazer had arrived. Was it a portent, she wondered? Had it heralded the start of her journey?

'Have you ever been to Carthage?' she asked the ship nymph.

'Of course,' she replied. 'I remember it well. I caught a glimpse of your aunt Dido before she . . .' Her sails flushed a little. 'I'm sorry. I shouldn't bring it up.'

'Don't worry.' Elissa stroked the ship. 'I didn't know her. She was a legend when I was little. They sang about her death as if it was some kind of heroic thing . . . They used to sing about her and Aeneas. Not much, though, about my mother . . . Did you ever see her?'

'Anna? I never did. But I do know one thing. She didn't die for love. She lived for it.'

Love. Elissa had not felt it yet. The feelings that burned in her heart for her mother and father were love, of course. But love for another, for someone who would be with her, share their life with her? None of the traders, or the boys in Lavinium, had stirred her thoughts.

The seagulls flocked around the figurehead, dropping offerings of octopuses and silvery mullets. Ruffler pounced on one and wolfed it down excitedly, whilst Silvius lit a fire.

It wasn't long before the great dark shape of the Peloponnese rose before them across the clear sea. Ruffler tried and failed to jump up and see, and Elissa lifted him up to show him.

A world she'd only heard of in stories, full of ancient families and blood feuds. The little wolf cub wriggled out of her arms, and she felt exposed. She was relieved when Silvius joined her, but wouldn't let it show. She had been reminded that his father had been the reason for her aunt's death, and it caused a shiver of resentment.

'Exciting, isn't it?' She quashed her feelings and turned to face him fully.

He merely smiled at her. The casket containing the Arrow-head had never left Silvius's neck, and he fingered it now, letting the light catch its chain. Elissa wasn't sure if she could feel an intention in those movements. What was he thinking?

'We are skirting the southern edges of the land of the Achaeans,' boomed the voice of the ship nymph.

'Should we send a message back home when we reach land?' Elissa kept imagining Lavinia, weeping over her spinning wheel, or Aeneas, angrily pacing the streets of Lavinium, dust in the reddish tufts at his temples.

'Yes.' Silvius crossed his arms determinedly. 'There will be enough time for us to find the rest of the Arrow without them catching up to stop us. No one can travel faster than a divine ship!'

All around them were other ships, the dark hulls of merchant traders speeding on their way, with cargoes of tin, bronze, pottery and silks. Every time one of them came near, Elissa strained to see if it was Carthaginian.

She'd never met one of her own people. Once she saw a boat that looked promising, with a dolphin as its figurehead, but the men on it were Achaeans, and called out amazed words of greeting before passing on. Silvius, looking up from his bow at the Achaean shouts, frowned.

Sometimes they saw fishermen, two to a boat, gnarled and ancient, taking the day's catch home to their families. These would stand in surprise and bow before the ship nymph – which obviously pleased her greatly.

A ship carrying priests, who were decked in white ribbons, engaged on some holy mission, came alongside them. They began a chant in praise of the ship nymph, which caused her sails to become almost red with pleasure. 'Hail!' they called across the waves. 'Hail, o beauteous example of the divine!'

Elissa, giggling, waved at them. Their chants continued until they were out of sight.

Only once did she see a ship full of warriors in the distance, surging onwards, the roar of drums and shouts racing across the sea; she shivered a little as she watched it disappear towards the scatter of islands that bore the easy prey of goats and cattle. Silvius, though, sprang to the stern, and looked out, eyes shining.

Later, Elissa stood by the figurehead, dolphins playing joyfully around their ship, their blue-grey backs curving and jumping.

'What do they say?' asked Elissa.

'It is very difficult to make out what dolphins say,' replied the ship nymph, a little testily. 'Most of it is about fish. But what they do ask is why a dolphin is sailing with a wolf.'

A dolphin and a wolf. The dolphin, she supposed, was the one around her neck. And the wolf – well, that was Ruffler, clearly. She fingered the pendant, and remembered what the Sibyl's obscure words had been. Dolphinlight. What light was that? And lionstone. The Sibyl's lion, perhaps.

Night fell, and the stars rose, spotting the waves, so that the sea resembled a mirror.

'I couldn't sleep,' said Elissa. 'Not now.'

'Me neither. We should think about what we're going to do when we get to Mykenai. What kind of people will they be? Will they welcome us? Will they hate me, as Aeneas hates them? Or send us away?'

'News will have reached them by now,' said Elissa. 'But they don't know what we want. I think they'll be welcoming.'

'We need to be as careful as possible.'

As predicted, Elissa could not sleep, and nor could Silvius. So they stayed awake, talking about what they might find, until the ship nymph, in a rather motherly way, ordered them to rest, as they were going to be coming up the eastern side of the land mass the next day, and would arrive at Nauplion, the port of the city of Mykenai, just before twilight.

'Will you sing to us?' Elissa asked.

The ship nymph agreed. 'What would you have? The flight from Troy? The harpies?'

'No. I'd like . . . I'd like the song of Dido and Aeneas.'

She settled into her bunk, and listened as the ship nymph continued her song. This time she reached the end of Dido's story. The queen, in her rage at being abandoned by Aeneas, killed herself. Looking at Silvius, it made Elissa wonder how stories became legends. How could you ever show all the sides? There was Aeneas, dutiful and plain-speaking, full of his love for his people. Had he done wrong?

It disquieted her, but then the ship nymph carried on singing, and this time she added a coda.

It was about how Anna, Dido's sister, left for Italia, seeking love, and how she found it not where she expected it to be.

Elissa went to sleep thinking of the last time she'd seen her mother. She could barely remember her, barely remember the curious accent she had when speaking the Trojan and Latin words that would feel so familiar to her daughter. How strange, she thought, not to speak the tongue of her own mother. She clutched the little dolphin pendant, and remembered the sudden seizure, the once bright eyes dulled. An ache of sadness stole through her.

She woke up into the dawn, feeling the ship speeding along like a swallow, and went on deck, leaving Silvius snoring behind.

The sun's gold rays seeped into the sky. Elissa played with Ruffler, and chatted to the ship nymph, whilst Silvius slept below. She didn't wake him, almost wanting to keep the sea and the sky to herself. She spent the whole afternoon in this way.

The port of Nauplion was ahead of them, a larger cluster of buildings than she'd expected.

'I can't believe it!' Silvius was clambering up the rope ladder to join her, looking serious and sleepy-eyed.

Elissa started jumping up and down and clapping her hands with excitement, Ruffler circling around her legs. 'We're here!'

'Almost,' said Silvius, arriving next to her.

The ship nymph, creaking with effort, dropped anchor. Elissa thought she detected a little waver in her voice when she said, 'We are here. Go, then, son of Aeneas and daughter of

Anna. Go now, Silvius and Elissa.' Elissa ran to the prow and threw her arms around the back of the figurehead, planting a firm kiss on her cheek.

'There's no need for that,' said the ship nymph, though the edges of her white sails were tinged with pink.

'I give you thanks, best of nymphs,' said Silvius, formally, and the ship nymph shivered with pleasure as she brought them into the shallows. Ruffler jumped into the water, his little tail wagging frantically, scenting already the wonderful smells of land.

It was about the midpoint of the day, and the shoreline was deserted. There were only a couple of other ships, and they had been pulled right up onto the beach. Elissa watched as Silvius checked everything twice. The casket around his neck. His bow and arrows. Their provisions; their water. The small amount of things they'd brought to trade. He looked nervous.

Elissa clambered over the side, making a small splash as she hit the calm sea, and, calling out one last goodbye to the ship nymph, waded to the shore.

It was good to stand on dry land, and feel the sand beneath her feet. As they stood ready to make their move inland, a movement caught their attention.

The ship began to shrink. The masts retracted into its body, and the bulging centre tapered inwards.

Soon there was just a shape which might have been the outline of a woman, long hair merging into the waves. She raised a hand.

'Be strong!' Elissa called out; but if the woman answered,

Elissa did not hear, as the sea nymph had already dived back into the waters, on her way back home.

Elissa and Silvius sat down on the shoreline, and shared the last of the fish. Silent for a while, Elissa took in her surroundings. This was the furthest she'd ever been away from Lavinium. This was Achaea, the land of Orestes. She glanced at Silvius, and saw that he was picking up pebbles and dropping them, as if getting a feel for the land.

They watched the late sunlight on the waves. It was getting dark. A gull shrieked, and they turned inland. Ruffler was keeping close to them, his little body tense.

'Let's press on to Mykenai. We can find somewhere to sleep along the way.' Silvius looked determined.

Elissa shook her head. 'It's too far. We should find somewhere now.'

'We'll lose half a day!'

'Better to go rested.'

Reluctantly Silvius agreed. But Elissa could see he was disappointed. He kept putting a hand to his temple and squeezing his eyes shut, as if he had a headache.

Walking side by side, carrying their bows and arrows and their other meagre possessions, they headed inland. They would rest for the night, before finding someone that could direct them to Mykenai.

They were lucky. There was a tavern right by the port, and it was full of life. A man stumbled past them as they came up the path that led to the front door, doubled over and was violently sick. Elissa held out the lip of her pack for Ruffler, who, used to it by now, jumped in.

The door of the tavern was ajar. Delicious wafts of roasting meats drifted to their nostrils. Inside was a lot of bustle and noise, the scraping of chairs and banging of tables. Silvius gently pushed the door fully open, and they entered as inconspicuously as they could, heads down, keeping to the wall.

There were about a dozen men inside, some sitting around low tables, others crouched on the floor playing dice. All were dark-haired and with the bronzed, toughened skin of sailors, and all had large wooden beakers to hand. A Molossian hound pricked up its ears and gazed right at them, but evidently lost interest, placing its massive head on its paws once more.

The friends slid round the edges of the room to where a thickset man was sweeping the floor. He barely glanced up at them, showing only an uninterested frown and some thick black eyebrows, until Silvius, gathering his courage, said, 'Be well!'

The tavern keeper put his broom up and gazed at them with hard eyes. 'Be glad,' he answered, using the Achaean greeting that Elissa had heard sometimes at the port in Italia. His voice, however, did not suggest welcome.

'A bed for the night?' asked Silvius, haltingly.

'From Italia, are you?' said the man.

Silvius nodded. 'We've come to visit our cousins.' The tavern keeper stood watching them for a long time, during which Elissa prayed to the gods that Ruffler wouldn't give himself away.

'Our uncle's a handsome man, like you!' smiled Elissa.

The tavern keeper grunted. He smelled powerfully of rank sweat and ale. Then he turned and walked to a door. When they didn't follow him, he sighed, and said theatrically, 'A room. You can have it. Two bronze coins, on the nose now.'

They sent each other relieved smiles, Elissa slipping the money into the palm of her hand, and scuttled after him. He showed them down a dark, mud-floored corridor, into a small, stuffy room with a straw pallet on the floor, and then stood too long at the door.

Elissa gave him the bronze coins, which he pocketed without looking at them.

'Well,' she said, when he'd gone, 'I don't fancy asking anyone in there about the best way to Mykenai at the moment. Let's wait till morning.'

Silvius glared at her. 'We could be on our way by now.'

Sulking slightly, he barred the door and piled up everything he could in front of it.

'I don't like this,' he said. Ruffler curled himself up at the end of the pallet. It smelt as if something might have died in it not long ago. 'You sleep. I'll keep watch.'

'I'll go first.'

Silvius nodded, reluctantly, and lay down on the bed. Within seconds, he was asleep.

Elissa took up her station at the door, alert to every movement. In the morning, they would begin their search for the rest of the Arrow. And what power the two parts would have when they came together, she shuddered to think.

Twenty-Four

The Trial of Tisamenos

MYKENAI, ACHAEA: KINGHOUSE OF THE LION

A tall, thin man, his lips bloodied, was speaking to Tisamenos. His voice was guttural, and Tisamenos could hardly understand his words. They were in a vast, dark room, and the man was pointing at something the boy knew was bloody and fetid, though it was just out of his sight.

He turned to look, but there was nothing. A groan called his attention back, and in the thin man's place stood another, broader in his chest and body, though his face was unmistakeably of the same family type; the same long nose, the same slightly pointed cast to the chin.

The ghosts of his ancestors filed before his dreaming mind, imploring, cajoling. They would never rest.

'The House Accursed ... we are all bound to it ... you cannot escape the curse ... Each one of us ...'

They were twined into the bones of the kinghouse, as much a part of it as the Fury that paced and snarled in the cellars.

Tisamenos's head was ringing with their cries, and he dragged himself up and out of sleep, feeling that their stone-cold fingers were snatching at him, that they might try to trap him with them for eternity.

His lips were parched. He was still in the same cell, lying on the same bit of earth. He was still waiting to be tried for a crime he did not commit.

He sat bolt upright. His body ached. A rough wooden beaker of water and some venison in a bowl sat within reach, and he took great pleasure in the liquid on his lips and the gamey meat filling his empty belly, tearing at it with his teeth and barely chewing.

Would the Swallows think him soft now if they saw him, trembling with hunger, cold and alone, lying in a dark, dank cell? Would they come and save him? He didn't think so. Perhaps this was what they had wanted all along. Without him, Orestes was weaker, his only other son a babe.

How stupid he had been to trust them!

The trial would be tomorrow. For plotting the death of the king, there was only one penalty.

Death.

His own father would have to sentence him to death. Maybe that was the only possible outcome for a member of the House of Atreos.

Maybe that was where everything had been tending towards, over all these centuries. The bloodied knife, making its way home.

So many had been killed before him by their own kin. He would be killed too, and Penthilos would take his place. Penthilos would end the cycle. There was nobody else.

Tisamenos placed his hands on the stone slabs of the walls. The kinghouse would help him. It had to.

His mind became still, a brief space in which he imagined the outline of his cell. Then an overwhelming clanging filled his skull.

The kinghouse was in uproar. He could not focus.

He tried again, but the clamour was too much, like a thousand smiths banging their hammers on vast anvils. It was too much. He knelt, hands tight over his ears, until the noise seemed to become the world.

A voice startled him, warm and lively. 'What have we got here then?' He opened his eyes and saw a young, cheerful-looking guard. He must have come in whilst Tisamenos was asleep. The handsome guard took his helmet off, revealing an unruly mop of springy, curly black hair, so black it gleamed. He winked at Tisamenos, and sat down on his haunches, sword clinking.

The cell seemed lighter. Tisamenos managed to sit up. The guard smiled at him, so infectiously that Tisamenos couldn't help smiling back. His eyes were shining with humour.

'Here,' murmured the guard, and passed a goblet to him. Tisamenos took it, noting that it was unusually rich for a guard to possess, and gratefully put it to his lips. It contained a strong draught of wine and honey. The young guard grinned widely as Tisamenos drank deeply. 'My mother makes that mixture. She always says to me, "Demos, that'll put curls in your hair."'

'It certainly does,' said Tisamenos, feeling stronger. 'I give you my most heartfelt thanks. I don't think I know you. I have not seen you in the kinghouse before.' He spoke formally, realising how stupid it was, but he wanted to honour Demos and show him that even if he was in a cell, he was still the son of Orestes.

'You do know me,' said Demos, showing beautiful, even white teeth. 'I've been here a long time. Always, in a sense.' He fingered the hem of his tunic, and polished his nails on his sleeve. 'But that's beside the point.'

Demos's voice took on a confidential tone. He looked over his shoulder, then back at him. 'She played a trick on you. Now you need to play a trick on her. Use what you have.' He tapped Tisamenos's head, then nodded once, as if in confirmation of the statement, and sprang upwards with the agility of a hare.

The light dimmed, and he was gone; Tisamenos was not sure whether he'd even opened the door or not.

Use what you have. He had a sliver of stone in his mind. He was becoming part of the kinghouse. He had been fighting it; he should try to make peace with it.

He breathed deeply, and calmed himself.

Now he closed his eyes, and laid his forehead against the stone. It was quiet now, and he wandered the halls of the kinghouse in his mind.

But this time, the halls were peopled. Some he recognised, and some he did not.

His mother Hermione was rounding a corner, her robes sweeping the floor, confiding something to a companion. He strained to hear what she was saying, but could not, and when he caught up with her she was gone. In the hall, Menelaus and Helen were enjoying a banquet. He was fatter than Agamemnon, and gazed adoringly at his wife, who had enough of Hermione about her to make Tisamenos stop and stare. There, in a corner, his grandmother Clytemnestra was gripping a sword, full of intent, and there marched Agamemnon, unknowingly heading towards his death at his wife's hands.

It was as if all time had collapsed into itself. This was how the kinghouse saw things. It was a great pattern, everybody moving about like pieces on a board. If only he could work out how the pattern formed. If only he could work out how to break it.

Deep in the cellars he focused on the haunting, dark presence of the Fury. He edged around her, feeling her terrible power.

As he walked, he caught sight of a face, handsome and smiling, flitting just out of sight. Demos. He began to know who Demos was. Sometimes he wore a helmet out of which poked two tiny wings. Sometimes he flew, alighting on roof beams and door lintels. Sometimes he was leaning against a clothes press, a staff in his hand, and around the staff, a snake twined with its twin.

Hermes, messenger of the gods, in human guise. He was sure of it. Hermes had come to him, to help him.

Everything was the same to the kinghouse, he understood. Wars, famines, raids, plagues. Everything that might devastate a city had happened to it, and it had lived through it all.

It knew Tisamenos now, and he knew it wanted to help him. He would channel its power into the right course.

He did not have to wait long for his trial.

His father came the next morning, carrying a bowl of warm stew and a fine horn of ale. Orestes ordered aside the guard, and came to sit by his son on the stone floor.

Tisamenos took the food gratefully, and smiled at his father. The cell was gloomy, but his father's features were distinct, lit by a small patch of sunlight. The wrinkles on his face appeared deep, the sadness in his eyes deeper. Nevertheless he held out his hand and grasped Tisamenos, and lifted him gently, leading him through the cell door out towards the trial chamber.

'I've done terrible, terrible things,' said Orestes as they came to the great stone door. Tisamenos knew. He had seen his father, barely older than he himself was now, gripped by terror in the courtyard of the kinghouse, facing the murderers of Agamemnon. 'We all act in ways that we think are right. It is this accursed family.' He paused, and gripped his son by the shoulder. His body heaved with a shudder, and Tisamenos grasped him back. He had the stones now, where his father hadn't. He would be strong.

They went in. The hall was huge and dark, with a circle of watching people, all fluttering fans and talking behind their hands, eating from gold and silver bowls of dates and grapes as if this were a piece of entertainment. Seated, veiled, on a wooden chair, whispering into the ear of a tall, grey-haired rhetor, was Erigone. Tisamenos knew that the rhetor was Erigone's cousin. Orestes, ignoring her, paced slowly to his throne at the top of a small dais at the far end of the room, where he sat, shrouded in shadows.

The entire concentration of the court turned to Tisamenos as he walked to the centre of the hall. His head was ringing, the stones now giving him strength.

There was another rhetor in the chamber, young and calm, standing by himself.

All too soon the proceedings began. Erigone's rhetor cleared his throat, and addressed Orestes in rounded, mellifluous tones, speaking lengthily about how the poison had been found in Tisamenos's room, and that Erigone had been told of it. The same slave was produced, who swore he had seen him put the silver garment into his chest, 'with my own two eyes'.

The watchers gasped, and Orestes frowned.

The rhetor bowed to Orestes, and then went to stand by Erigone, who clasped his hand.

The young rhetor took his place. He had a sweet, calm voice

that penetrated the depths of the hall. Tisamenos was young, said the rhetor; he was full of misguided energy, and should be shown mercy. He finished abruptly, as if there was more that he wanted to say; but that was the sum total of his speech, and he took his place unhurriedly. He had been paid, thought Tisamenos, by Erigone.

With heavy voice, Orestes thanked the rhetors. He stood slowly, his hand placed on the hilt of his sword, which hung at his hip. He looked around the room, until everyone was silent.

'What do you have to say, child?'

'I know what is true,' said Tisamenos stiffly. 'You always taught me that.' His eyes flickered to Erigone, across all the watchers, all the faces that he knew. 'The truth will be known. I have never plotted to kill you, or anyone else. The poison in my room was planted there.'

'Lies!' shouted Erigone. 'We have proof!'

'Silence!' called Orestes in return. 'I am not sure about this. Something stinks, but I do not know what it is. An accusation has been made in this room. The law of the land is just. The law of my ancestors and my people. Those who attempt the life of the king will be killed.'

Tisamenos closed his eyes, ignoring the confusion of shouts around him, feeling the hardness within him.

'But because I am uncertain, I am adjusting the sentence. There are penalties for perjury, too,' he added, with a sideways look at Erigone. 'Tisamenos – though it grieves me deeply, I must obey the laws. I therefore sentence you to exile. By sundown you will be beyond the city gates; you will not be allowed within the bounds of Mykenai again.'

A cold emptiness pooled itself through Tisamenos's mind. He had feared this exile. He would now have to wander through the world, like the bards. But what would he sing of? His own family? Perhaps he would tell the truth.

He barely glanced at his father, who was still standing upright, hand resting on his sword hilt; he hardly registered the satisfied smirk on Erigone's face as a guard came to lead him away, and pushed him out into the corridors of the king-house, driven from his own halls.

Twenty-Five

Lion, Dolphin, Wolf

THE ACHAEAN MAINLAND

'I'll take you to Mykenai.' The broad, barrel-chested man, who had introduced himself as Paulos, was only a little taller than Silvius. He wiped his nose with the back of his hand, and hawked up a globule of phlegm, which he spat onto the dusty floor. Silvius raised an eyebrow at Elissa, who looked as if she might want to spit back at him.

They were in the main room of the tavern, where one man was fast asleep in a drunken stupor, sprawled on his front and snoring very loudly.

During his watch, Silvius had heard all sorts of footsteps and quarrels inside and outside, and he was still edgy. His hand kept straying to the casket around his neck, and he kept wondering if others could feel its pull. It was certainly stronger now, as if it knew it was in the land of its origin.

'I'm going there anyway – got a cartful of fish to take up to the kinghouse.' Paulos studied his thick, stubby fingers.

'Kinghouse?' said Silvius, tongue running over the rough edges of the unfamiliar word. 'Is that like a palace?'

'It's where Orestes lives. He's the king round here. Just had a new son.' Paulos leered unpleasantly, and began picking the wax out of his ears.

Elissa was poking Silvius in the ribs, and hissed into his ear, 'I don't like him.'

'I don't like him either,' said Silvius through his teeth.

But there was nobody else around who had a cart.

So a short while later, Silvius, Elissa and a very grumpy Ruffler were perching uncomfortably, jolting with the steady movement of the donkey's hooves as it set out across the plain on the wide road, and trying not to breathe in the fishy stench that came from the pottery jars all around them.

Silvius could see the citadel of Mykenai rising up in the near distance, poised in between two mountain peaks as if it were the nest of some giant, terrible bird. These were Achaeans, Silvius remembered. The ones who had burnt his father's city to the ground. And he was going right into the centre of their territory.

Yet it was so different from the wooden walls of Lavinium that Silvius couldn't help gazing up in awe. His own city was so new, everything freshly hewn, buildings going up all the time. This place looked like it had been there since a time before the gods. Soon the stones of the walls themselves could be made out. They were massive – so massive that no human could have placed them there.

'Who built the walls?' asked Silvius.

'The Cyclops, they say,' answered Paulos.

Silvius imagined the giant one-eyed monster dragging stones across the plains. It must have been a fearsome sight.

The road was dusty and well-travelled, and there were one or two other carts going along it also. Paulos exchanged greetings with a few foot travellers coming from the direction of Mykenai. One of them said something that made him hesitate; as he started up again, he called back over his shoulder to them. 'King's exiled his own son, so they say.' The memory of Aeneas struck Silvius forcibly. He'd disobeyed him. Would he be exiled when – if – he returned?

'What for?' Silvius turned round on his knees and leaned on the edge of the cart.

'Trying to kill his own father, apparently,' said Paulos, as if he were telling Silvius the way to the market. What kind of son would do that, he wondered?

'They're cruel, these Achaeans,' Silvius said, adjusting his position so that he could see Elissa. She was tickling Ruffler's head, and looking back at him with her eyes narrowed. 'We must be on our guard.'

'We don't know if it's true. We need to ask Orestes at the kinghouse.' Elissa scratched Ruffler under his muzzle, and the little wolf shook himself free and went to curl up in a corner.

'And so we will,' answered Silvius. The news they had heard troubled him. But they had little choice.

There was a shout from Paulos, and the donkey brayed, coming to a stop. Silvius sprang up and made sure his bow and arrows were to hand. 'We're surrounded!' A group of men in dark tunics was encircling the wagon. Elissa, wide-eyed, was already drawing her bow.

The bandits' leader, tall, with a white, pocked face and a nose that ran straight and long, was brandishing a large club. On either side of him loomed heavyset men with daggers.

Ruffler bared his teeth.

'That thing doesn't scare me,' scoffed the leader. 'Now get off the cart. You're coming with us.'

There were six men in all. Paulos had jumped off the driver's seat and was on his knees, begging not to be killed in voluble tones. Silvius exchanged a quick glance with Elissa. Her bow was braced, but she shook her head almost imperceptibly. It wasn't worth fighting these bandits. They were big and tough, and would kill them easily. There was only one thing he could do: try to negotiate.

'Sir . . .' he began, and the leader laughed.

'First time I've ever been called sir,' he said, and tapped his club on his hand.

'Sir,' continued Silvius, biting his bottom lip, 'I must reach Mykenai. I'm on a special mission—'

But the leader cut him off with a blow to the head, which left him reeling, and he was dragged from the cart before

Elissa had a chance to loose an arrow. Two of the other heavies grabbed her as she kicked and bit fiercely.

The leader threw a gold coin to Paulos. 'Thanks for the tip, Paulos,' he spat. 'Now be on your way.'

'Told you,' said Elissa, fiercely. 'That pig betrayed us. A curse on you and yours, Paulos!'

One of the men advanced on Ruffler. The little cub leapt at him, biting him on the calf; the man shook him off, and Ruffler sped off, away into the distance.

Neither Elissa nor Silvius had time to shout after him. They were dragged in the opposite direction, forced to walk in front of the band of robbers, burning with indignation.

After a while they came to a crossroads, where the leader paused and looked Silvius up and down, grabbing the chain around his neck. Silvius instinctively put up his hand to stop him. A shiver of its power coursed through him. 'Don't touch it.'

'Knew you had something special on you,' hissed the leader. 'Heard two young ones had come from Italia on a magic boat. I'm surprised you're still alive. What is it that you have here, anyway?'

'Listen,' said Silvius, in quiet desperation. 'If you take us to the king, unharmed, I'll make sure you're well rewarded.'

The leader's stumpy fingers, blackened with dirt, closed around the chain.

'Don't touch it,' begged Silvius.

'That was the wrong thing to say, boy,' answered the leader, grinning.

And he grabbed hold of it, lifting it over Silvius's head. The casket rippled with light.

'I beg you,' said Silvius. 'Give it back to me. Please. It will only bring you harm.'

The bandit leader held the casket up close to his eye, and swung it.

'Heavy,' he smirked. 'Who knows what price this will fetch?' He caught the box in his palm. Silvius held his breath, knowing what was to come, feeling a perverse mixture of anticipation and horror.

A moment later the scream the leader uttered was so intense it pierced the air.

The other bandits gripped their weapons. One tried to prise his hand free. He let go, and the casket fell to the ground. With a stab of hunger, Silvius leapt to grab it, but the leader kicked it out of his way.

'Keep them away from it! Whatever in Hades that thing is, we need it.'

'No!' Silvius kicked against the bandit restraining him. 'It's more important than you can possibly know!' They scuffled, and Silvius elbowed his opponent's stomach, which only made him tighten his grip.

Silvius tried to throw him over, but he was too heavy, and Silvius found himself on his back, with a dagger pointing at him. He scuttled backwards, and struggled to his feet, ready to fight, but the bandit pinned him to the ground.

'Why do you need to bring that to the king?' It was a different voice, softer, lighter than the bandits', the words enunciated more carefully. And yet there was a haughty grit in it that Silvius had not heard before. It commanded attention.

A boy about Silvius's age, resting on a staff, was standing by the side of the road. He was wearing a rich-looking white tunic, and gold glinted at his neck and on his arms, but he was not attended by anyone. He had very long golden hair, and curious marks on his otherwise blemish-free skin.

He was also carrying two bags, one slung across his neck and one on a stick which he was currently pointing at the casket. Silvius realised that he was missing a finger on his left hand.

'We have a sacred message,' blurted out Silvius. 'We must bring it to the king. Orestes.'

'This isn't your business,' snarled the bandit leader.

The boy looked like he might be from the palace. He might be of use. Silvius said, 'These men attacked us. We are making for Mykenai, to look for help in a mission.'

'Release him,' said the traveller, in a tone that suggested he was used to giving orders.

'I said,' snapped the bandit, in between dipping his hand into a skin of water one of his men had given him, 'this is not your business.'

'And I say,' continued the traveller, in cold, measured tones, 'that it is. Release him.'

The bandit holding Silvius looked at his leader in confusion. Silvius took advantage of his momentary lapse in attention and slipped from his grasp, jumping to the casket and landing on it, covering it with his body. He felt relief, as if he had slaked his thirst after a long journey.

'Just kill him!' shouted the leader.

'I wouldn't do that.' The stoniness in the traveller's voice was stronger.

The bandit sneered. 'You going to stop me?'

'Oh, not me. I wouldn't do that. No.' The traveller put his staff down, carefully, and reached into the bag around his neck. 'She will.'

He pulled something out of it. It was a woman's severed head, stuck in a terrifying grimace, with a rim of dead snakes, lolling and drooping. A bandage was covering the eyes.

The traveller pointed the head at the bandit leader.

'You foolish boy.' He smirked, showing broken yellow teeth. But the traveller whipped the bandage off, and the smirk rapidly became a circle of pain and terror. What was happening? Silvius scrambled to where Elissa was standing.

'What is that?'

'I don't know . . .'

The leader looked down aghast. He tried to run, but his feet had become blocks of stone. He began to scream, far more terribly than he had done before, as if a whole slaughterhouse of pigs were being killed at once.

'Could it be the Gorgon's head?' Silvius whispered. They should flee now. But if they did, he might turn it on them.

The transformation did not last long, and when the bandit's whole body had become a rock, the traveller carefully bandaged up the severed head's eyes, and placed it back into his sack.

The other bandits had already fled. Silvius, on edge, backed away, beckoning to Elissa.

'Don't fear me,' said the stranger. 'I would not harm those who don't deserve it.' He tied the ends of the rope around the sack in a tight knot, and then placed it back around his neck. 'It is the head of the Last Gorgon. I won it. She was locked into her own gaze, and I tore the shield from her grasp.'

Silvius trod warily to pick up their belongings from where they had been dropped. Elissa paused by the stone man, a look of compassion etched into her face.

The traveller watched them, not smiling, and studiedly picked up his staff and his baggage once more.

They faced each other in a triangle, the sun not quite at the midpoint of the sky, the strong breeze rushing through their hair, the stone that had only moments before been a person right next to them. He had helped them, this long-haired Achaean. It was Silvius's duty to acknowledge that.

'I give you thanks, stranger,' said Silvius. 'I am Silvius, son of Aeneas.'

'And I am Elissa, daughter of Anna Perenna,' Elissa spoke in an undertone.

'We owe you our lives, I am sure of it.' Silvius extended a hand. 'I have only this to give you.' He rummaged for the silver amulet, and proffered it to him.'

The stranger eyed him for a moment, ignoring it, and Silvius put it away. 'Son of Aeneas?' asked the stranger. 'Son of the Trojan? The enemies of the Achaean people?'

'You defeated us!' said Silvius, retracting his hand. 'You burned our city.'

The stranger smiled, and gave a low bow. 'We are not our parents. My instinct to save you was right. I am Tisamenos, exiled son of Orestes.'

'You tried to kill your father!' Silvius's voice was sharp. 'We heard it from the other travellers. How can we trust you?' He crossed his arms fiercely.

'Well,' said Tisamenos, idly, looking at his nails then smoothing down his tunic. 'I tell you that I did not. You can trust the word of travellers. Or you can trust the son of a king. You have a choice. Either you make your own way to Mykenai, and get robbed and killed by any of the number of brigands who seem to have heard about you. Or you go with me, by the secret ways, and I take you directly to the king.'

'But you've been exiled! They won't let you back into the city.' Silvius was still suspicious.

'I have been,' answered Tisamenos. 'But now, I have this.' He indicated the sack containing the Last Gorgon's head. 'I will bring you to Orestes with your sacred message. And my father will have to listen to me.'

Elissa studied him. 'You're strange,' she said. 'There's something odd about you. There's a flintiness in your eyes. What happened to you?'

Tisamenos let out a harsh chuckle.

'You would not believe me if I told you.'

'But,' she continued, 'I trust you. You seem to be telling the truth.'

'I don't know,' Silvius spoke softly. There was something in this boy that gleamed, hard and bright. 'But you say you can get us in the back ways. That might be useful.' He held out his hand once more for Tisamenos to shake, and the strange boy took it. Silvius was shocked to feel the stone stump of his finger, but managed to hide his surprise, and nodded.

They turned towards the black citadel of Mykenai, its outline stark against the sky. Elissa was looking around, concerned.

'Are you all right?' Silvius asked in an undertone.

'I can't see Ruffler anywhere.'

'He'll be fine. He's a clever thing, he'll find somewhere to hide and then he'll follow our scent.'

A little mollified, Elissa agreed. A crow soared down and settled on the stone that had once been a bandit. It began searching the crevices for insects, as if it had been there for centuries, baking under the beating sun.

Tisamenos strode ahead, aloof, whilst Silvius kept pace with Elissa just behind him. They were walking across the plain in a curve, away from the road, and the ground was hard and scattered with thorny bushes which tore and scratched at their legs. It was thirsty going, and more than once they had to stop to drink from their diminishing water supplies.

The Achaean boy didn't utter a word. Silvius felt a tug in the Arrowhead, as if it knew where it was going, and he took this as a good sign.

He led them round the eastern side of the citadel, up a winding goat track which was barely visible to the human eye. Above them were some structures shaped like beehives, nestling together outside the vast city walls of Mykenai.

'What are these?' Silvius asked as they came underneath their spreading shadows.

'My ancestors' tombs,' answered Tisamenos. 'And here, we halt.'

Silvius and Elissa took refuge in the shade of one of the tombs, whilst Tisamenos remained standing, arms folded, long golden hair falling to his shoulders, regarding them as if they were not humans at all, but simply objects. The golden circlet around his neck gleamed. What use did Tisamenos have for them? Silvius thought there must be something he wanted.

'We're outside the city walls,' said Tisamenos. The rasping quality in his voice was stronger.

'You can't take us inside,' said Silvius, running his hands through his thick black hair. 'You've been banished. It'll pollute the city if you do.'

'You're right.'

'So you need us to help you,' continued Elissa.

Tisamenos this time simply nodded. 'The stones tell me that you have something. An arrowhead, belonging to Apollo himself.'

Silvius said sharply, 'What do you mean? How can stones talk?' He wondered if Tisamenos was going to trick them. Did he think they were stupid? But then, they had seen so much already – stones talking was not the least of it. And besides, he knew about the Arrowhead.

'I know it sounds mad. But I can't explain it,' answered Tisamenos. 'I can only tell you what happened. I was tainted by the Last Gorgon, and since then I hear the stones . . . I know that Orestes has something of use to you.'

'We were meant to meet,' said Elissa.

'You've seen it?' said Silvius. 'Where is it?'

'In the kinghouse,' answered Tisamenos.

'Then we're almost there!' That hunger again, and a pulling in his chest.

'Tell us, then, what we can do,' said Elissa, draining a water skin.

'It is guarded by a Fury. She will only let Orestes past. You need Orestes on your side.'

'And you would help us with that?' said Silvius. 'After you tried to kill your father?'

Tisamenos laughed, mirthlessly. 'I tell you again. I did not try to kill my father.' He unfolded his arms and leant against the stone door of the tomb, and suddenly he looked more natural, more like a boy Silvius's age, and less like some hardened soldier. He continued in a tighter tone, 'I was framed. My stepmother Erigone set me up. She wanted me out of the way.' He told them about Hermione's death; about the poisoned garment, and the pig, and the trial, and by the end of it he was clenching his fists, and he beat one against the stone so hard he grazed his knuckles.

'I'm sorry,' said Elissa, moving towards him. 'I know how it feels not to have a mother.' She stretched out a comforting hand, but he pushed it away.

'How do we know what you're saying is true?' Silvius asked.

'We need to work together. You have to trust me.'

There was no other choice. Either they tried to go in on their own, or they took Tisamenos's help. There was a pride in his eyes, unwavering, which Silvius recognised.

'We are agreed.'

'First find Hero. She will be in the courtyard with Erigone and the other women. She will help you. Elissa, you must go to the women's quarters and befriend Erigone. Go to her with a tale that I will give you, and she will follow you. Silvius, you must find Orestes, and also bring him here. But you must not tell him that I am here, or he will send guards, and I will be escorted away, and maybe even killed.'

The shadows of the tombs were lengthening. Overhead, clouds passed over the sun, cooling now. A lizard, poised, leapt across a small gap in the stones, and scuttled away out of sight.

'Will you help us afterwards?' said Silvius. 'Whatever we find in the box, we will need help to defeat this evil . . .'

Tisamenos lifted his eyes up from the ground. 'I will help as much as I can. But I can't escape my destiny.'

Elissa kissed him on both cheeks, then Silvius held the strange boy in his grip for a moment, and felt the stone stub of his hand again. After Tisamenos pointed out to them the way to the Lion Gate, Silvius looked back and saw him staring after them. He lifted a hand in farewell, but the Achaean did not respond.

Then feeling the pull of the Arrowhead, he went onward, up the winding path.

Twenty-Six

Among the Lions

The shadow of the Lion Gate spread across the road towards Elissa. She paused, holding Silvius back. A sleepy-looking guard was standing at the left side.

The two companions halted just a little way from the gate. The guard, who was young and clearly very bored, batted a fly away from his face and sighed heavily.

'Still not a good idea to alert him,' whispered Elissa, pulling Silvius into the lee of a rock.

Laughter floated up towards them, and around the bend came a group of women following a wooden cart drawn by an old mule, on which were piles of freshly dried clothes.

Elissa acted quickly. She slipped in behind a pair of young girls, and twisted a cloth off the cart. Then she draped it over Silvius, hiding his short hair, and took him by the arm, leaning in as if telling him a secret. They followed the women a few paces behind the ones in the rear.

They were singing and chattering as they went, some in pairs sharing a shawl, some carrying toddlers and babies.

'The clouds are massing,' a tall, long-haired woman called to the guard. 'The Skyfather is angry! There will be a storm later.'

'At least the Skyfather could wait until my watch is over!' answered the guard. 'Any of you girls got a kiss for a lonely soldier?' There was a gust of laughter, and Elissa and Silvius were through.

Up the dusty ramp they went, now within the encircling citadel walls, the great plains of Argos rolling beneath them. They passed a collection of stone buildings, but it was obvious where the kinghouse was.

Within the city, Elissa began to feel the weight of the stones pressing down on her. She had loved the openness of the sea. But here she was constricted, the walls like a prison.

The kinghouse seemed to her to have erupted from the ground itself, a living thing that had decided, for reasons of its own, to crouch here and wait. Its huge bronze doors were open.

Inside all was shadowy. They watched as people thronged in and out, busy, hurrying, boys off to wrestle and hunt, men and women talking, arguing, carrying jars and clothes and weapons and all the things that made up life.

It was far less ordered than Lavinium. Everything was crumbling and ancient; nobody seemed to be in charge. It made Elissa feel a little less nervous. In all this chaos, it would be easier to stay unnoticed.

Elissa turned to Silvius. He had a peculiar expression on his face, and he was fidgeting with the chain around his neck.

They had to get on with their mission. She had been worrying about the effect the Arrowhead was having on Silvius. Was it making him forget their purpose? Now, she took his arm gently. 'We're nearly there,' she said.

His eyes focused on her, and a smile formed. 'Yes. Let's find Hero.'

She approached the kinghouse up a flight of enormous dark stone steps, Silvius behind her.

At the threshold, the brightness of the sun made the inside seem as if it might engulf them both.

A small boy ran past them, being chased by his sister, as Elissa entered the cool gloom of the kinghouse. Her eyes adjusted, and she noted the layout. Four corridors led off from this hall.

'He said at this time she would be in the courtyard with Erigone,' said Elissa.

'Where do you think that might be?'

'Probably off the main corridor. That one looks like the biggest, doesn't it?' There were more people coming in and out of the one that led straight on. 'Let's take that one, and then we can always come back here and try the others.'

Silvius nodded. Soon enough the light of day spilled onto the ground ahead of them, and they came out into a large open space, bathed in sunlight, with an olive tree in the centre of it. Underneath the tree was a wooden chair, and in it sat a woman, bony and swathed in a rich purple robe, with a baby on her lap. Around her were many ladies, busily weaving at looms, whilst two soldiers stood at attention on either side of her.

'That must be Erigone,' Elissa whispered to Silvius. 'And Penthilos, the baby.'

Erigone was listening to a pair of women who were apparently looking to her for judgement.

'Please, my lady, Xanthe's son lamed my donkey, and now my husband cannot carry his wares to market.'

'It was an accident!' cut in the second. 'I owe her nothing!'

She waved them away, their pleas unanswered, and continued playing with Penthilos, who gurgled and yowled. As if she'd been bitten by a wasp, she thrust the child at a waiting woman, who took him and started to nurse him. Erigone called another to her, and whispered in her ear.

Standing far back, half in shadow, was a young woman with dark skin. She wasn't dressed as the others were, in robes and sandals, but in a hunting tunic and boots. Her black hair was tied neatly back, and her hand was resting on a dagger that she kept at her belt.

Something sparked in Elissa. She looked like a wolf, lazily keeping an eye on a herd of deer. She was of the space, and yet not of it. Like Elissa. Suddenly she wanted to run to this girl, to take her by the hand, to talk to her for hours.

'It's her,' said Elissa. 'I know it.' They crept round the courtyard, keeping quiet, until they were right next to her. Elissa leaned casually against the wall, and said, as Tisamenos had instructed her, 'The swallows return tonight.'

A tiny ember of recognition burned in Hero's eyes. Without looking directly at them, Hero said, 'Wait until that fat man starts speaking to Erigone.' She indicated with her chin a large, perspiring steward who was waiting to say his piece. 'When he does, go out of the north-eastern corner of the courtyard. And then, whatever happens, do not be afraid.'

She slipped away to the south. A few moments later, the steward, who was carrying a goose, came forwards. He dropped the bird, and, hissing, it waddled away among the women, who all started flapping their robes and shooing it. 'Can't you get that thing out of here?' Erigone was shouting.

Quietly Elissa sidled to the north-eastern corner, and entered into another dark corridor. There she paused and looked at Silvius. The space between them was alive with anticipation. He was frowning, again fingering the chain.

Elissa sniffed. 'Something's tickling my nose.' She grabbed at whatever it was, and gazed at it in the dim light. 'It's a feather . . .'

Before Silvius could reply, she was bombarded with them, as if someone were plucking a goose right next to her. She caught sight of Silvius's astonished expression, before it was submerged in a whirl of blackness.

'Silvius!' Feathers were stuffing her mouth, so she kept it shut, and closed her eyes tight, feeling now that she was spinning round and round, into a vortex, and then being lifted bodily upwards. She uttered a silent prayer to the gods.

There was silence, and she was now standing on hard ground. Cautiously Elissa opened her eyes. They were in a large stone chamber, obviously underground, and she was relieved to see Hero waiting for them. Silvius was looking on with suspicion.

'I think it's all right,' Elissa whispered.

'Don't be afraid,' Hero said. 'You were brought here by the power of the Swallows. Silvius, you are my kin – I am also half-Trojan, though I never knew my mother, Cassandra.' She half bowed to Silvius, who acknowledged it. 'My grandfather was King Priam, your father's cousin.' Then she looked carefully at Silvius and Elissa, and seemed to acknowledge something to herself.

Elissa could not help feeling a little jealous of this family connection, but she did not show it.

'And you have come to this place,' Hero said. 'The whole kinghouse reeks with slaughter. And now it is time to purify it.' Her eyes glowed with a deep passion that Elissa found frightening.

Hero brought a grey robe from a wooden chest, which she held out to Elissa. 'Erigone wants nothing more than to rid the city of Orestes. She burns with revenge for her father's death. So you will go to her and explain that you are a new servant sent from Crete, with designs on Orestes's life, to help Crete expand its power. You will offer her an alliance with the king there, and tell her to come with you to the beehive tombs.' Elissa took off her own stained tunic and put on the soft grey robe. Hero gave her a ring, too, engraved with the bull insignia of the kings of Crete.

'Silvius. You must go to Orestes himself. Since Tisamenos was exiled, he spends his time with his sister Electra. They sit in silence among the ashes of their past. Find him, and tell him that you suspect a plot against his life, and bring him to the tombs at the same time as Erigone.'

'Why will he trust me?' Silvius bit his lip.

'You will have to persuade him. When both of them are by the tombs, Tisamenos will know what to do. And then we can cleanse the citadel.'

There was something about the fire in this girl that made Elissa uncomfortable. She was part Trojan, though, living in the heart of the enemy. How she must have suffered.

'Return to the kinghouse through the streets.' She led them through a series of small, dark chambers, before reaching a blue-painted wooden door which opened out onto a dusty thoroughfare.

'May the gods that remain go with you,' she said, and ushered them out.

It wasn't far to the kinghouse, but they were certainly dustier and hotter when they arrived.

'Here we split,' said Silvius when they came within a few steps of the great bronze doors. He took Elissa's hand. 'Be careful.'

He felt hot, and she thought she could detect trembling. She nodded, and then kissed him on the cheek, which made him blush. She thought she saw a brief flicker of need in his eyes, before he regained his composure.

Just as she was about to disappear around a corner, she turned back to acknowledge Silvius.

He was standing, half-facing away from her, determined.

She raised a hand, and then she set off into the depths of the kinghouse.

Twenty-Seven

The Throne Room

Silvius waited, listening to the echoes and footsteps around him. Tisamenos had said that Orestes would be in the throne room after noon, attending to problems of law. He reminded himself that Orestes was the son of the killer Agamemnon.

What would Aeneas be thinking of him now? He felt a sudden shiver of hatred as he watched the complacent, well-fed kinghouse inhabitants going about their business. They had never known hardship, never known what it felt like to be at the mercy of raids and wolves.

But he had to discard all of that. There were more important things now.

Python's threat was bigger than old quarrels. Even now Silvius could feel the Arrowhead pulsing with power against his chest.

Two men came past, one gaunt and hollow-eyed but sleek-looking, the other shorter and sturdier, talking animatedly about a field whose boundary stone had been moved. That sounded like the right sort of thing for Orestes to be presiding over, and, resolutely, he fell into step behind them, trying to look as if he knew exactly where he was going.

His instinct proved right. As they came to a large door, the two men clasped each other's hands. He entered with them into a great hall, where, seated on a raised platform, a large stone throne overshadowed the room. On it was a slumped figure.

Could this be Orestes, King of Mykenai, greatest king of all the Achaeans? Surely not.

This man was glugging from a goblet of wine, and laughing as he spilled a little of it on his robe. Beside him, standing with her arm resting on the back of the throne, was a pale, black-clad woman. Her eyes were half-closed, and she swayed a little, as if dancing to some tune that nobody else could hear.

A woman came scurrying away from the throne, and she whispered at the two who'd just come in. 'Don't try Orestes now – he's in his cups.' So it was him. She scuttled off. The two men faltered for a moment, then after a few muttered words went back out. The door slammed behind them.

Silvius had heard all the stories about Orestes. That he had killed his own mother. What would stop this man from killing him? Though at the moment, it did not look like that was possible.

The king raised his left hand, and a servant came forwards with a wineskin, filling the heavy gold goblet that Orestes held in his right. He drained it, and smacked his lips, then stood up, leaning heavily on a stick.

'All of you – all of you. Go. The king commands you. All of you get out of this room – except my sister.' So that was Electra beside him.

A councillor stepped forwards to whisper something in his ear, but Orestes waved him away. 'No more today. No more.'

There was a great murmuring and a movement of feet as they all streamed away. Silvius hung back in the shadows until the last person had left, and the door clanged to.

Orestes sat on the steps. Then, much to Silvius's surprise, he began to sob. His sister Electra joined him, embracing him with her slender arms, and though she did not weep, there was a great sadness in her eyes.

When Orestes finished, with one final, racking rasp, there was a luminous silence in the room, and the king stood up; he regained his throne carefully. Electra lifted herself up by the arm of the throne and steadied herself. Orestes cleared his throat, looked directly at where Silvius was skulking and said, 'Child. Come out.'

Gathering his strength, Silvius stepped into the circle of light that came from the light well above.

'What a handsome boy,' said Electra. 'That skin, and that black hair.'

'Tell me, child, why are you spying on the King of Mykenai? And tell me why I should not have you killed?' There was a coiled power in Orestes, Silvius felt. He had to tread carefully.

'If you kill me, the world will be in danger,' said Silvius. He knew that he could not lie to this man. There was something about him, something haughty and damaged and strange and wild.

The chain around his neck was heavy, the Arrowhead throbbing with energy.

'You speak oddly, child,' said Orestes. 'Where are you from?'

'Our king was Priam,' continued Silvius. 'Of Troy.'

The names hung in the air, javelins about to hit their mark. Electra turned sharply to study him, and Orestes straightened, eyes narrowing.

'You were all defeated,' said Orestes. 'My father Agamemnon razed your city to the ground.'

'A new Troy rises again in the West,' said Silvius. 'In Italia, where Aeneas has built the city of Lavinium.'

Orestes gripped his sword handle. All trace of the drunk had gone, and in his place was a fierce soldier.

'No.' Silvius removed the chain from his neck, and held up the casket so that they could see it. 'I am not your enemy. My father's battles are not mine. In here is the Arrowhead of Apollo.'

A groan escaped Orestes's lips. He placed his head in his hands. 'Then it is true, the message from Italia. I thought that I would rest, now . . .' He looked up. His eyes were hollow.

'Give it to me, child.'

Electra, silent, burned into him with her gaze.

'I can't,' answered Silvius. He steeled himself. He was now a messenger of Apollo – he had to tell the truth. 'Apollo is offended by some lies that have been told. Some lies that affect you directly. And until those lies are revealed, he will not allow it.'

'You are brave, child, to face the lion in his den,' said Orestes. Was this the lion of the prophecy, then? He didn't look very lion-like to Silvius.

Silvius had seen the stone lions above the gate of the city. And while Orestes might have his lion, the people of Aeneas had the wolf.

'Why shouldn't I run you through right now, and seize the Arrowhead?' Orestes hobbled towards Silvius, and suddenly drew the edge of his sword along the boy's cheekbone. Cool and sharp, Silvius felt its bite. He quashed down a shudder.

'I am the son of the wolf,' said Silvius, voice strong as the bronze grazed his throat. 'You will not take it from me. When the truth is known, we will reunite Arrowhead and Shaft.'

The eyes of Orestes, haunted and ravaged with sorrow, rested on Silvius's. The weight that they carried was like a physical force.

'You are the age of my Tisamenos,' said the king, softly. Electra, eyes bright, merely glared at him.

'Meet me at the tombs, when the night is still and the watchman calls the fourth watch.'

Orestes withdrew the sword. 'Well then, son of the wolf. The King of Mykenai will see what you have to show.'

And Silvius, bowing deeply, backed away, fearing that at any moment Orestes might change his mind. He reached the door, turned and stepped out into the corridor.

As soon as he had done so, he ran. He did not think he could stand Electra any longer.

The moon was a pale disc hanging low in the darkening sky. Among the shadows of the beehive tombs, Silvius stopped to wait, turning everything over in his mind.

He had been alone with his thoughts for quite some time now. Would the plan work? Would Elissa be successful with Erigone?

More than ever he missed Lavinium; its clean newness, and the forest glades of his early life. He wanted to wake up and see the sun dappling through soft green leaves, and hear the pounding of his brother's horse nearby, not this terrible black stone citadel.

A low whistle made him look up. Instinctively he put his hand to his dagger. A figure approached that resolved itself into the familiar shape of Elissa, and he relaxed. She threw herself down next to him.

'Erigone is not an easy woman,' she said, and hugged herself. 'I wish I had Ruffler here.'

'Was she suspicious?' asked Silvius.

In the moonlight he could make out her furrowed brow. Elissa tossed her hair back from her forehead, and shook her head. He was very pleased to see her.

'I don't know, but I told her how important it was to be secret – she said she would be here at the appointed time.' She sighed once more, the air blowing away some strands from her face. 'And how was he?' The way she intoned 'he' made it very clear that she meant Orestes.

Silvius did not want to tell her what he had experienced. The terror of death, the strangeness of Electra and the ancient power of that royal house. He had felt the blood feuds between them, and also the lines that bound them across the years and generations like a huge web.

If you pulled at one strand, it might threaten to catch you in it too.

So he simply nodded, and said, 'I told him what I had to. Now we have to wait, and hope that all goes as Tisamenos planned.'

'It will.' That flinty voice, coming from nowhere, startled them. Tisamenos appeared slowly from behind a rock. He took his place slightly apart. 'That, I promise you.'

They sat in silence as the moon rose and silvered the tombs.

They heard the watchman cry out the fourth watch; and then their moods became more tense. Silvius kept drumming his hands on his knees, whilst Elissa looked up sharply at every movement. Only Tisamenos was still; eerily so. It made Silvius uncomfortable.

Every rustle, every sound, might be someone approaching. It occurred to Silvius that either Erigone or Orestes might bring guards, and they might be discovered very quickly.

At last, a woman, muffled up in a long cloak, appeared at the end of the path that snaked between the beehive tombs, carrying a single torch. She paused in front of the door of the second tomb on the left, and placed the torch against the wall.

This was the signal. Elissa gulped.

Silvius flashed Elissa a look of encouragement. She had to keep Erigone here until Orestes arrived. If he didn't, they would have to overpower Erigone, and that would lead to all sorts of complications.

Elissa approached her softly.

Erigone, on the other hand, did not waste any time. 'Tell me, then, young Cretan, what your plan is.' Silvius thought she spoke like somebody who was used to getting her own way, whatever the cost.

'First you must agree to our terms,' said Elissa, firmly.

'Foolish girl,' snapped Erigone. 'I will not agree to any terms without knowing what your plan for Orestes is. Or have you brought me out here on a phantom chase?'

'Not at all,' answered Elissa. 'I have what you want.'

'Then don't play games with me, young girl. You do not want me as your enemy.'

'Crete's power is waning in the Middle Sea,' said Elissa, stalling. Silvius admired her confidence. He saw Tisamenos watching her carefully. It made him feel protective of her. 'We need an ally we can trust. Orestes will never make terms with us. But you . . .'

'I . . . as queen, ruling, of course, in place of Penthilos until he is old enough . . . Yes, I understand. But you see, I have a problem. And that is what to do with Orestes.'

'Yes – what to do with Orestes?' A flare of torchlight, and the hollow face of the King of Mykenai was illuminated.

'Treachery!' cried Erigone. 'I tricked this girl here into revealing her plot against your life!' It was a shocking lie. Silvius wanted to rush out immediately, but Tisamenos restrained him.

'I go first,' he whispered.

'The boy was right,' said Orestes, his voice heavy with weariness.

'The boy was.' Tisamenos now stepped into the torchlight, walking stiffly, head erect, his mutilated hand held aloft as if it were a trophy. 'I, Tisamenos, was right. Your son.'

Twenty-Eight

The Fury

Tisamenos approached the King and Queen of Mykenai in a circle of tawny light. 'I was right, Father.' He saw Elissa, standing proudly beside Erigone. How brave she had been, entering into that nest of vipers.

'Traitor!' cried Erigone. 'He's called us both here to murder us with his foreign friends and take the throne!'

Silvius placed his dagger on the ground. 'Not I.' This rough Italian had something noble in him, Tisamenos thought.

Tisamenos felt his sinews stiffen. 'Father – *Mother*. I have to show you something. It is time for the truth to be known.' He laid a palm on the stone door of the tomb, and then took Erigone's hand. She flinched, but he held it tightly. 'Father, please put your hand on your wife's.' Orestes, gazing anxiously at his son, did so.

The stones were part of him now. They were in him, and they spoke through him. In the cold halls of his mind, his father and his stepmother now appeared, and they saw what he saw.

He felt an insidious sense of power dancing ahead of them in the corridors, shouting, 'Follow! Follow!' They had no choice but to do so, pulled along by the force of the stones, as Tisamenos closed the way behind them.

The stones showed them everything. First, the wicked Tantalos, grinning in his foulness, standing triumphant before a table groaning with slaughter. Then Atreos and Thyestes, clothes and faces spattered with blood.

What came next was closer to home. They paused on the steps of the kinghouse.

It was a hot afternoon. Flies buzzed above an old dog who slept, whimpering slightly, in the shade. A soldier, back from the war, was greeting his daughter, his weary face relaxed at last, marvelling at how she'd grown in the ten years since they'd sailed for Troy.

King Agamemnon was entering into his bathhouse, followed by Cassandra, her Trojan robes bright. He took off his war gear, let himself gently into the bath, allowing Cassandra to wash the back of his neck, his shoulders. Tisamenos saw war being eased away from his grandfather. Cassandra began to sing something, a Trojan lament, and Agamemnon grabbed her hand as if to stop her.

The door opened, a wedge of light spilled across the floor, and then a net was thrown over the king and his concubine. A dagger, and a sword, and the bathwater dripping red.

Tisamenos heard Orestes sob.

But they had to go on.

And now, years later, a boy not much older than Tisamenos, in armour that didn't fit him properly, was standing in the hall of his ancestors. His sister Electra was goading him onwards. He stood, irresolute, before making a decision and marching into Clytemnestra's chamber.

There was a terrible cry, and it was Clytemnestra, and it was Orestes too. 'Snake!' came a shout from the queen.

A moment later, the boy was staggering out of the room, a bloody mark on his face, his expression aghast; then Aegisthos was rushing into the hall, unarmed, and Orestes was blindly, furiously, slaying him.

'You've seen it now,' said Tisamenos's father behind him. 'You've seen what I did.'

Then they saw the daughter of Aegisthos, Erigone, sole survivor of her family, always in the shadows, watching as Orestes married the beautiful Hermione and bore him a handsome son, nursing revenge in her heart.

Erigone, now slipping into Hermione's chamber, handing her a goblet; Hermione drinking, and choking, foam spattering her gentle mouth; Hermione slumping onto her dressing table, knocking over a jug of clear water.

The stones were relentless. They were now in Erigone's chamber. They saw her meeting with an old wise man who passed her a bottle of poison. They saw her spreading the poison on the tunic. They saw her putting it into the chest in Tisamenos's room.

That was enough.

Tisamenos, drained, released his grip on Erigone, leaving her holding hands for a moment with Orestes. He left his palm on the door, his lips moving in thanks.

Husband and wife parted.

Erigone was trembling, like a tree in the breeze. She lifted up her skirts. 'I will go back to the kinghouse now, and I will raise the alarm. These are enemies, helped no doubt by those who hate us. What we saw was some kind of trick, some vision made by a dark wizard.'

Orestes regarded her. He said, softly, 'I took you in. I married you. I wanted an end to all this! Our son Penthilos, he would be a sign of peace between our branches . . . But you killed my wife, you exiled my son . . .'

'It's mine,' said Erigone, unexpectedly softly. Tisamenos saw that her expression had altered. Gone was the pleading inno-cent; now there was something harder. 'This citadel, this king-house. By holy right, it's mine. Aegisthos was king here, and I am his daughter! I did only what our family has always done.'

'It has to stop!' cried Orestes. 'It's like a slaughterhouse . . . Every day I battle with it . . .'

'It cannot stop. Kill me, and in time Penthilos will take his revenge on Tisamenos.'

'I will not kill you,' said Orestes.

'I don't understand.' There was a stillness, and both seemed to Tisamenos to be trapped by the weight of the past, by the horror of the present.

In a moment she had turned, and was running out of the tombs.

'Quickly!' Tisamenos sprang after her, and the others followed along the stony path.

'She'll try to raise the kinghouse against us,' called Orestes.

They were catching up with her. Soon she was stumbling up the broad steps of the kinghouse, and into its dark, torchlit corridors.

'Keep her from her women,' called Orestes.

'I know where to take her.' Tisamenos blocked her off from the women's quarters. She headed down the dank-smelling corridor that led to the cellars. The logic of his mind was taking over, pushing them onwards towards the only possible ending. His kinship with the kinghouse now felt total, as if it was inside him, as if he was also at the same time the house itself, leading Erigone on and on.

Filled now with a kind of exultation, Tisamenos herded Erigone into the hidden corner with the secret door. Erigone, at bay, turned to face her pursuers, Silvius with his sword raised, Elissa poised to block her way if she tried to run.

Erigone's eyes glinted cruelly in the torchlight. Straight and tall, she did not waver.

'If you kill me now, in this place, my ghost will haunt you,' she said.

'I will not kill you,' said Orestes. He pressed the spring that opened the door. 'Go down.'

'Exile me. Send me away. I will go to the furthest north.'

'You must go down.' Tisamenos's voice was cold and hard now.

She had no choice. She went into the room where the black cube sat, its terrible pictures stark in the flickering flames. This time Tisamenos struck the mechanism, and opened a panel in its side.

'Down,' said Orestes.

'What is beneath?' Erigone was still proud, and did not betray her emotion.

'Your fate,' said Tisamenos. A stench reached their nostrils, rank and strong. Silvius spluttered, and Elissa coughed.

Tisamenos went first with a torch. He could hear the clink of the chain as the beast sensed them. Then Erigone followed him, stiffly, but holding her hands over her mouth against the smell. Orestes followed her, and Silvius and Elissa, looking suddenly small and young, came after.

This was what the stones wanted, and this was how he would end the cycle of horror that had haunted his house.

The chamber below was black as the night sky. Erigone, pride still ringing, said, 'You cannot do this to me!' Orestes seized the torch from Tisamenos.

'See, Erigone,' he said, 'see the curse of the House of Atreos.' Tisamenos watched Erigone as the torch lit up a recumbent form. His stepmother let out a terrified moan as the light touched the Fury, as it unfurled wings, leathery and huge, and twisted round to face them, a terrible distortion of a woman, a lizard, a dragon, a monster, its teeth huge and dripping, its eyes yellow and pitiless. It sniffed the air, and screamed, pulling on its chain.

'What is that?' Silvius's horrified face was like a mask.

'It is from the Underworld . . .' Elissa spluttered.

'So it is true . . .' Erigone gasped. The Fury pawed at the ground, its claws scraping. 'They said there was a Fury here . . . I did not think it possible . . .' Her voice was trembling now, betraying her fear.

She tried to run up the stairs, but Tisamenos grabbed her by the elbow. She snarled at him, scratching with her long nails. He held firm.

Orestes approached the Fury. With a low growl, it slunk aside for him, its huge shape retreating and coiling round like a snake. Releasing Erigone, Tisamenos saw his father take the box from its place on the ledge. He lifted it up in triumph, and showed it to Erigone.

'This is what they seek. I do not know what is in it, but this is what will save us. I have the trust of the gods. I have kept it, as a mark of my pride, and as a mark of my shame. The Fury will allow anyone pure in intent to take it from its place. Erigone, I challenge you. I challenge you to take the box.' He returned it, slotting it back, and then stepped aside. 'If you do it successfully, you will be pardoned. If not – then death.'

'And if I refuse?'

'A public trial, a public shaming, a public execution.'

'I will take the box.'

Determined but trembling, Erigone slowly approached the Fury. It curled its lips, showing its sharp, pointed teeth. But it remained still, only pawing slightly at the ground.

With a quick lunge, Erigone went for the box. She closed her hands on it, and an expression of cold pride passed across her features. 'It's mine! I have it!'

The Fury drew back.

But it was only gathering its strength. Quick as a hawk, it reared, its wings eclipsing everything, and Erigone barely had time to shriek once as it enveloped her with its snapping teeth and tearing claws.

There was a terrible moment of hideous movement.

And then there was silence. The Fury, slowly, furled its wings along its back, and turned its head to regard Orestes and Tisamenos.

'The pattern is broken . . .' it hissed. 'The curse is lifted.'

Then it bowed its head, once; and where there had been a Fury, there was suddenly nothing but an empty space.

Silence gripped the room like a fever.

They stood, unable to move, gazing for what seemed like an eternity. Tisamenos rested his hands gently against the stone wall. He was met by a sense of peace.

'The Fury has gone,' said Tisamenos. 'Our house is free.'

Orestes was weeping. He grasped Tisamenos and buried his

head in his shoulder. 'Can it be true?' he said, voice muffled. 'All those years of blood, everything, it has finished?'

'It has, Father,' replied Tisamenos. 'It has. We did not kill Erigone – the Fury did. The cycle is finished. Penthilos has no cause.' He was just a little baby, sleeping innocently in his wooden cradle.

And now Tisamenos, the weight gone from his mind, wept too, clutching his father as he had not done since he was a tiny boy.

Twenty-Nine

The Bearer of the Bow

Elissa watched the Achaean king and his son, together in their embrace. The darkness around her seemed less threatening now. She could make out the outlines of the stones in the walls, pools of water collected in the cracks of the floor, moss growing tenaciously.

Elissa felt a sudden pang. She couldn't remember ever having met her father, let alone hugging him. She felt awkward, but at the same time wanted them to stay together, and sensing Silvius's impatience, she placed a gentle hand on his.

Father and son parted. Orestes, standing back a pace, stroked Tisamenos's cheek, and paused when he came to the stone part of his head. A frown passed over his features.

'What's this?'

'I have a lot to tell you, Father,' said Tisamenos. There was a note of pride in his voice, but also a quiet respect. It seemed to Elissa that Orestes was looking at his son with new eyes.

'But first we must do what we came here for,' Silvius cut in, stepping forwards and taking the chain from his neck. 'What is in the box?' His eyes were glistening brightly, and he looked feverish and flushed.

'I do not know. But I know that it is for you.'

Orestes solemnly opened the lid, which shone now with a white light.

Elissa edged forwards to look into it and for a blissful moment she felt the beauty of Apollo's light. She heard Orestes gasp, and then her eyes adjusted.

There it was.

Looking like an ordinary wooden thing, feathered by an expert fletcher, yet thrumming with divine power, was the other half of Apollo's arrow.

Elissa's heart quickened. The king held out his hand, but Silvius shook his head. 'No. I will place it back with the Shaft.'

There was a perceptible shift in the air as the two caskets were positioned next to each other, and a glowing arc of white light sprang from one to the other.

Elissa sensed another presence in the room, a joyous one which charged the atmosphere.

There, lit by the whiteness, apparently as yet unseen by the others, was the god Hermes.

He had slipped into her sight in the curious way that gods had, as if he had always been there but she just hadn't noticed, with his warm smile and glossy black, curly hair. He was eating an apple rather studiedly, a quiver slung over his shoulder. The god swallowed the last bite of the apple, nodded mock gravely to Elissa and tossed away the core.

'My lord Hermes!' Orestes had seen him, and now the others were aware of him, his bright essence lighting up the clammy chamber. Silvius bowed his head, whilst Tisamenos gazed in wonder.

The god, without seeming to move through space, was now bending over the Arrowhead and the Shaft. 'Such power,' he murmured. Tenderly he lifted up the Arrowhead's casket. Silvius flinched as he opened the lid. But of course Hermes did not ask for destruction, and instead stroked it with his finger.

'A pretty thing.' Hermes toyed with the Arrowhead, turning it up and down, admiring the sheen of colours rippling over it. 'And now, I bring together what has been separated.'

Elissa felt a surge of Apollo's clarity. She grabbed Silvius by the hand, and saw his face was lit with joy. Tisamenos was kneeling, and Orestes, awed by the presence of the god who had absolved him, was prostrate on the ground.

'The Arrow of Apollo!' Hermes called, voice ringing and echoing through the chamber. 'The weapon that will lay Python low once more. Tisamenos, son of Orestes; Silvius, son of Aeneas. You have brought them together. And now you must find the Bow.'

Elissa remembered the vision she'd had when she'd first touched the Arrowhead. She knew the god would have a message for her.

'Where is it?' Elissa asked.

238

'The Bow lies across the waves.'

Another journey then. Another chance, perhaps to see someone from her own country.

'You will find it in the ruins of Troy.' Elissa's eyes lit up. She saw a worried expression pass over Silvius's face. 'Apollo placed it in his temple there, and when Troy fell it was forgotten. Now you must retrieve it. But it must be done by one who is neither Achaean nor Trojan.'

Hermes replaced the Arrow in the quiver, and presented it to Elissa. 'Silvius carried the Arrowhead. Tisamenos led you to the Shaft. And now, Elissa, it is your turn – to bear the Arrow and find the Bow.'

Elissa held the quiver, trembling, as Silvius and Tisamenos looked on.

The air was suddenly tinged with sweetness, then Hermes was gone; there was only blackness where he had stood, and a lingering scent of wine and honey.

Silk-covered couches lined the walls of Orestes's inner chamber, which was now lit by dozens of torches whose light gleamed off the surfaces of gold and silver vessels and the bronze armour that stood always at the ready by his dressing table. Elissa had never seen such luxury. The King of Mykenai was resting in a carved wooden chair with a soft cushion behind his back. Electra was next to him, her eyes blank, her gaze steadily but not unkindly on Elissa, her fingers interlaced.

Seated on three smaller chairs in front of Orestes, each inlaid with golden enamel, were Tisamenos, Silvius and Elissa. Elissa had gulped down three tall beakers of cool water, and was now devouring some cured and salted hams, whilst Silvius and Tisamenos regarded each other warily, each picking off bits from a roasted partridge. She finished the ham, and then took a sweet, juicy date from a silver plate.

The delicious taste of the food overwhelmed her, making her forget for a moment about the unaccustomed weight of the quiver on her back and the power of the Arrow it held. An Arrow that had brought down a monster, that had been wielded by a god, that now she, and she alone, was carrying.

Tisamenos had told his father about the stones, and the head of the Last Gorgon, though Elissa felt that he was being evasive about something. And now they were discussing how to reach Troy. She could see that it was difficult for Silvius, that despite all his efforts to pretend it didn't mean anything to him, it was still his city. As a result, he was being a little possessive.

'We need to go as quickly as possible,' Silvius was saying tightly. 'Just the three of us, so we will be fast. I wonder if the ship nymph would help us?'

'I think we should wait,' Tisamenos said. 'We still don't really know what this threat is. What if this Python of yours has taken the cities near Troy? Do we have spies there, Father?'

'We do not, but I have heard nothing from Thessaly.' Orestes addressed them all now, clearing his throat. 'I have considered it. My information from Italia was pressing, and it is clear that the Bow must be found. Tomorrow, you must leave immediately. I will send you to Troy with a full crew and in my fastest ship.'

Silvius gave a small nod of satisfaction.

'We must act with all speed.'

'Yes, Father,' Tisamenos answered. But Elissa could tell that he felt his pride was injured.

There was a noise outside, and Electra went to the door to listen, bending her head slightly. Her brows drew together with worry, and, her black garments flapping, she came hurrying back, hands clasped together, fingers twisting. 'There's fighting in the kinghouse,' she said.

'Impossible! Our guards would have seen anyone approaching.'

'Then it must have begun inside . . .'

A servant boy rushed in, the air from the door shifting the tapestries on the walls. He was clearly terrified, his forehead gleaming with sweat. 'Orestes, my king – it's the Swallows!' Elissa saw Tisamenos look up suddenly, part guilty, part fearful. 'They're slaughtering us! The guards were not ready – there's a dozen of them in the main hall, and they're spreading out into the rest of the kinghouse.'

Slowly Orestes stood up. He went, limping slightly, to where his breastplate and his sword were laid out. His eyes glinted. 'I will lead the fight.' He buckled on his breastplate. He turned to his son, whose hand was already grasping his sword.

'You go now.'

'But, Father! My place is here with you, helping to defend the kinghouse!'

'No. This is my kinghouse, my battle. You, all of you, go now, to Nauplion, and ask for my sea captain, Andros. You have the Arrow, and the head of the Last Gorgon, your wits and the favour of Apollo and Hermes. You will succeed in your task, I am sure of it. Go, go now.'

Tisamenos wavered. Then he ran to his father and embraced him tightly.

'This mission from Apollo. It's a way to atone for the past,' he said.

'Yes, my son,' answered Orestes. 'It will heal us all.'

Orestes then gripped Silvius by the shoulder. 'Son of my enemy,' he said. 'The feud between our houses has ended. I call you now Silvius, friend of the Achaeans.'

'And I accept your friendship.' Silvius bowed his head formally.

The King of Mykenai turned to Elissa. 'And you, your part to play is yet to come. Play it well.'

Elissa could not help flinging her arms around the old warrior and burying her face in his neck, as she might have done her own father.

Armed and ready, Orestes hurried away into the fray, a lion defending his pride. Just as he reached the door, Electra called him. 'Brother – I will fight with you. It is my house too.' Sister joined brother, and they clasped hands. Elissa noted the steel in her eyes, the strength in the veiny hand that took up a sword. The two of them marched out into the corridors of the kinghouse.

Elissa would be like Electra. She would be strong, too. She would find the Bow, and deliver the world from Python.

Thirty

The Fall of a City

Tisamenos took the lead, bringing the half-Trojan Silvius and the Arrow-bearer Elissa behind him, through the beehive tombs that now seemed full of shadows watching them, and down the winding mountain path.

He pressed onwards in the darkness, down the hill, aware of the ravine to their right, aware that there might be those who meant them harm. 'Stay close to the side!' he ordered them, knowing one misstep could be fatal.

All the time he wondered if he should turn back.

They soon reached the plain, and the wide road ahead of them to the port of Nauplion. The sky was tainted with orange, yet it was not the right time for sunrise. Flames were licking all over the kinghouse. Tisamenos stopped, heart pounding.

'I have to go back,' he said, and started up the path again.

'No!' Silvius called.

'You have to come with us,' said Elissa. 'We need you!'

Torn, Tisamenos heard the cries of battle above, and the kinghouse of his ancestors burning down. If he returned to the citadel, he would fight with honour, but maybe die. If he went with these strangers, he would face unknown dangers.

'Please!' Elissa was by him now, her gentle hand on his. 'The Shaft was kept here for a reason. The Lion of Mykenai will be a great part of this!'

'What do you mean?'

'The Sibyl,' said Elissa. 'She gave us a prophecy. I don't understand half of it, but now I know at least some. The dolphin is me. And Silvius is the wolf. Lion, dolphin and wolf – they are the parts of the prophecy that must come together. So you must be the lion.'

Breathing deeply, Tisamenos acknowledged the grave look in her eyes, and he nodded. 'Then the three beasts that Hero mentioned . . . she was wrong! They did not foretell my death. The three beasts – it's us.' A new resolve came over him. 'I will come with you.'

The road was hard in the dark, and they tripped and stumbled. 'It's not so far,' Tisamenos was saying. 'We'll be there before dawn.' But it was far, he knew. He had to keep the others going. They had only one water skin between them, and they eked it out, but even so their lips were soon parched.

'There'll be water when we get there. The ship will be ready for us, I'm sure of it. We'll be on our way soon.' Tisamenos was filled with an energy that came from knowing he was going to live.

When Elissa, missing her footing, stumbled and almost fell, hands reaching instinctively for the quiver on her back, he caught her. She smiled her thanks, clear in the starlight. Silvius, who had been lagging behind a little, gave him a curt nod.

How Tisamenos wished they had stopped to get horses. But there had been no time. Soon he recognised a curve in the road, and knew that they would be approaching Nauplion within an hour or so. They shared out the last of the water. Elissa shifted the strap of the quiver around her neck. It had clearly been weighing on her. Tisamenos offered to carry it, but she refused.

There was a strange brightness in the air, though it did not feel like dawn. They reached the inn where Elissa and Silvius had stayed. Not a light was on in the house.

'Don't,' said Elissa. 'They tricked us.'

'But the captain might be in there. They will listen to me, the son of Orestes.' Tisamenos banged on the door, but nobody stirred within.

Undaunted, Tisamenos led the way down to the shore.

And now he understood the lightness in the sky. Ranged in front of them were six ships. The sea was scarlet, burnished by the flames that licked all over them as they lay at anchor.

Somebody had set fire to them all.

It was hard for Tisamenos not to collapse – torn, bleeding, thirsty – and sink to his knees.

Hero. Hero and the Swallows, all this time, had been wanting to destroy him and his family.

She had betrayed him. She had simply used him to get rid of Erigone, and then had attacked when she knew that he and Orestes would be occupied. And now his city was burning.

His father was probably dead.

'What can we do?' They were all covered in sweat and soot. Silvius coughed as a plume of smoke passed over them. Crumpling to the shore, Elissa cradled the quiver in her lap. A mast toppled into the sea, blazing.

'The ship nymph can't help us now – she's gone home.' Elissa held her hands together as if in prayer. 'And I am glad that she did. She would have been killed if she'd stayed.'

'We'll have to go by land, reach another port ...' This journey was the only thing left for Tisamenos. He had broken the curse of his House, but now it was destroyed.

He couldn't show his emotions to the others, though. He had to keep going. 'We can find horses, somewhere. There must be some.' He picked up the Last Gorgon's head, and turned away from the flames. 'We must get as far away as possible. The Swallows may still have spies here.'

He hadn't, in the end, been able to save his blood family. But he would help Silvius and Elissa.

'Let's get off the shore. It will be cooler.' He took them behind the rocks, and gasping, they pressed on, limping, woozy, leaning on each other. 'We'll make our way round the bay until we have to stop. Then we'll rest somewhere high up, and in the morning we can go on.'

This time he walked in between the two, sometimes helping them, sometimes exhorting them onwards.

Climbing up the hill was the worst. A path made for sure-footed shepherds was only just visible in the starlight. There might be wolves or bears out on the hunt. Silvius slipped once, and almost seemed to lose consciousness, but Elissa pulled him upwards. Tisamenos slung Silvius's arm around his shoulder, and helped the boy to stumble on.

It seemed to take an eternity, step by faltering step, but eventually they were at the top of the hill, and the breeze was cool and fresh. Tisamenos placed Silvius gently down. Elissa, too, looked drained. 'We'll stop here. There's shelter, and a spring.'

The first thing Tisamenos did was bring a helmet-full of water to Silvius's lips. Silvius sputtered awake and went to kneel by the stream, drinking deeply.

There was a hollow under the brow of the hill which was not quite a cave, but large enough to accommodate all three of them. Tisamenos threw a rock into it to scare out anything that might be using it as a home. Nothing emerged, except a tiny lizard, which skittered away.

'We'll sleep now.' Gratefully Elissa and Silvius crept into its protection and lay down, slumbering almost immediately.

Tisamenos, just outside the cave, did not. His body was aching and he had a stiff neck, and he was hungry. His thoughts ran over the same patterns, again and again, and he hurled a stone away down the mountainside in silent rage.

Just after dawn, the sun was pushing itself up from the lip of the sea. The other two were still asleep, and he felt a stab of unaccustomed envy when he saw that Elissa's arm was draped over Silvius.

He stumbled away, blearily, to relieve his bladder behind an outcrop, and then went to drink from the stream.

A thin plume of black smoke was rising from the citadel of Mykenai. The whole kinghouse might have been destroyed. The cruel head of the Last Gorgon rubbed against his skin through the sacking, and he felt a sudden revulsion. What had he won it for?

A cough made him turn round. Silvius was behind him, black hair lank.

'I give you thanks,' said the half-Trojan, in that formal way he had; so stiff and yet so unpractised, like a rustic trying to be polite. 'You didn't have to help us.'

'I should be there.' Tisamenos indicated the citadel.

'I left my city too,' said Silvius. 'I left my father, my mother, my little brother. But this mission is from Apollo himself.'

'If Mykenai is weak, the other cities will hear of it. One of them is probably already mustering an army – Argos most likely. It was always a better positioned city.'

Silvius took hold of Tisamenos's arm. 'Python's danger is real, and more terrible than any army from Argos. I've seen it. I've seen the people Python controls. They're terrifying – unstoppable. They might even have destroyed my own city.'

'We must go to Troy to find the Bow.' Elissa joined them, the quiver on her back. 'My people are near there. It is all meant to happen. An Achaean, a Trojan, a Carthaginian – lion, wolf, dolphin. It makes sense, doesn't it? We don't know what we have to do yet, but it's us three who have to do it.'

'The children of enemies, seeking to make a greater peace . . .' Silvius paused.

Trembling, the son of Orestes gazed across at the burning citadel. They were right: Apollo's mission was a greater one. That had been what his actions were for. The cleansing of his house so that he could join in this deed for the god.

Clenching his fists, Tisamenos turned to face them, and he was matter of fact once more. 'And how in the name of the Skyfather do we get there? Over land is thousands of miles.'

'If only we could fly,' Elissa said, thoughtfully, watching the buzzard. 'How did Hero move us with those feathers?'

'Spells. Some terrible dark spell. I don't trust that kind of thing.' Tisamenos frowned.

There was a rumbling sound, like rocks falling, and he placed his mutilated hand with its stone stump on the ground. His face wrinkled in concentration as he struggled to understand the harsh speech of the rocks. They were trying to warn him of something, some gathering darkness.

His anger was too loud; he could not make out what they were saying. There was only the hissing and clattering of thousands of harsh tongues.

Watch out, one said. Watch out. From the Nine Rivers. Darkness. World. Watch out. Under.

It was too late.

He saw that something was coming out of the hollow where the others had slept, something shadowy and huge.

It crawled out into the light and unfurled, pulling itself into an upright position so that it looked like a very tall man wrapped in a billowing black cloak. It seemed to flicker in and out of existence like a candle, and had a long white face, with black glowing spheres for eyes.

Something else came with it too. A sense of terrible loneliness, of an echoing, empty space.

The creature took a step towards them.

Tisamenos, trembling in every part of his body, unwrapped the head of the Last Gorgon, but the long white face merely laughed darkly, and came further towards them.

There was no escape from this being. It seemed to stretch until it was bigger than the hill, whilst at the same time remaining what it was, a giant moving forwards.

Silvius called, 'What about the Arrow?'

'I don't know what will happen!' Elissa stepped forwards, her hand behind her back, ready to pull it out.

The creature sniffed the air, and halted a few hands' breadth away from them. The solitude radiating from it was almost overwhelming, and Tisamenos was all but ready to give in.

Then, to his astonishment, it bowed, its great forehead brushing the ground.

'Stones told about you,' it hissed, raising its head, black eyes glinting. 'What you carry. Where you must travel.' It wrapped its black cloak around itself. 'Sun rising. Come with me. I take you to Troy.'

Across the plain there was a cloud of dust, and armour glinting in the sunlight. An army from Argos, marching on Mykenai, about to attack his city when it was at its most vulnerable. Feeling a pressure in his mind as if he were about to split in two, Tisamenos resolved to treat this being with the utmost courtesy.

'Who are you, lord?' asked Tisamenos.

'I live in darkness,' the creature answered. 'And I take you through darkness.'

Tisamenos felt the hairs rise all over his body. Something strange was happening to him. The Nine Rivers. The Darkness. 'Is that – is that the Underworld?'

'You have no choice.' As if he were nothing more than thistledown on the wind, it lifted Tisamenos onto its shoulder. He saw the horror-struck eyes of Silvius and Elissa as it bundled the other two under its arms.

Its touch was like snow. A sadness consumed Tisamenos. He did not want to even look at the others, and all he could think about was the blackness of the creature's robe, and then the cave's entrance, and he was falling down a long tunnel.

They were leaving the dawn light behind, and the breeze, and now there was nothing but shadow.

Thirty-One

Into Darkness

Silvius recognised the coldness. It drew him back to the vision of Python. The feeling lasted for a long time. He was dizzied, and fragments flashed in front of his eyes, confused and confusing.

The whiteness of a long fang. The smoke from a funeral pyre. Red-eyed enemies, rushing towards him, death in their hearts. All the time the creature sang to itself, a low rumble.

He fell and fell, until he could not tell what was up and what was down, and his head felt as if it might never stop spinning.

Without a bump, the falling simply stopped.

The creature released them.

Silvius rolled into a patch of boggy ground, the other two falling beside him. He lay disoriented for a second, sensing emptiness around him. With relief, he saw Elissa was near him, and then the Achaean, Tisamenos, helping her up. He jumped up too, his feet sinking into mulch. Above was a small, faint orb, and his eyes could only make out outlines.

In the far distance there was a red light, as if from a huge fire.

'Python . . .' Silvius tensed. 'Where have we been brought?' He moved closer to Elissa, able now to make out her worried features. He saw the Arrow on her back, and had a sudden longing for the light of Apollo. 'Could you take it out?' He reached towards it.

'I don't think so.' Elissa moved away resolutely.

'She's right.' Tisamenos came forwards. 'The light of Apollo is not for this place . . .'

'This is not what I thought the Underworld would be like.' Elissa's voice echoed loudly, making Silvius flinch. When Tisamenos put his arm around Elissa, Silvius turned away.

The white-faced creature that had brought them walked on, expecting them to follow. Silvius bent down to the ground, and his hand came away covered in some kind of slime. Walking through it was like wading through wet sand.

He trudged onwards, at the rear of the straggling procession. Blackness was all around them. At every step, his heart felt heavier. He began to wonder what it would be like to hear the trill of a bird once more, to feel the light broken by forest leaves on his cheek.

The glowing orb above them did not move. Time itself did not exist in this place. There was nothing to mark their way, and it seemed as if every pace was the same, that he was stuck in an endless loop, and would never be able to escape. The freezing air got into his eyes, his nose, his mouth, filling him from the inside with the touch of death.

When he thought he would not be able to move his foot again, the air around him subtly shifted, and became almost imperceptibly lighter.

'Ahead!' Elissa's voice was faint but clear.

There were two dim spots, like stars in the night sky, shrouded in mist.

'Light!' Elissa spoke again, stronger now.

It was coming from two lamps which were set on either side of a jetty, and at the end of the jetty was a boat, bobbing up and down gently.

Elissa embraced Tisamenos, then, looking at Silvius over his shoulder, she beckoned him, and gratefully he joined her.

The creature hissed at them, 'No delay.' Its voice was so cold and powerful they had to obey.

It creaked past them and flowed into the boat, taking up position at the helm. The boat was an unpainted thing that looked as if it might be full of holes. Silvius was suddenly terrified in that blank space where nothing grew or lived, with only the dull sound of black water washing against the muddy banks and the featureless face of their companion, white in the lamplight.

'You are the ferryman,' said Silvius quietly. 'I will not get on your boat. You take souls into the Underworld.'

'Safe passage,' hissed the ferryman. 'I take no gift.'

'How do we know?' Silvius said. 'You brought us here against our will.'

'Look here.'

From out of the shadows, a figure emerged. The lower half a beast, the upper part human. For a moment Silvius thought it was Stargazer's spirit, come to help them in the Underworld. It came further into the light. A mane, glowing with health and colour. A woman, clothed in white, pearl-eyes staring.

Riding on her lion, it was the Sibyl.

Silvius felt a great rush of relief.

She greeted them; Elissa had already buried her face in the lion's mane in welcome. 'I came from Sicilia through the dark ways to aid you, as my mother did your father Aeneas when he came to the Underworld. Python gathers an army. He will consume everything in his path, including those that remain here.'

'We are few . . .' said the ferryman. 'King and queen long gone, through a gap in time. I saw them go. World of ice. I stayed. I ferry the souls. They come still, sometimes.' It was the longest Silvius had heard him speak, and there was a desperate, dull sadness in the words.

'Where else do they go?' asked Tisamenos.

The ferryman shrugged. 'I know the river, the two banks. The stones and the earth.'

Dismounting, the Sibyl deftly embarked. With a leap, the lion followed her, and Silvius was relieved to see that the boat remained steady.

'We go this way,' said the Sibyl, 'and bring you out by the ruins of Troy. You cannot return, as the ghosts will only let you pass once – until it is your time.'

'I do not wish to come back here,' said Silvius.

'I want to see the sea again,' replied Elissa.

'And the sun.' Tisamenos held his hand out to Elissa, and she took it gratefully, clambering onto the boat beside the lion and immediately burying her face in his mane again. The beast flicked his tail in response. Silvius, however, ignored the other boy's gesture, and jumped on by himself, sitting a little way apart by the Sibyl.

Once they were all on board, the boat seemed to have expanded. The lion's head was raised, but even he was subdued, his eyes dulled.

The ferryman pushed off, and rowed them out into the dark, swirling waters of the River Styx. The blackness was infinite, the oar strokes were slow, and the water that splashed them was freezing.

Hollow booms sounded in the distance. The monsters of the Underworld that Silvius's father sometimes spoke of – might it be them? Or might the ancient Titans be tortured still for their crimes? He shuddered, and snuggled into the lion, which kept him warm as the boat made its way steadily onwards into the darkness.

Soon the lights of the jetty behind them had gone, and ahead was only the water and the blackness and the cold and that terrible loneliness.

Silvius did not dare to speak. The space around them might steal the words from his lips, might suck his life out through his mouth, pull him into watery oblivion.

Tisamenos clutched the Last Gorgon's head in its sack between his knees; Elissa clamped onto the quiver as if it were a branch and she a drowning girl. Silvius stared out into the blackness. He didn't miss the Arrowhead, but he still hadn't quite made sense of the vision that it had given him, and now that Elissa had the quiver, he wondered what role was left for him to play. Was he needed, now that Tisamenos had come along? Would Elissa be able to carry the Bow and Arrow by herself? The Sibyl's sightless eyes seemed to glow in the gloom as she stroked her lion's mane. All the time the ferryman rowed, his oars slipping in and out of the water.

And at last lights appeared ahead of them, beacons in the murk, and the boat cut on through the sluggish waves, until it bumped against the shore, and the ferryman slipped out.

As Silvius passed him he bowed again, and whispered something that sounded like, 'Go well.' But Silvius thought, for a moment, that he might have been saying, 'Save yourselves.'

He slid back into his boat and cast off, and soon he was gone, the companions alone on the far side of the Styx, in the depths of the Underworld. The ground was harder here, and the light was now a kind of grey shimmer. Even the Sibyl and her lion looked insubstantial.

From ahead, rumbling and loud, came a sound like a great roar.

'What was that?' Silvius looked around. Through the gloom in front of them appeared the outline of a beast. He gripped his sword, and realised that it would be as effective against this thing as a pin.

It was vast, and it was angry. It reared upwards, higher than the ferryman, and it had many heads at the ends of long necks, some like snakes, some like wolves, some like lions. All of the heads were spitting and foaming with rage.

'What is it?' asked Silvius, trembling.

'One of Python's children . . .' The Sibyl's fingers tightened their grip on her lion's mane.

With a growl, a wolf's head came rushing towards Silvius. Panicked, he jumped out of the way, the head missing him by a knuckle's breadth. Tisamenos had bashed away a lion's head, but it was already springing back. And Elissa was running from a snake, fangs exposed. There was no escape from those jaws, those huge, terrible appetites.

Snapping back, the wolf head faced Silvius once more, and gritting his teeth, he stabbed it in the cheek. His sword came out bloody and steaming, but the wolf's head simply shook itself from side to side. And then it paused, looking down at Silvius, as if considering how exactly it was going to destroy him.

It was about to strike. Whichever way he turned, he would not escape it. Desperate, Silvius pointed the sword upwards, hoping that as it came down he would be able to get its throat.

The wolf's head gathered its strength. It had yellow eyes, its mouth open revealing sharp fangs that dripped with slobber.

A beam of light, hurtling through the darkness, struck the wolf on its skull, and it whimpered and withdrew. Silvius saw the Sibyl with a glowing golden staff in her hand, the aura expanding and surrounding him in a shield of brightness.

Fangs dripping with venom, the many-headed monster shrieked an unearthly cry from all its heads.

'This light will keep us safe,' shouted the Sibyl. 'Keep close to me.'

Roaring with frustration, the monster flung several of its heads towards them. Silvius tensed.

But the light protected them, and the beast gave one last howl of rage as they rushed away.

Once they'd gone some distance, they slowed to a walk. The golden light made a circle around them, flickering and bright.

Outside its reach, Silvius sensed movement. Once he thought his name was being called, and he turned around and saw something like a person, but wispy and insubstantial. Tisamenos was looking about from side to side, whilst Elissa had her hands over her ears. Only the Sibyl walked calmly, straight and unerring, and the lion kept up the rear.

Again Silvius thought he heard his name. His hairs were standing on end, his arms covered in goose pimples.

'What is it?' he asked.

'It's the Underworld,' answered the Sibyl. 'Do not listen. It will drive you mad.'

His name again. That shade, slipping away just out of his vision. Was it one of his ancestors? He paused, and turned.

And then Silvius, tripping over his sandal, fell, and landed outside the light.

Within moments terrible cold hands were clawing at him. Faces surrounded him, distorted by loneliness and hatred, their features locked into grimaces of pain. They whispered his name.

He felt his life ebbing away from him as the hungry ghosts began to feed.

Thirty-Two

The Choice of Achilleos

'Silvius!' Tisamenos gasped as the black-haired boy sprawled on his back, and almost immediately vanished under a crowd of spirits.

Without even thinking, and ignoring the Sibyl's cry, he rushed out of the circle and grabbed Silvius by the shoulder, plunging through the freezing spirits to drag him back, Elissa now helping too, until both were within the bounds of the light once more.

Around the edges the ghosts prowled. Silvius, eyes flickering, sat up weakly.

'I give you thanks,' he whispered. 'I thought I had died . . .'

'And you could have died too,' intoned the Sibyl. 'We must not dally in this place.'

Hefting him up, Tisamenos said, 'We can't lose you.'

Elissa gently took Silvius's other arm, and the three of them hurried on behind the Sibyl, linked now, moving as quickly as they could.

More silver orbs appeared above, Tisamenos saw. In the distance on the tops of hills, huge shapes like fortresses rose up. They even passed a wood, and the banks of a stream that flowed sluggishly back to the water it had come from. It was like a ghostly parody of the world above.

Soon Tisamenos felt the way underfoot become smooth, like marble. When he stopped the group to place his hand on the surface, he heard thousands of dark voices that spoke of things he did not understand. The endless echoing that was always at the edge of his mind was now magnified. They were warning him of something, too, something about Troy ... Terrified, he quickly removed his hand. It seemed that only in Achaea, his own land, could he touch the stones and be able to bear it.

They were now passing through a hall, echoing and vast, and here some torches were alight, torches that, Tisamenos shuddered to think, no mortal had set, and no mortal could put out.

'This is the hall of the King and Queen of the Dead,' said the Sibyl. 'They have many names, but Hades and Persephone will be known to you.'

'Hades?' said Silvius.

'You call him Pluto,' answered the Sibyl. 'Though he and the Queen have long since departed.'

Two huge thrones, carved out of solid granite, gilded with

silver, dominated the space. In front of them were gathered a group of souls.

They rustled like a billow of leaves, and turned as one, rushing to the light of the Sibyl like a swarm of moths. Silvius shuddered, and Elissa shrank closer. But Tisamenos looked outwards because he thought he caught a glimpse of something, shining among the grey and gloom.

Nearer she came. White robes, gold at her wrists and her neck.

Tisamenos let go of Elissa. He gulped.

It was Hermione.

Tisamenos's mother, as golden as he remembered her. She reached out towards her son, her long hair drifting about her neck, her bright blue eyes smiling. She was wearing a necklace that he remembered, one given to her by a Thessalian king.

'Don't touch her!' The Sibyl's warning was swift.

Tisamenos could not help himself. Suddenly he was a tiny boy again, just wanting to be picked up and comforted, wanting the warm security of his mother's embrace. He came as close as he dared to the edge of the light, showed her his mutilated hand. His mother held up hers in return, and they almost touched, a hair's breadth of space between them.

'Mother . . .'

'My little lion cub . . . my son . . . What has happened to you?'

He had to tell her. She could be at peace; he could release her from this shadowy place. 'You have to know that Erigone has been punished for what she did. Your death has been avenged, and the curse has left the House of Atreos.'

Hermione lowered her hand, and relief spread across her face. 'I have been waiting here for judgement for I do not know how long. You have given it to me in this terrible place. Oh, my darling Tisamenos . . . now I can be at peace. Sometimes it is all I can remember, her face.' She frowned for a moment. 'My son, no longer a lion cub, but a lion of Mykenai. I give you blessings . . .'

She began to fade from view, but just before she vanished, she smiled.

'Seize life,' she said. 'It is short, and you must take it and live as fully as you can. Do not make the same mistake as Achilleos . . .' Tisamenos let out a sob.

Then there was nothing where she had stood. 'Where has she gone?'

'She has returned into the rushing of things. We must not stay,' said the Sibyl. On they hurried, and it felt to Tisamenos as if they were walking into the wind, the souls of the dead swirling around them, calling, stretching out for comfort and love. Was Achilleos among them? He'd been the greatest warrior of the Achaeans, and had chosen a short life full of glory.

Tisamenos was glad when the empty thrones of Hades and Persephone receded into the distance, and the ghosts fell away, moaning and bewailing their fate.

It was silent once more. The incline was steep, the path rocky, and beside them tramped a huge figure, pushing a rock upwards, and when they reached the top of the hill, the rock rolled back down, and the figure, silent and grim, plodded back down to retrieve it.

'Sisyphus,' said the Sibyl.

The wicked king, still carrying out his punishment, trapped in his futile action. Tisamenos shuddered, and remembered what had befallen his ancestors. Were they still here?

The weight of the atmosphere was getting to him. He was feeling listless and strange. Elissa was drooping, and Silvius was even paler than he had been.

At the summit Tisamenos could see out across what seemed to be a black plain. In the distance were two shimmering beacons.

'Those mark the gates. One of those leads to the ruins of Troy,' said the Sibyl. She seemed to falter, and the light from her staff flickered.

'What is it?' asked Tisamenos.

She sniffed the air, as if sensing something, and whispered to the lion, which leapt forwards down the hill. At the edge of the blackness it turned back, scrambling up to join them, tail drooping and head slung low.

'Something has changed. As Hades departs, so his world seems to shrink. There is nothing here. We cannot walk on nothing.' The lion roared, and his roar reverberated in that vastness, vanishing into the silence.

This was the end, then. They could not stay here. But Tisamenos could not bear the thought of crossing back through the halls of the dead. And hadn't the Sibyl said they would not be allowed again?

Something harsh sounded, distant at first. Tisamenos felt an eerie thrill of recognition.

Three huge shapes swooped down upon them, dark and stinking, three winged beasts that landed in front of them, creatures like women.

Instead of skin, however, they had scales, and leathery wings that thunderously clapped behind them. They scraped their talons on the ground and roared, eyes flashing with fire.

It was the Furies, all three of them, and they had come for him after all. Tisamenos, terrified, prepared himself to fight.

The middle Fury lifted up her head. Her eyes were yellow and bright, with huge dark pupils, and she stared right at him.

'Peace, child. I give you my name. Tisiphone.'

Her name. Like the Gorgon, Tisamenos now had her name. And he did not like the fact that it chimed so nearly with his. Trembling, he inclined his head.

'We have not come for you. I returned here, to my home. But I found that we are not wanted now. Our king and queen have vanished, and we cannot find the way to where they have gone.' She flicked her tail, and it cracked like a whip. 'This is all that remains to us, this hall of lost souls. Python will destroy even us.'

'We have the means to destroy Python.' Elissa spoke, though she was shaking. 'You could help us.'

'What are you doing?' Tisamenos turned to Elissa. 'These things will kill us!'

'We will not help you.' It was the largest who spoke. Her breath was foul.

Tisamenos knew it. How could these creatures be of use to them? He shrank from them, not knowing where to turn.

'But it is in our interests that Python be destroyed.'

This could not be true. 'And so we will fly you to the gates. Climb on our backs. You will be the first and only mortals to have been so close to a Fury, and lived.'

Elissa flashed a grim smile at Tisamenos. He could not hide his astonishment.

The three Furies crouched down, facing the distant gleam of the gates. The Sibyl said, 'I thank you, great goddesses. But there is no room for me. You three will go alone. I will return through the dark ways to Sicilia.'

'Don't leave us now!' Elissa threw her arms around the Sibyl's neck, and the Sibyl bent to kiss her on the top of the head.

The Sibyl said, 'Go through the golden gate – it will take you to the ruins of Troy.'

'Will the lion go with you?' asked Elissa. Tisamenos could tell she was missing Ruffler.

'The lion is me,' said the Sibyl, and for a moment, confusingly, it seemed as if the two were as one, not joined together like a centaur but taking up the same space, superimposed on each other.

And then they separated, and were lion and woman once more, the Sibyl's white sightless eyes stark in the darkness. She drew the folds of her white robes apart, and placed her golden staff back beneath them. The lion roared, and his roar dispersed into the echoes and booms of the Underworld.

'Sibyl, I give you thanks,' said Silvius. 'For me, for my father, for my people, for the whole world . . .'

'And I too,' Tisamenos joined. 'You have been our guide and our comfort. I wish that you would not go.'

'I must. You do not need to give me thanks. I am the mouthpiece of Apollo, and I must help him. Just go, and do what you must do. Python must not retake Delphi.' She kissed each of them in turn.

With a few bounds, she and her lion had vanished, leaving Tisamenos and his companions facing the Furies alone.

Trembling, Tisamenos neared the first Fury. The stench was unbearable, like sulphur and rotting flesh. Her back was slimy and scaly, her wings leathery and huge, her black hair long and lank. Her claws were curved like a hawk's. He gulped, and, carefully holding the sack behind his back, clambered on.

The other two had mounted. He looked to see if Elissa was safe, and she shot him a glance of determination. Silvius was holding on, knuckles white. Each Fury began to lumber forwards, and then with a horrible lurch they were in the air, soaring above the shadows, bellowing like bears.

Tisamenos held on tightly to the Fury's neck, encircling it with his arms. He tried not to think too much about how the Fury had consumed Erigone. As her powerful shoulder muscles pumped her wings, he found himself being bumped up and down.

The twin lights were now near, one silver, one gold, both framing arches that became clearer and clearer, seemingly made out of light, opening into the fabric of the shadows.

The Furies, circling the gates, cawed and boomed, and swooped in to land. They did so remarkably lightly, almost like cats.

Tisamenos scrambled off as quickly as he could. Elissa leapt down neatly, whilst Silvius followed a little more cumbersomely.

The Furies hissed, and spat, and clawed at the ground.

Tisamenos bowed low to them. He was still terrified of them, but now as he looked he saw that their eyes were deep and sad, and that their faces were expressive of a sorrow he could never hope to understand. These elemental beings had haunted his house for so long. And now they had helped him.

Wings beating, the Furies took off. He had not had time to thank them. Somehow, they were beyond those courtesies.

Tisamenos faced the archway. Behind him were the pulsing shadows of the Underworld. Elissa grabbed his mutilated hand, and he squeezed hers in return. He took Silvius in his other hand, and said, 'We've passed through the Underworld. Nothing we face now can be as hard. We will find the Bow, and then we will bring down Python.'

He led them through the golden arch.

As if the sun were blazing out its rays, there was a flash.

The shadows were gone. And now there was air, sweet air, and the smell of the sea.

Thirty-Three

The Ruins of Troy

The shore was long, the sand they stood on deep gold. Behind the three companions, the foamy sea was drawing out, leaving long strands of seaweed and dark wet sand behind it. There was a bright whiteness to the air, the sun high and dazzling, and the sky unclouded. Gulls swooped low over the surface, catching silvery fish in their beaks. No boat swam on the waves. Silvius was in the place his father had fled, fifteen years ago, the pain of it still burning in Aeneas's heart, the place where his ancestors had lived and fought and died.

Silvius watched as Tisamenos stretched out his limbs on the sand and yawned with exhaustion; meanwhile, Elissa was standing, letting the waves wash her feet, gazing thoughtfully out towards the horizon, looking, Silvius knew, for the Phoenician trading ships she longed to meet. Silvius envied them, knowing that soon he would have to turn and confront the destruction of his city.

The stink of the Furies was still in his nostrils. He took a deep breath, and listened to the shriek of gulls and the sucking sound of the tide. At his feet lay a shell, white and pink, spiralling to a point. Whatever had lived in it had long gone. He picked it up and hurled it away.

When he could breathe freely, and the only thing he could smell was the sea, Silvius pulled himself upright. He would look now.

There, across the broad plains, was a hill. A river ran by it, reaching the sea near to them, its mouth wide enough for two ships to pass through.

This was it. This was the place Silvius's family had been torn from, their once proud and royal city. But now there was nothing but a rubble of black, scorched stones.

Once, his father had told him, the towers of Troy rose into the sky. It was the richest city, grander by far than anything the sheep-stealing Achaeans could manage. The sight of it made Silvius clutch his head in sadness, and he could not help the tears that followed. Here, his cousin Hector had been slain by Achilles. King Priam himself had been murdered at the altar. How many thousands of Trojans had died? How many had been slain and left unburied, how many enslaved and taken captive?

His father was right. The Achaeans were monsters.

Tisamenos joined him, placing a hand on his shoulder, and he shuddered involuntarily, pushing it off. 'Your city has burnt,' said Tisamenos, 'but you're building again. I don't know what's happening to mine.'

'This was your fault. Your family.' Rage blinded Silvius.

Elissa got up too, dusted the sand off her tunic and squeezed his arm. 'At least you have a city,' she said. 'I'm neither one thing nor the other.'

She was right. And Tisamenos was right, too. Mykenai might be in ruins by now as well, or captured by enemy forces. He had to put all that behind him.

'Let's go,' said Elissa. 'There's a river over there. We can get some water.'

'The Simois.' Silvius knew the name. They set off towards its banks. 'I know the warrior Achilles fought the river god before he slew Hector.'

'Achilles? We call him Achilleos. He was killed by a Trojan,' answered Tisamenos.

'So an Achaean killed a Trojan and was killed in turn by a Trojan.' The spiral again. He wondered if he could ever get out of it.

Once they'd drunk from the clear waters, and filled their water skins, they turned towards the ruins.

The whole plain was deserted, covered in scrub and weeds. They could walk straight up the hill and find the Temple of Apollo, and there the Bow which could shoot Apollo's Arrow and slay Python.

Tisamenos clicked his knuckles together, making Elissa laugh, but Silvius frowned and pressed on.

'We're almost there,' Elissa said. 'Almost at the Bow!'

'And then how will we get back?' Silvius could not bear the thought of being stuck here.

'We'll have to deal with that when we come to it,' said Tisamenos, confidently.

The Last Gorgon's head was slung across his shoulders; Elissa had the quiver.

But Silvius had nothing.

He looked up, and saw there were many birds circling around the summit of the hill of Troy, and as they neared he realised these were crows and vultures. He shuddered to think what they might be feasting on. Clouds were scudding across the sun, sending huge shadows across the stark plain.

They reached the slopes. Scrub was growing over the stones. Already it was looking as if there had never been a city here at all. The landscape itself was consuming his history, and soon nobody would remember.

Would Brutus care about Troy? Would his children know? Would their stories become mangled, changed by many tongues, until they were nothing but shadows of memories?

Something golden, glinting among the sandy soil, caught Silvius's eye, and he paused to look. He knelt to brush the earth away with his fingers, and revealed a breastplate, engraved with wolves. Holding it up, he realised that it was almost exactly the same size as he was. He shivered suddenly. Had it belonged to one of his young cousins? Out of King Priam's fifty sons, only one, Helenus the seer, had survived. Carefully he laid it back where it had been, leaving it for the dust and the sun.

'Try it on,' said Elissa.

'I can't – it would be taking something that isn't mine. I don't know whose it was – his ghost could be around here . . .'

'Try it.' She smiled at him encouragingly. 'Pour a libation first.'

So Silvius knelt, poured out some water on the dust and prayed to the shade of his dead kinsman. A breeze ruffled his hair, and a seagull shrieked.

He lifted up the breastplate. The leather straps were in good condition. He placed it over his neck, and Elissa fastened the buckles. It fitted. It might have been made for him.

'Thank you,' he said.

Tisamenos eyed him with a keen glance. 'Looks good on you,' he said, a little grudgingly.

Ahead was a ring of rubble that must have been the walls of the citadel of Troy. Tisamenos strode in front, with Elissa half-skipping to keep up, whilst Silvius picked his way over the stones more carefully.

A road wound in a circle, slabs of coloured marble blocking it occasionally that might have belonged to houses or temples. Once they passed what was unmistakeably a human skull. Silvius paused, whilst the others went on ahead. Kneeling, he stroked it lightly with his fingertips, sending a message of comfort to whatever ghost might still be haunting it. It occurred to him that he could not tell if it were Achaean or Trojan.

A voice made him look up. 'Did Aeneas ever talk to you about Troy?' Tisamenos was there, standing loosely, with his arms crossed over his shoulders.

Silvius stood up. 'All the time. But only about what happened here. Not so much about the layout of the city itself. I only know that he gathered his followers by some tree. And there aren't any trees left.'

'How on earth are we going to find the Temple of Apollo?' Tisamenos was squinting into the sunlight.

'We know what his statues look like,' said Elissa. 'We'll have to look for one. It might have fallen near his temple.'

Silvius led the way, continuing on the road into the heart of the citadel. There was rubble everywhere. Some of the stones were too large to move. As they searched, he began to wonder whether the gods had really left this city once and for all.

There was no sign of a statue, or an altar of any kind.

After about an hour, during which they found nothing but an old battered helmet, Silvius turned to Tisamenos. He was beginning to get desperate. 'Talk to the stones.' This Achaean, whose grandfather had wasted the city, he had to make reparation now.

Tisamenos slumped and put his hands on his face. 'I can't. It's too much. It's too painful. The stones – they don't like me here. They know who my grandfather was. In the Underworld, it was awful. And here I can sense them, their hatred.'

'I don't see that we have any other way,' said Silvius. The heat was getting to him. He was thirsty. 'You do it by touching them with your hand, don't you? I've seen you. Does it work if someone else makes you touch them?' He moved forwards, his shadow falling over Tisamenos. He was trembling a little.

'I wouldn't want you to try that,' said Tisamenos. He tightened his grip on the neck of the bag in which the Last Gorgon's head was kept.

'You wouldn't dare.'

'Wait!' Silvius turned to see Elissa, standing proudly by a large block of marble. With her back to the sun, it looked as if she was outlined in light. 'I've found a statue!'

Ashamed of his anger, but now feeling a jagged sense of annoyance that it was Elissa who had found it, Silvius went to look.

Lying on its side, toppled from its pedestal, was a larger-than-life statue of a young man. Its bright colours were still there, though now faded. It was a youth with golden hair, carrying a lyre. 'It must be him,' said Elissa. 'Apollo, Lord of Light, Lord of the Lyre. So his temple must be near here.'

With renewed energy, Silvius began to scramble around, looking for where the temple might have stood. He would find it first, he was sure of it. The others dispersed to different parts of the small square.

He searched and searched. He had finished the last drop from his water skin.

After a while, Elissa came to him. 'I've found nothing,' she said gently.

Tisamenos approached from the other side. 'I'm sorry,' he said, clasping his hands to his chest.

The sun was beginning to set, and it was almost twilight. Bats zigzagged about above their heads.

Silvius threw himself down in frustration, grazing his hand on the stone. 'Oh, Apollo . . . if only you could help us now!'

But there was no answer. Only the wind in the stones, and the last rays of the sun.

Their situation became clear to Silvius. They had not much food left, and no way of returning home. They didn't even know how far the nearest settlement was. Had any of the Trojan allies survived the devastation, or had they all fled to the interior?

They had to find the Bow of Apollo, or they would surely die.

The Trojan breastplate bumped against his chest. Whoever had worn it, he reflected, would be ashamed of him. He had to show himself a true Trojan. Resolute now, he decided that he would lead, like his father.

Elissa was scratching in the dirt with a stick. Tisamenos was leaning against a wall. Silvius called them together. 'Let's rest for the night. We can drink water from Simois, and we've still got some provisions left. Tomorrow maybe we can catch a bird or a rabbit.' Though he hadn't seen any evidence of rabbits. His heart began to sink again.

'Let's do one more round,' Elissa said, her voice falsely bright. 'We might have missed something.' She looked askance at Tisamenos, but he shook his head. 'I would do it for you, if I had the power.'

'It's not power . . . it's dark and strange and I wish I didn't have it . . .'

Pain shone in Tisamenos's flinty eyes. Silvius caught the look. It might be painful, but he would have to try.

Elissa grasped Tisamenos by the hand and felt the stump of his finger. 'I can't possibly know what it's like to be you. But you have to do this.'

'Sometimes I wonder why,' said Tisamenos, gently. 'One city falls, another rises. What will there be left for me when I return home?'

Elissa looked up. 'Why do you have to go home? You could come with me. Then the stones will not haunt you any more. The curse on your house is ended. When this is finished, you can start again.'

Silvius felt his cheeks burning and the anger dissipating into something else.

The stars were beginning to appear. A breeze rushed over them, making them shiver slightly. Silvius watched as the son of Orestes looked out across the darkening plain, and said, 'I'll do it. If we can't find it tomorrow, I'll do it. And then, Elissa, I'll come with you, wherever you go.'

Elissa and Tisamenos embraced, and Silvius stood at the side, angry at himself, full of confusion.

When they released each other, he nodded his thanks, suppressing his emotions. 'Now let's find somewhere sheltered to sleep.'

A stone fell to the ground, as if it had been knocked over. A snarl, like a dog. Silvius whipped round, sword already out of his scabbard.

A red glow appeared, lighting up the stones with scarlet, the same kind of scarlet that shone in the eyes of those possessed by the Enemy, that had stained the sea crimson, that had dispersed into the air above Lavinium.

'Elissa!' called Silvius. 'The Arrow! Tisamenos, ready the sack!'

From behind a large boulder appeared three men, each bearing torches, and a large dog, heavy and slinking.

'Attack!'

Silvius ran forwards, sword raised.

But a deep voice simply laughed, and said, 'Three young ones in the ruins of Troy? We've seen no ship land here for years. You are no traders from Tyre.'

Stopping in surprise, his sandaled feet skidding, Silvius looked more carefully at the men. Their leader, who had spoken, was old, with long grey hair bound by white priestly bands, and an amused look on his deeply lined, long face. The other two, who appeared equally old, wore red bands that fluttered in the breeze. Though frail, they moved with purpose. The dog bounded straight up to Elissa and put his paws on her shoulders; she pushed it off, smiling, and it lay at her feet, presenting its pink belly to be rubbed. Tisamenos kept his hand in the lip of the sack.

'Who are you?' Silvius demanded, weapon still poised.

'Young man,' said the leader, 'I might well ask the same question of you.' He gave his torch to one of his companions. 'Except that I do not need to.'

'What do you mean?' Tisamenos approached carefully.

'The birds told us.' The man began busying himself with something he drew out of a casket, a powder that he threw into the air, mumbling beneath his breath. The other two men imitated the actions and sounds he was making. The dog came to the leader's side, tongue hanging out.

'The birds told you in the auguries,' said Elissa.

'You are right. They tell us the future in their flight. I am Chryses, priest of Apollo. And we know all about you. I know what you are carrying in that quiver.' Chryses cut over their exclamations. 'And we can show you what you are looking for.'

'How do we know this isn't a trap?' Silvius asked.

The priest smiled, and pressed his gnarled, liver-spotted hands together. 'You can't, of course. We could be anyone. But do you have any other choice?'

Silvius glanced at Tisamenos and Elissa. It was true. They would have to stay on their own for a whole day tomorrow, and hunt for food, if they did not go with the priests. And they had no idea how to get back.

'We will go with you.'

Chryses bowed and mumbled a few words of prayer.

'Now, you must follow me. Come along, then.'

He went straight through the middle of his companions, and stopped a few paces away from them. For a moment he seemed lit by a sun that was not there – and then he was gone.

'What – where did he go?' The priest had simply vanished.

'Come with us,' said the other two priests, 'and you will see.'

The second of the priests went to where Chryses had stood. Now it seemed as if he too were lit by a different sun. Silvius squinted.

Chryses was there and yet he was not there. If Silvius was simply looking around the space, he saw a line of broken stones and the statue of Apollo on its side. But if he stared and narrowed his eyes, he saw something else entirely.

As Silvius followed the priests, the world around him shifted.

The sky was now bright, with the sun high above them. It felt as if here the sun never went down, the sea was eternally clear, the shore untouched by warships or raiders. This was the Temple of Apollo at Troy, a beautiful high altar before the steps of a large pillared building, and a statue of the god himself, presiding.

He had come home.

Thirty-Four

The Temple of Apollo

In front of Elissa rose a tall altar, before which Chryses was now kneeling. A sacrifice was burning, and the smell of roasting ox filled her nostrils, tinged with the lighter scent of cedar. Behind the altar was a large marble-pillared building with a huge stone flight of steps leading up to it, cut smoothly out of massive rocks. The building was painted in lively crimsons and golds, and it shone as if lit from within.

The other two priests joined Chryses in kneeling, adding their voices to his prayers. Elissa watched Silvius kneel with the priests, eyes shining, and Tisamenos for once looked at peace, resting his load and closing his eyes. She herself joined them, thinking of Apollo and his light, and letting the sun warm her.

Chryses finished his prayer, and stood up to welcome them, opening his arms out wide. 'The Temple of Apollo,' he said. 'Still here in the ruins of Troy, if you know where to look, hidden in a fold of the world. We worship the Lord of Light, coming here as often as we can, and will do as long as we live.' A flicker of sadness crossed his eyes. He knew that would not be long, thought Elissa. Then he cleared his throat, and banged his stick once, sharply on the ground.

'An Achaean, a Trojan and a Carthaginian,' said Chryses. She knew it. She had been right about that. They were meant to be together like this. 'Now I cannot see what happens next. I cannot enter the temple, and I do not know what is in there. You must go in and see what Apollo has prepared for you.'

He gestured to them, as if shooing away birds.

Elissa took to the stone steps, leading the way to the shadowy entrance above.

This was what she had been looking forward to. The sense of Apollo himself was filling her, his light, his brightness, his purity. She paused in the portico. It was dark inside. But impelled, she went on, and the others followed.

Inside the temple a huge expanse of gleaming white marble floor spread out in front of them.

Right at the far end, Elissa was delighted to see a statue of Apollo looming above them, holding his lyre. The paints were bold and bright, his hair shining, the lyre too.

'It must be there,' she shouted, excitement brimming in her voice. 'Let's go!'

She set off towards it. Tisamenos caught up with her, and then Silvius was overtaking them both. Laughing, they turned it into a race, and Elissa put on a spurt of speed.

But when she looked up, the statue was still as far away as it had been when she'd started.

Puzzled, Elissa stopped.

Tisamenos had paused too, and was staring at the statue in befuddlement. Silvius was pacing back and forth, nonplussed. Elissa started again, slower this time; after ten steps she stopped and looked back.

Still she had made no progress. Each time she ran, she would only end up in the same place, just near the portico.

Annoyed, Elissa peered outside where she could see the sky and the priests.

'What's happening?' Tisamenos asked.

'I don't know. It's some kind of magic.'

Tentatively she tried to step outside. There was a barrier there, something she could not see. She pushed harder, and some invisible force knocked her back.

They were stuck.

'Don't panic,' said Elissa. 'Think carefully. We're in the Temple of Apollo. He wants us to be here.'

'But there will be safeguards around the Bow, to stop the wrong people,' cut in Tisamenos. 'Like the Fury guarding the Shaft.'

'The temple won't let any of us approach the statue. We must be thinking about this in the wrong way.' Silvius's brow creased.

Elissa unslung the quiver. 'I think I should open it.' She glanced at Tisamenos, who nodded. Silvius thrummed his fingers uncertainly.

'I think,' said Tisamenos slowly, 'that we should all do it.'

'If something goes wrong, we all die,' said Silvius.

'I'm prepared to take that risk,' answered Tisamenos.

'Apollo will not let us die,' said Elissa.

It was decided. They stood in a line, Tisamenos and Silvius on either side of Elissa, facing the statue of Apollo. Each of them clasped the quiver's cover, fingers touching. Elissa spoke. 'Apollo, Lord of Light. We bring you the Arrow that laid Python low. We need the Bow that can shoot it. We need your help.' As one, they lifted the cover of the quiver.

For a moment, there was nothing. Then Elissa felt the quiver shaking, and a great golden light issued from it.

The force of it was so powerful that it pushed the three of them backwards. Silvius and Tisamenos let go, but Elissa held on to it, until she could do so no longer.

The arrow shot out from the quiver. Elissa watched in astonishment as it trailed a bright stream of light, which spread out into a wide bridge, leading towards the statue, where the arrow lodged.

The bridge of light remained.

'It's for us!' Elissa called. 'Apollo is showing us the way . . .'

Elissa was about to step on it, when Silvius shoved past her, and began to walk. He called excitedly to his friends, 'Come on!'

Elissa sprang up after him. The bridge was solid, though it seemed to be constructed from light beams, woven together like a tapestry. With a few excited bounds, Silvius reached the end of the bridge, and jumped off, landing at the feet of Apollo's statue.

Elissa landed confidently behind Silvius, and Tisamenos a little more tentatively. As soon as they'd done so, the bridge of light disappeared. Looking back, Elissa saw the entrance to the temple now vanish into shadows.

'It's gone – the entrance. We can't go back that other way.'

Silvius grasped the Arrow, and pulled it out from where it had stuck into the statue's pedestal, placing it back in Elissa's quiver.

'Now what?'

Elissa cast around. There was only the statue, and a ledge above it. A gleam of something golden alerted her.

'I think that's it – up there!'

'Can you climb up and get it?'

'I think so . . .' She attempted to get a grip on the statue. There were many holds, but it was slippery. Tisamenos came to help her.

Then a hissing sound made Elissa jump.

'It can't be . . . I killed the Last Gorgon . . . I have her head . . .' Tisamenos was clutching the sack, trembling with fear.

A huge shape slithered out from behind the statue, as long as a man, its fangs dripping venom. A snake.

'Python? Here?' It was Silvius, and Elissa saw that he too was overcome with terror. She begged Apollo for an answer.

'It is not Python,' came a voice. A young, curly-haired man was there, leaning casually against the folds of the statue's robe.

Hermes. Delight coursed through Elissa. He reached up and took the Bow from the ledge, and looked along its length as if appraising it. 'But you must still fight it.'

The snake reared its crested head and spat, showering them with hot venom, hitting Silvius in the arm and Elissa on the cheek. It stung, burning painfully. Tisamenos, thinking quickly, crouched and placed his shield above his head. 'Get behind me!'

Shuffling across the floor, Elissa managed to reach him, and Silvius joined them a fraction later, just before the snake struck where he had been standing.

But the snake was too fast, and like a bolt of lightning it hit the shield Tisamenos was holding, and the three companions tumbled away from each other, out from its safety. Tisamenos lost his grip on the Last Gorgon's head.

Now the snake was looming above Tisamenos. Silvius had fallen to the right, arm bruised, and he scrambled to pick up his sword.

Elissa was on the other side of Tisamenos. She hadn't been hurt. She had to deflect the snake's attention from him, so she grabbed a torch from its bracket, hurling it at the snake's head. It turned to look at her. In its eyes she saw cold death, an inhuman power that made her shudder all over.

Silvius jumped at the snake, and he stuck his sword into it; it recoiled immediately, and narrowly missed him as the creature swooped back to deal with what was irritating it. He yanked his sword out and toppled backwards.

Elissa swooped in from the other side, and gashed the snake with her own sword. It was the first time she'd used it. Dark blood spilled out, and she slipped on it but did not fall.

Angered now, the snake began lashing about.

'The Gorgon's head!' called Tisamenos. Elissa swiftly threw it to him. 'When I say go, run straight in front of me!' he cried, catching it. 'And don't, whatever you do, look at me!'

The snake was swaying from side to side, sizing up each of them in turn, judging which one to go for. Its long forked tongue flickered in and out of its deadly mouth.

'Run!' shouted Tisamenos. Elissa and Silvius sprinted across between him and the snake, and the snake, confused, gazed right at Tisamenos, who pulled out the Last Gorgon's head and ripped off the bandage.

As Elissa and Silvius tumbled to a halt and turned, ready to help Tisamenos, the snake tensed all its muscles, and began to swing its head from side to side again.

'Tisamenos! Run!' called Elissa. But he remained firm, and the snake readied itself for the final attack.

Trembling now, Silvius called too. 'Tisamenos! Run! You'll be killed!'

Elissa thought quickly. 'Do what I do!' she shouted to Silvius. Then, remembering how she'd been told to pick up snakes, she jumped onto the beast's body just behind its head. Silvius immediately joined her.

'It's working!' shouted Tisamenos.

There was a strange cracking noise, and the snake's tail began to turn grey, stone rippling up its spine. With a powerful lunge, the beast pushed forwards, throwing off both Elissa and Silvius. It happened so fast Elissa barely had time to register it. One moment she thought that Tisamenos was about to be bitten. The next, the creature had turned entirely into stone, just near Tisamenos's head.

Exhausted, Tisamenos bandaged the Last Gorgon's eyes, and then sank to the floor. Elissa was the first to reach him, and she quickly put a water skin to his lips. Then Silvius arrived, and, shivering and bloodied, Elissa held her old friend in a tight embrace.

The atmosphere in the temple altered a little. Elissa looked up to see Hermes before them, a small smile on his lips. In his arms he held the Bow, a thing of golden beauty, its radiance dispelling any shadows.

'You know what that snake was,' he said, quietly.

The fight had been a test, Elissa thought. It was a way of showing them that they could only defeat their doubts and fears when they worked together. 'Was it the snake inside us?' asked Elissa.

'It was. You have now slain it. Tisamenos,' he continued gravely. 'You must not use the Last Gorgon's head, except in times of great need. Or else you risk becoming like her.' Tisamenos bowed his head.

'Silvius. You have felt the power of Python and withstood it.

You will now carry the Arrow.' He gave the quiver to Silvius, who took it gently.

'And, Elissa.' The god turned his gaze to Elissa, and she felt the warmth of his beauty coursing through her. 'You have the most important task of all.' And suddenly she was holding the Bow, and gazing all along its golden length, and the light of a thousand suns shone all around her.

'For now,' said Hermes, 'the fight begins.'

Thirty-Five

Return to Achaea

All Tisamenos could think about was the snake. In the last minute before it had turned to stone, he had gazed deeply into its eyes, and he had seen something there that frightened him. His own reflection, staring back. And then all he could remember was Elissa, her soft voice calling to him, her gentle touch. She was now thanking the three Trojan priests, Silvius carrying the Arrow beside her, grinning.

And what did he have? A monster in his bag; a monster who had saved them.

He cradled it as if it were a baby.

'Go to the mouth of the river Simois,' Chryses was saying, 'and you will find someone there who will carry you home.'

Elissa was striding ahead, Silvius walking alongside her like a puppy, whilst Tisamenos brought up the rear. When the hill of Troy had become a small thing in the distance, Silvius turned for a moment to look at it.

Then he swung round, determined, and marched on with Elissa. Tisamenos dawdled. What was home now? Had the kinghouse been razed to the ground? Had his father and Electra been slaughtered? And if he did return to Mykenai, what would the Swallows want with him?

They followed the Simois until it reached the sea, and they found there a dark ship, and a small group standing in front of it.

Dark-skinned and in shining robes, they bowed, and spoke in a language that Tisamenos had not heard before. But Elissa gasped in amazement, before running towards them as fast as she could.

She was almost jumping up and down with excitement. She spoke a few words to them, and they answered her with delight, and then she embraced each of them in turn, and they kissed her on the cheek and smiled and teased her as if she were their own daughter. She called back to Tisamenos and Silvius, and said, 'Phoenicians. They're from Tyre, and Chryses has asked them to take us back to Achaea. They have a cargo of silks they want to sell, but they will give us free passage.'

'We know of this Python,' said one of the Phoenicians, a tall man with a long handsome nose, and hair that gleamed with oil. He had gold on his arms and a quick smile, and his name was Batnoam. 'We call him Lotan, the serpent. The priests sent to us that you were coming. You are of great importance, and it is an honour for us to carry you.'

'Thank you,' Elissa was saying, and then she clambered on board, as if she had always been with them. Silvius nodded and shook their hands, whilst Tisamenos followed more stiffly afterwards, noting that the traders looked at his bag with curiosity. He kept it close to his body.

'Come!' Another tall, smiling man beckoned to Tisamenos and Silvius, and led them to a cabin. A large bronze bath stood in the centre of it, filled with hot scented water.

Tisamenos glanced at Silvius, and then they were both tearing off their dusty, dirty clothes, and racing to get in first.

It was big enough for both of them, and they washed and splashed until Tisamenos had almost forgotten about the horror of the snake, and his other worries were melting away too.

The tall man brought hot sweet drinks, and Tisamenos barely noticed the boat leaving the river and entering the open sea.

'In Lavinium we don't have baths like this,' said Silvius. 'We wash in cold water, or the river.'

Tisamenos blushed, thinking of his nurse and the servants who would attend him whilst he had a bath. But all of that was behind him now, and he would go with Elissa and find somewhere new.

'Do you think your city has survived?' he asked.

Silvius's face grew grave. 'I don't know. I looked for my father in the Underworld, but did not see him. But then the ferryman said that souls don't go there any more. So I do not know . . .'

'Let's not think about it for now,' said Tisamenos. And he sipped his warm spicy drink, and sank deeper into the bathwater.

When the water was beginning to get cold, Tisamenos got out first, and dried himself with white linen, then dressed in a soft white robe. Silvius did so too, and for the first time Tisamenos saw how alike they were. They both had the weight of expectation and family on them; they both were trying to make their own way in the new world. He smiled at the Italian, and Silvius returned it.

Wondering if Elissa had also been treated so well, and thinking that she probably had, Tisamenos led the way to the deck, where waiting for them was a veiled figure in a dark blue robe tinged with gold.

The figure spun round elegantly, performing arabesques, and laughingly came to a stop before the two boys.

The veil was torn off by a hand, and there, grinning, was Elissa. Gone was the determined expression, and in its place was a relaxed, happy smile. She seemed so at ease among the traders. 'Not bad, don't you think?' she said. Tisamenos thought it was better than that. 'Now we feast!'

Tisamenos sat awkwardly cross-legged under the stars on a rich silk cushion whilst flutes and a strange stringed instrument he'd never heard before played quietly. Elissa, who'd been picking up words and phrases with ease, was chattering, playing dice, and drinking wine and eating fruits that had been kept cool in ice. He was happy just to sit and listen, and sometimes Elissa would turn to him and explain what she was talking about.

Tisamenos picked up the stringed instrument from its player and began to strum it. But the only sounds he could make were melancholy, so he put it aside. Elissa all the time was talking excitedly to the traders, hearing about what had happened in Tyre since her aunt Dido had left, and whether they traded with Carthage, and what news there was from there. She could hardly stop moving about, dancing from one foot to the other.

Tisamenos soon fell asleep where he was sitting, to the sound of Elissa as she continued chattering throughout the night.

As they journeyed over the days that followed, Tisamenos avoided talking about what lay ahead of them, and there seemed to be an unspoken agreement with the others to do the same. Instead, he simply enjoyed the unusual sights of the ship and the cargo it carried. Reams of beautifully coloured silks, and spices that made his tongue tingle.

A few days into the journey, Batnoam told them that they would be approaching Euboeae on the morning of the next day.

Tisamenos called Silvius and Elissa together. They had both been bronzed by the sun, and seemed happier than he'd ever seen them. He tried to hide his own feelings as best as he could.

'We need to plan,' he said. The sea was bright all around them, white breakers appearing and disappearing.

'We'll find news when we reach land,' Elissa said. 'We need to get back to Aeneas.'

'To my father,' said Silvius. 'If he is still alive . . .'

Early the next morning, the port of Histiaea on the island of Euboeae came into view. Tisamenos went below deck, and changed from his soft white robe back into his tunic, once fine, now stained. Then he examined his weapons.

The Last Gorgon's head was sitting waiting. And now he

picked it up again, and felt the same thrill of horror and power.

Tisamenos was glad to feel Achaean soil under his feet once more. Here the stones knew him, here he could talk to them and not go mad. He went down onto his haunches and touched the earth, and hearing the voices of the stones, he was both comforted and alarmed. They were quiet and gentle, but he could make out a word that kept returning. 'Father ... father ... father ...'

His father. Perhaps they were telling him that he was really dead. He stood up slowly, and let the rich loam fall from his hand.

The Phoenicians, after taking on provisions, would sail later that day. They said their goodbyes. Elissa hugged all of the sailors in turn, who pinched her cheek and made many promises to see her again. Batnoam grinned at Tisamenos when he shook his hand, but there was a look in his eyes that said, *Be careful, my friends, and may the gods go with you.*

'Who's going to get news?' Tisamenos asked when the three of them were sitting alone by the harbour, backs against a low wall.

'I'll do it,' said Silvius. 'I'll attract the least attention.'

'He's right,' said Elissa. 'A blond-haired stone-handed boy is going to get people talking. And I'm a girl, and how many girl Phoenician traders have you seen?'

Silvius darted off.

Tisamenos and Elissa waited for him by the harbour, whilst the business of the port went on around them. Some merchants were unloading timber, and one of the captains was having a long argument with the harbour master which ended with him walking away, throwing his hands up.

Tisamenos watched Elissa, her quick movements, her eyes that lit up when they caught his. He took her hand gently, and said, 'I meant it. I will go with you, wherever you go after all this has finished.'

'I want to see Carthage, and Phoenicia. I want to know more about my mother. I know you will come with me.' She squeezed his hand, and they sat, not speaking, but leaning in to each other, until Silvius reappeared, and they sprang apart.

'I'm sorry, Tisamenos,' he said. He looked dejected, head bowed, shading his eyes from the sun. 'There is news from Mykenai . . . it has fallen to Argos.'

Tisamenos had guessed this, but hearing it confirmed was a blow. He would not be welcome in his home city now. He was an exile once more. 'And my father?'

Silvius shook his head. 'There is no sign of him.'

Then he was dead. If he was alive, there would be someone who had heard of him, drawing up an army with him at the head to retake his city. Orestes would not go down without a fight.

The loss of his father hit him deeply, and he turned away from the others, letting his body heave with sobs. He allowed Elissa to comfort him, finding warmth in her soft touch.

There was only one thing left, now, for him. Python, and his destruction. The thought filled him with a cold kind of resolution, and he stopped his tears.

'What more news? What of Python?'

'In Italia, they say, a great army of the Enemy has taken the northern cities. Lavinium still stands, but the army encroaches. We must hurry back.'

'We can't rely on the ships of Orestes now. And I cannot go to Argos and ask them for help,' said Tisamenos. 'They'll kill me as soon as look at me.' He hoped that Penthilos was safe.

And so, dejected, they went back to the port. But none of the ships' captains was heading to Italia, and between them they had not enough goods to buy passage or commandeer a ship; not even Silvius's amulet could persuade.

The day was reaching the midpoint, and they filled their bellies with bread and olives from the tavern using one of the silver coins.

Tisamenos was turning everything over in his mind, trying to see a way out for them. Looking at Silvius reminded him of Troy, and then he thought of Achilleos, the great warrior, and then his mother Hermione, and the necklace she'd been wearing from the Thessalian king.

Thessaly. It hit him like a bolt of lightning from the Sky-father. 'We have a guest friendship with the Phthians, north of here in Thessaly. Neoptolemos, the son of Achilleos, still rules there, I believe. We are not so far from there by sea. If we go there, he is bound to help us reach Italia.'

'But it's in the wrong direction! And how long will it take? What if Lavinium is attacked and destroyed? What do we do then?' Silvius's voice was cracking a little. Tisamenos knew what he was fearing: the loss of his father.

'Your father is a good leader, isn't he?' said Tisamenos. 'He is prepared for this danger. We can only hope.'

'I know Aeneas,' said Elissa, firmly. 'He's survived so much already. He'll do everything he can to defend the city and your family.'

'We will go to Neoptolemos and tell him what is happening. He will call other kings to join him, and we can gather an army together and attack Python from behind. We'll have to march overland. And . . .' Tisamenos paused. He owed it to Silvius to be honest. 'Hope that your father doesn't fall to him from the south.'

'It's the only way,' whispered Silvius. Resolved, he stood firm, eyes glinting with purpose. 'We will do it.'

Tisamenos found a small skiff that was sailing north to Phthia, and booked passage on it. The boat was leaving at dawn the next morning. They decided to sleep under the spreading branches of an oak tree. Elissa placed her bow carefully underneath her head, whilst Silvius cradled the quiver. Tisamenos went to sleep with his hand tightly around the neck of the sack.

He woke every time he thought he heard movement. Once he saw a squirrel scampering away from them. Another time he opened his eyes to see a fox regarding him with implacable blue eyes.

All too soon it was dawn. Before the sun was fully above the horizon, they were all in the stern of the skiff, moving at a steady pace to the city of Achilleos.

Tisamenos searched for dolphins, but none played around the bow. Elissa tried to engage the skipper in conversation. He was a fat, lazy man with crooked yellow teeth, and he deflected her questions with nods and grunts. So Tisamenos watched the sea in silence, and soon even Elissa stopped trying.

They landed in the full heat of mid-morning. A haze glimmered in the sky. Ahead of them was a wide, fertile plain, a herd of horses galloping in the distance. It was a lush, rich landscape of a kind Tisamenos had not seen before. He had heard of the grasslands of Thessaly, and the famous horses that were meant to be bred by the North Wind. Watching them vanish into the horizon, he felt a thrill.

'How far is the city?' asked Silvius.

'I don't know. But we Achaeans never build our cities that far from the sea. We will go inland.'

The shoreline became grass very quickly, and there was only a narrow road, barely paved, leading away from it. The skipper simply shrugged and pointed, as if the way was obvious, and then carried on with his own business.

They had only been walking for a short while when they heard the sound of tramping feet coming towards them. Regular beats, like a group of soldiers marching.

Suddenly, they were facing a patrol of armed men. Tisamenos counted six of them, in full armour, carrying spears and shields, with swords at their waists. They were tall and strong, and the three of them were no match.

'What business do you have here?' barked the commander, bringing his men to a halt behind him.

'We come to seek Neoptolemos,' answered Tisamenos.

'Neoptolemos is dead, this long time,' continued the commander. In a sudden flurry, the six guards surrounded them, spears pointing. 'And you will come with us.' The impulse to use the Last Gorgon's head was strong. But Hermes had told him not to do so. They would have to march with these men, and perhaps whoever was king now would help them.

'We will go with you to the kinghouse,' said Tisamenos, in as regal a manner as he could, and he was pleased to see the men glance at each other in surprise.

The heat was making them sweat as they marched. He caught a defiant look in Elissa's eye, and warned her with a quiet gesture that now was not the time to bring out the Arrow and the Bow. She agreed, with a little nod.

Soon a city rose up in front of them on the grassy plain, encircled with a white wall. Many soldiers stood watching from the ramparts, and as they were herded through the broad, pleasant streets, lined with white houses of two or more storeys, they saw many soldiers at work.

Tisamenos's heart was sinking. They could not afford to waste time here. They would probably be taken prisoner, until they could get a message through to Aeneas and maybe ransom Silvius. But by then it would be too late.

Nobody gave them a second look.

They reached a large stone hall, were pushed into a wide antechamber hung with tapestries, and left with a guard. They sat on a hard wooden bench, a table laid with cool bronze jugs filled with clear water by them, and a plate of soft goat's cheeses, which they fell upon eagerly.

'I'm sorry,' said Tisamenos when the men had gone. 'This was a mistake. I should have listened to you, Silvius.' He felt dejected.

'It's not your fault,' said Silvius. Tisamenos looked gratefully at him.

'We'll find a way,' said Elissa. 'We got out of the Under-world. We'll get out of here.'

They would, thought Tisamenos. They would find a way, even if he had to use the Last Gorgon's head.

After a long while, there was the sound of footsteps, and the door to their room opened. Two men entered, engaged deeply in conversation. Tisamenos looked up at them. And then his heart began to race.

For a moment, he couldn't be sure.

One of the men was darker skinned, and had long black hair. He wore the long robes favoured by the Trojans. He was handsome, and he had a long nose and a thin face, with dark eyes flashing kindly, and he bore the white bands of a priest in his hair.

The other was taller, and limping slightly, looking at Tisamenos with an expression that he knew so well.

All of a sudden Tisamenos hurled himself at the man, and was embracing him and crying for joy, saying, 'You're alive, you're alive!' He was overwhelmed, and clung to him.

'My son,' Orestes whispered, 'my son. You are so changed . . .'

After a while, they came apart.

'I came to the right place! The Fates were with me!' Tisamenos was exulting. Everything seemed brighter.

'We have much to discuss,' said Orestes. Tisamenos saw his father looking at him with both respect and love. He indicated the man with him. 'This is Helenus.'

'Helenus?' Now Silvius could not contain his excitement. 'The Trojan priest? My father's cousin?'

'I am indeed,' answered Helenus, smiling broadly. 'You must be Silvius. Your father is very anxious about you. I will send word to him immediately.'

'What do you mean?'

'When you left Lavinium your father dispatched messengers to wherever he could to track your whereabouts. Of course the first place he thought of was here.'

'But how did you get here? And what happened to Neoptolemos?' asked Tisamenos.

Orestes said, 'My son, Neoptolemos died some while ago. You know he had been married to your mother, Hermione? I reclaimed her from him, as we had been betrothed first. And when Neoptolemos died, his kingdom was split up, some given to Helenus here.'

'A Trojan prince, now ruling in Achaea,' said Helenus. 'You see how everything changes, and everything is reborn.'

Everything, thought Tisamenos. Then maybe there is hope for me, and hope for Mykenai.

'But we can't rest,' Silvius was adamant. 'Python's army is massing. My father—'

'Is holding out still,' interrupted Helenus. 'He has all the armies of the south with him, and those who managed to flee Python. There has been no skirmish in recent days. We think that Python is massing for a major attack.'

'So we have to go there now,' said Silvius. 'We have the Bow and Arrow of Apollo.'

Silvius showed them the quiver, and Elissa, with great seriousness, displayed the Bow so that they could admire it.

Tisamenos knew that he should tell them about the Gorgon's head. Reluctantly he told his father he had it.

Orestes looked sharply at him. 'My poor son ... Such a weapon. We must guard it carefully.'

'No,' said Tisamenos. 'I will keep it. Until I have to use it.'

'You have undergone great hardship,' said Helenus. He touched each of their faces in turn with his long, thin fingers. 'And we will go to Italia. Come with me.'

The kinghouse of Phthia was made of white marble. Tisamenos lightly touched it as they went, and heard the quiet voices of the stones, more gentle than in Mykenai, but still whispering and foreboding.

He concentrated instead on the sun as it glinted off the polished surfaces. He marvelled at the rich tapestries fluttering in the breeze, and cool fountains playing in shadowy courtyards.

Everyone they passed was moving with some purpose, carrying a message or a burden, and they all bowed respectfully to Helenus as they went. He brought the three friends out into the main agora.

And there, Silvius gasped in joy, and Elissa jumped up and down. And Tisamenos could not help but be awed.

Rank upon rank of soldiers, polishing armour, practising sword play, their banners and standards fluttering in the breeze, horses with gleaming flanks and high steps, chariots at the ready, spears and swords being forged, the clank and clangour of a people preparing for war.

'We have an army. Two armies, as Orestes brought what he could from Mykenai. We sail tomorrow. Tell the men to ready themselves!' said Helenus.

He called out to the agora, and the whole mass of soldiers roared in reply.

But Tisamenos was thinking that it was not enough, and though his father was cheering, he could not join in. Instead he turned, and leant against the marble, the weight of the Last Gorgon heavier than it had ever been.

Thirty-Six

To Italia

The harbour of the city of Phthia was rammed with huge beautiful warships, and men were loading them up with barrels of provisions and bronze armour. There were a dozen or more, and every time that Silvius tried to count them, he became distracted.

He kept thinking about the coming battle, and about getting to his family. He knew that he had disobeyed Aeneas.

But this was greater than that.

Tisamenos and Orestes were standing by the shoreline and looking out to sea, father's hand on son's shoulder. He couldn't wait till he could stand with Aeneas like that again. Once this was all over.

He heard a sigh, and saw that Elissa was gazing at Tisamenos. He'd realised over the last few days, that they needed each other in a way that he didn't need Elissa. There was a gap inside Tisamenos which she could fill. She was his friend, and ally, and they would stay like that. Silvius said quietly, 'It's all right, you know. I know that you love him.'

Elissa blushed, and said fiercely, 'You don't know anything.' But she looked at him gratefully from under her eyelashes. 'Look!' she cried, changing the subject. 'Helenus!'

Silvius thrilled as his cousin, the Trojan priest Helenus, came striding out onto the shore, dressed for battle, and he raised his silver staff and roared, and all the men answered, their shouting and the clashing of metal on metal filling the skies. Joining in, Silvius banged his sword against his shield, the sound throbbing through his body. He'd polished the breastplate until there were no marks on it at all, and he wore it now snugly.

As they were embarking, a messenger reached Helenus, and he listened to him with brows furrowed. It was a man of about Iulus's age, and he had been riding hard.

When Silvius asked him what it was, he simply said, 'They have lost another city,' and moved onwards to check the final loading, and to make a sacrifice to Apollo.

'Is it Lavinium?' called Silvius, running after him.

Helenus shook his head. 'No. But they are close.'

The news hit Silvius hard, like a blow to the stomach. Mouth dry, he went to join the others. He wished he could hurry things up. They were fortunate that the wind was in the right direction. Helenus was now preparing the final sacrifice for Apollo. He called to Silvius, and he was only too glad to help. The priest, the white bands in his hair shining in the sunlight, blessed him. 'My kin,' he said. 'The Lord of Light will guide you in this.' Then he touched Tisamenos on the head briefly, his hand betraying just a shiver of anxiety. And finally, he muttered words to Elissa that Silvius could not hear. But Elissa stood up, looking stronger and more determined than ever.

An hour or so later, the ships sailed out of the harbour, a good wind in their sails. Silvius listened to the navigator describe the route: through the Gulf of Corinth, and then hugging the coast until they were opposite the northern part of Italia.

He enjoyed hearing the name of his homeland in the mouth of an Achaean. If only he were returning in triumph, crowned and bearing gifts, not adversity.

Although the sky was clear, dark clouds hovered at the edge, and sometimes the breeze would shift and bring with it something cold and frightening.

The sailors would look at each other and make the sign against the evil eye. Helenus kept checking the sky, as if scanning for auguries. Elissa pulled the Bow nearer to her body, as if seeking warmth from it, whilst Tisamenos was stony and distant.

Silvius lingered by himself in the prow. Tisamenos and Orestes eagerly talked together about things that he did not understand, and he did not feel that he could join in with them. Elissa spent more and more time with them.

He had chosen to take this path. Nobody had forced him to steal his father's horse; nobody had forced him to take the ship nymph's offer – he had made the decision himself. He'd sensed the light of Apollo in the Arrowhead, and he'd been drawn in by the visions of Python. Often as he watched the foam he would remember Stargazer the centaur, and how lonely it must have been for him with all his brothers and sisters gone.

Now, the Arrow whole and safe on his back, he knew that he would not have been able to withstand its pull without Elissa and Tisamenos.

He would make sure that he honoured Stargazer and his sacrifice. The darkness would not prevail.

Sometimes the foam would shift into the shapes of the hungry ghosts he'd seen in the Underworld, and then he would shiver and draw the cloak around himself. He remembered the prophecy of the Sibyl. *One will die.* But what did it mean? Lionstone? Dolphinlight? And would Python die, or one of the three of them?

The soldiers of Helenus were the Myrmidons of Achilles, and they were strong and purposeful. They worked continuously, making sure the ship was sailing true.

When they were not working, they were exercising, wrestling each other on the broad deck or throwing spears, or sword fighting. Silvius watched them, envying their togetherness and their camaraderie. But they mostly ignored him, and he felt useless.

One day a dagger landed at his feet. He looked up to see one of the younger ones, Callias. 'Teach you hand combat,' said Callias, his blue eyes glinting. Unlike most of the Achaeans, he had very pale skin and eyes that were the colour of the unclouded sky; his hair was flame red, and he kept it very long. He was proud of his long red hair, and was often found combing it.

So Silvius passed the time learning how to fight with Callias. He was a good teacher, and let Silvius make mistakes. Silvius felt his muscles hardening, and his skills growing, and soon he could twist and turn and stab and parry so well that one morning he took Callias unawares, and laid the young man low.

Callias simply laughed, and said, 'The wolf cub is turning into a wolf!' Silvius blushed, but he was pleased, and wished Elissa had been there to see it.

Elissa spent her days doing target practice with the archers. Once an arrow thudded into the wood of the deck just by Silvius, and he looked up to see a laughing Elissa. 'I meant to do that!' she said.

'Sure you did,' smiled Silvius, and threw the arrow back. She caught it with one hand, and made a little mock bow. But she was improving, and he watched as she hit the bullseye dead in the centre.

Tisamenos was practising fighting with the Last Gorgon's head around his neck, and sometimes he would face Silvius for a bout.

One afternoon, as they were circling each other, Silvius lunged, and managed to knock Tisamenos to the ground. The sack fell from his shoulder and the head fell onto the floor. The bandage slipped from its eyes and a gull, which happened to be sitting on the rigging met its gaze and dropped, stone now, to the deck, before Tisamenos could grab the head and shove it back into the sack.

It unsettled everyone. Helenus consigned the stone gull to the waves, with a prayer to Apollo.

Day and night merged quickly into each other on the warship. The drums kept the rowers going, and they rowed throughout the night, taking shifts. Silvius rather liked the way that the beat filled his mind, but he could see that Tisamenos found it difficult, and was jittery and pacing. Elissa simply danced to the beat, making them laugh with her contortions.

At last, they came to Corinth. Helenus beached his ship and went to parley with the Corinthian king. Silvius sat with Orestes whilst he was on shore. Tisamenos and Elissa were with them, side by side on the floor, hands intertwined.

'We hope that the Achaean cities will send us troops. They all know of the threat.' Orestes was gazing out towards the land.

'We will need as many men as we can.' Tisamenos sounded grim.

'I hope they'll help . . .' Silvius said.

They waited.

Soon, Helenus returned. 'Corinth has given us ten ships!' he announced. 'And Athens has sent fifteen!'

'And what about Argos?' said Orestes, gruffly.

'We have had no communication from Argos,' answered Helenus. So the Argives would not send men to help. They were holed up in Mykenai, waiting for the storm to pass.

312

Even so, a larger fleet made its way through the Gulf of Corinth, and into the Tyrrhenian Sea, where not long before Silvius and Elissa had caused the sea nymphs to look on in wonder as their ship that had once been a nymph sailed by. Then, the sea had been all but empty, and he had been an excited boy, hurtling into something he did not understand. Now he was returning with a fleet of Achaean ships, a Trojan priest, the Bow and Arrow of Apollo, and the head of the Last Gorgon.

He had never imagined it would turn out like this.

Standing in the stern one morning, Silvius's nostrils pricked. There was something on the breeze, something pine-scented and woody, so unlike the plains of Achaea. He turned and called to Elissa, 'I think I can smell it. Home! I can smell Italia!'

She came running to join him, her face lit up with joy. 'I can smell it too!'

He felt a tug in his stomach as he remembered his mother Lavinia, and his little brother Brutus, and the look of disappointment he imagined he would see in Aeneas's face when they were finally reunited. He had, after all, disobeyed his father, and that was something for which the penalty was severe.

And there was the bigger fear, too. The fear that Lavinium might no longer be standing. That the new palace built so carefully by his father might be destroyed, and his whole family with it.

The watchman sang out, 'Land!' And in the distance a dark line grew gradually more distinct, and soon Silvius could see hills and harbours, and the drummer drummed faster, and the men cheered, and Elissa danced on the deck and whooped, and Silvius leapt up and down, whilst Tisamenos looked on, a small smile on his face.

There was a broad bay ahead, and the thirty-five ships, each with their two hundred or so soldiers, drew up onto the shore, and the men pouring out of them were like ants rushing from their nest. Silvius remembered how he'd longed for battle, with the spears shining in the sunlight, and now he realised that would soon be happening.

'We camp by the shore tonight.' Silvius caught up with Tisamenos and Elissa. 'And we march tomorrow.'

Tisamenos merely nodded, whilst Elissa looked serious.

'Come on,' said Silvius. 'Let's go and hunt a deer.'

As they were sitting round a fire eating freshly killed venison that night, a messenger arrived from the Trojan settlements in the west. He was panting, and grimy, and he gulped gratefully at the water he was given. He was thin, and his eyes were black with lack of sleep. But when Silvius saw him, he rose up and embraced him.

It was Drusus, the boy who shared his watch in Lavinium on the day that Stargazer had arrived in the city with the Arrowhead.

'Silvius! You're back! They talk of nothing else in Lavinium. And Elissa, too!' Drusus greeted them excitedly.

He told them the extent of Python's conquests. 'They've taken all the lands as far east as Spoletium, and they are encroaching on the Latin cities.' That was most of the north of Italia. But Silvius was not deterred.

'How many men have we lost?' asked Silvius.

'Don't fear – they hold out well. I was told to come and meet you, and lead you the safe way. Python is concentrating his power on Lavinium, massing for an attack. We have retreated to Alba Longa, where we have joined with Iulus's forces.' At the mention of his brother, Silvius looked up, remembering how he'd left him on the shore. He found he wanted to see Iulus again, that proud, distant figure.

'And the remaining Etruscans,' Drusus continued. 'We're backed up by the Achaean colonists in the south, though they are few. We are very grateful to see you.'

'Does Aeneas have a message for me?' asked Silvius eagerly.

Drusus shook his head. 'He was hunting when I left.' Silvius observed him closely, but it did not seem as if he was hiding anything. Then he must be alive. His heart swelled, longing to see his father once more.

That night, he bedded down next to Drusus.

'Do you remember when the blacksmith's boy overslept, and Blaeso was so angry he chased him all round the city?'

Silvius laughed. It was good to talk about Lavinium as it had been.

'And he got so red and hot I thought he'd burst!'

There was silence for a moment. 'Things are different,

though. We're all under siege. We're crammed in together . . . I've been patrolling all day, every day. I leapt at the chance to come here with the message. I envy you, Silvius.'

Silvius was surprised. 'Why?'

'You've seen the world.'

'Some of it . . .'

'Tell me . . . is it true the Achaeans eat their children?'

Silvius could not suppress a snort of disbelief. 'Of course not!'

The two whispered late into the night, talking of things they'd done back home, until Silvius heard Drusus's deep breathing, and then he slept too.

The next day dawned cloudy, the sun's rays peeking timidly through a thick mantle, and the mood on the beach was grim. 'Has Apollo removed his favour?' asked Silvius, anxiously.

Helenus prepared a small sacrifice. In his care and duty, in the diligent way he laid the thigh bones on the fire, he reminded Silvius of Aeneas as he led the men in prayers, and when they had finished, the sun appeared, giving them hope. Helenus's silver staff blazed, and he seemed surrounded by an aura as the men cheered and roared in praise of the god.

They left the ships with a small guard, and went onwards, following Drusus, who was at the front of the vanguard. Helenus strode purposefully, and Orestes, despite his limp, went with him, Tisamenos by his side, gaze hard and down-cast, whilst Elissa and Silvius walked in tandem behind them, bearing the Bow and Arrow of Apollo. There was comfort in the Arrow on Silvius's back, and in the breastplate, though it rubbed against his skin.

'An Achaean army,' said Elissa. 'Coming into Italia not to conquer, but to help.'

'War makes strange bedfellows,' answered Helenus as they went. 'To think that our parents were busy slaughtering each other not long ago . . .'

Silvius agreed. The bigger evil was to come. They had to face it together, as one.

The way was trackless. Here Silvius began to help, as his forest skills were equal to Drusus, and they were able to find a path ahead.

Often they had to scramble down steep banks, or ford streams, where some soldiers were detailed to construct wooden bridges for the carts to follow with provisions. The army marched in small units, and behind them straggled the supply lines to the beach.

After splashing through a ford, Silvius came up against a thick tangle of bushes. So thick that the army would not be able to pass through it. The entire army came to a halt behind them.

'It's no good,' said Helenus. 'We'll have to retreat and find another way.'

He began to make the orders to turn about.

But Silvius could not risk losing another minute. There had to be a way through. The quiver struck his back as he faced the problem, and it gave him an idea.

'No! Wait! Elissa!'

Elissa came bounding to his side.

'There's a blockage here. We'll have to go back unless we can find a way through it.'

She immediately understood what he meant. Carefully she unslung the Bow. 'I think I can aim the Arrow through it.'

'We've not tried before. It might be a good way to see how far it can go.'

Elissa nodded. 'And show the men, too.'

'What are you doing?' called Helenus.

'Watch!' Elissa notched, and shot the Arrow. It burst through the tangle in a burning furrow, like a meteor, clearing a way for them, and Elissa ran after it, Silvius following, until the Arrow came to a rest in a clearing. Elated, Silvius placed it back in the quiver.

The astonished army caught up with them, cheering and exclaiming, 'Apollo is with us! Apollo is with us!'

But it didn't get any easier after that. There was a steep hill to climb, and the rest of the army was snaking its way up to join them. When they reached the summit, Silvius felt that he was so exhausted he might collapse on the spot. Below he could see across a wide grassland where they would camp for the night. Firmly Helenus called down to the men, and the word was passed along: 'Rest soon. Rest soon.'

The beat of the soldier's feet became part of Silvius's mind, and he turned to Tisamenos. 'Is this what it's like to have the stones in your head?'

Tisamenos answered, 'Yes. Like a never-ending thump.'

'I'm sorry I made you promise to speak to them in Troy. I can't imagine how much it might hurt.'

For a moment, Silvius thought he saw anger flicker across Tisamenos's flinty eyes. But then the Achaean smiled, and Silvius returned it.

Something tapped him on the shoulder, and then he saw Elissa sprinting ahead. He skidded down the hill after her, Tisamenos too, and suddenly Silvius was enjoying the simple pleasure of being with friends, and running in the wind, until they all tumbled down onto the grassy plain, and the army spilled out around them, setting up camp. Tents were put up with surprising speed.

Silvius found Helenus and Orestes supervising the provisions. Drusus was with them already, swallowing down huge chunks of bread as if he hadn't eaten for days.

'We're now only a day's march from the Enemy domains,' he said, face serious.

'Then we will set double watches,' commanded Orestes.

Silvius relayed this back to Elissa and Tisamenos, and they decided to share the watch themselves, keeping guard over the weapons.

But even as they settled, after they had eaten a simple supper of hard bread and cheese, they did not sleep, for a messenger came from Helenus.

Helenus called them into his silken tent, and they found

him there with Orestes, both seated in wooden chairs, sharing a beaker of hot wine. The two men looked serious.

'My children,' said Helenus, setting the beaker down in a gesture that reminded Silvius so completely of his own father that he was almost thrown. 'I wish that it were not so. But we must plan the attack.'

'We three have to go together,' said Silvius. 'Tisamenos and I will be the guard for Elissa.'

'Tisamenos can use the Last Gorgon to cut through the Enemy army,' Elissa said, leaning forwards on her knees.

'And I can fend off attacks from the side and back,' added Silvius. 'Where does Python himself lurk?' he asked Drusus.

'There is something in the middle of their army, some strange blackness, but they have never advanced fully on us, so we have never seen it.' His words hung in the air.

'And that's the blackness we have to defeat,' said Silvius. 'The blackness that threatens the world.' And even the terrors in the underworld.

The flames flickered long in their braziers as they talked, until they slept where they lay, and when the morning dawned still grey, they were ready for the march towards Python.

Thirty-Seven

Python's Army

Within half a day they had crossed the plain, and were now facing the domains of Python. The fear in Elissa was growing stronger as the air took on a sickly tinge, as if the breath of Python himself were polluting it.

Her unease remained even when she touched the Bow for support. Fogs and mists wrapped around her like damp cloths. Though it was summer, the trees were fading, their leaves edged with brown, and nearer the Enemy camp they even began to lose their foliage completely.

Soon the forest was bare. Elissa began to feel nauseous, and she had to stop to cough as if the miasma was infecting her, creeping into her lungs and bones. She saw Silvius struggling too, and pressed on, urging him to keep going. Tisamenos was next to her, and she was reassured by his hand on her shoulder.

The vanguard emerged from the forest, and once more Elissa saw there was a plain in front of them, ringed by mountains to the west, and the forest on the east. In the far distance was the glimmer of fires.

'Python's army,' said Drusus, quietly. 'They massed here, where a star fell a while ago. There is a crater. We have not got much time.'

A star. The Sibyl's prophecy came back to Elissa. Starwolf. Lionstone. Dolphinlight. Had the meteorite fallen here? Was that what it meant? The fall of a star. Her heartbeat quickened with the imminence of the upcoming battle. The rest she did not understand, though she knew that the dolphin might have something to do with her.

'The men need to rest,' said Helenus.

As he said this, Elissa heard a rustling, and looked up, horrified, as something dropped from a tree beside Helenus, and the red glow of the Enemy spread on the ground. A man was standing there, half-naked, his eyes beaming with scarlet. His face was handsome and young, and he was wearing the loose breeches of a goatherd. But he was carrying a sword, and he swung it at Helenus.

Helenus was too quick, and parried it. The Enemy soldier was too strong, pushing Helenus down. Two Myrmidons pounced on the Enemy as Helenus jumped nimbly to his feet, and the Enemy simply shrugged them off and went for Helenus again. Elissa was already primed, Silvius by her side, and she put her forefinger to the string of the Bow.

The Enemy paused, as if he'd heard something, and turned to examine Elissa. Once more it was as if instead of a man there was a long, snaky creature, hissing in and out of existence. It was terrifying, and Elissa was hardly able to hold still. But she said to Silvius, 'Give me the Arrow.' The red glare of the Enemy's eyes washed over them.

'What is this?' The Enemy approached where they were standing, pushing aside Tisamenos, who tried to block his way. 'You have something that stinks. Give it to me now!'

'No!' shouted Silvius, fumbling with the quiver. Elissa thrust at the Enemy with her sword, but did not harm him.

'Python rises, fools,' snarled the Enemy. He was surrounded now by a ring of soldiers, facing Elissa and Silvius. 'Give that bow and that arrow to me, or face the consequences. Python will take back what is his.'

He was too near now to shoot. Elissa and Silvius together went for him. Tisamenos scrambled. Suddenly there was a fletch sticking out of the Enemy's eye. He merely grinned.

'Give them to me, or I will take them from you.'

Shaken, Elissa swung blindly at him, meeting flesh; the Enemy still grinned.

And as arrow after arrow sank into him, he called, in a strange, hissing noise.

From beyond, from the camp of Python came an answering hiss, filling the sky.

'They are coming,' said the Enemy, as he sank under the

arrows; and then, as Silvius stood above him, sword raised, he simply laughed as the blade cut into his neck.

The red light in his eyes dimmed, went out, and he slumped, toppling to the ground. Silvius was shaking, and Elissa ran to comfort him. He was stricken, staring from the corpse to his sword. 'You had to do it. It wasn't a man, remember that. It was something else.' Still trembling, he knelt to wipe the edge of his sword on the grass, until it was clean of gore.

Tisamenos shook Silvius's hand. 'There will be more. We have to keep going.'

But from across the plain, Elissa saw a greater crimson light was growing.

Helenus paled. 'Rally the men. Get them formed up. Pass the message along.' The front ranks began to line up. Orestes was to command the rearguard.

Elissa heard Orestes calling her and the other two. She saw how tired he looked, and yet resolute. 'Python attacks. Get ready, now.'

Orestes pulled Tisamenos towards his chest, whispering. 'I have made mistakes, my son. Now go well, and fight well.'

Helenus blessed the three of them, touching their foreheads in turn. 'By the light of Apollo, go well.' Tisamenos stood upright, hands clasped behind his back. Silvius could not conceal his trembling. Elissa bowed her head and prayed to the god. This was their final attack. If they did not succeed, then Python would take the Arrow and the Bow, and he would be unstoppable. The white bands on Helenus's head began to shine with the radiance of the god. 'Apollo hears!'

It was a joy to Elissa to see the god's light, and she felt the Bow humming gently with his power. In the darkness there was still light. And she knew she was the bearer of that light. She, and Silvius, now gripping the quiver, ready to pass her the Arrow; and Tisamenos, flinty and strong beside her.

There was a great mass in the distance pushing over the plain, and a terrible sound like a thousand snakes.

'Ready!' Helenus's voice rang above the clamour. 'Front ranks – march!'

The forces of Achaea moved forwards in unison, shields and swords clanking, leather armour chafing them, helmets clamped down. The rank smell of people facing a terror unknown.

Onwards they marched, javelins bristling, and in the centre of the second rank were Tisamenos, Silvius and Elissa, grimly in step.

The opposing army seemed to be a long way away. For a few moments it was as if the two would never meet. In front of Elissa was a dark mass of ragged rage: rank upon rank of men, women and children, all possessed with the power of Python. Around her, determined, fighting for life and light, were the Achaean soldiers.

The white bands on Helenus's head gave out a burst of light.

Elissa held her breath. Then, just as she exhaled deeply, like two waves crashing together, the two armies met.

The Enemy struck.

It was chaos. Elissa took her position behind Tisamenos as a hundred red-eyed soldiers raged into the Achaean front line. Tisamenos immediately unveiled the Last Gorgon's head, and the woman rushing at him turned to stone, mid-run. 'Come on!' he called. Focusing on him, Elissa followed. Silvius was just a pace behind her, sword out. Somebody fell across her path, and she had to jump over the body, turning to make sure that Silvius didn't trip either.

Three soldiers swooped on them at once.

Tisamenos petrified the one in front of him. But the other two kept coming.

The Last Gorgon's gaze only worked on one at a time. Elissa hadn't thought of that. Three more were coming from the sides, and Tisamenos was not quick enough. One rammed into Elissa, taking her by surprise and knocking her to the ground. She rolled over, and Silvius stopped to help her up, swiping at the Enemy at the same time and gashing the soldier in the neck.

It was enough time for Tisamenos to turn the Gorgon's head, and as the Enemy soldier recovered, his eyes solidified in his sockets, and he was nothing but stone.

'What can we do? I can't turn them all!' Tisamenos was panting.

A fat man with a permanent grin, lit up by the red glow of his eyes, charged at Elissa, and she found herself in hand-to-hand combat.

That was not supposed to happen. The Bow was now

vulnerable. He was strong, full of the power of the Enemy, and he was gaining the upper hand.

As the fat man swiped at her, Silvius came in from behind, and sliced at the back of his neck, making him falter for a sliver of time, enough for Elissa to jump backwards out of the way and regroup her strength. The onrush was relentless. Another woman soldier leapt at Silvius.

Elissa saw Tisamenos was faced with a desperate choice. He could not be sure, if he turned the Gorgon's head, that he would not catch Silvius or Elissa with its gaze, and then they would be stone for eternity.

Silvius laid a stinging blow on the woman's arm, and she dropped her sword, and at the same time, Elissa leapt at the fat man, knocking him to the ground. Tisamenos petrified him, and Silvius stabbed the woman in the stomach.

'There are too many of them!' Silvius croaked.

The Achaean forces were surging around them, the front ranks fighting as hard as they could. Helenus was at the forefront, pushing through the Enemy in the heat and rage of battle, the light of Apollo shining from his forehead. The Enemy were wary of the priest, who was like a torch burning in the night, and Helenus was pressing further ahead than the rest, with a few young fighters. Callias was with him, bloodied but unbowed.

'Get behind him!' yelled Elissa. 'I have a plan!'

They fell in with the soldiers around Helenus. There was a moment of calm. Shouts came from all over the plain, and the hissing of the Enemy was loud.

'Lock shields! Two above.' She held hers above her head, and Silvius, getting the idea, did the same, so that they had protection above them, and Tisamenos went in front of them with the Last Gorgon's head in his left hand.

The Enemy were concentrating on Helenus and his band, and Tisamenos turned the gaze of the Gorgon on them as they attacked. As each one became stone, Tisamenos's face seemed to harden too, his eyes glazing over. It made Elissa fear for him. But they had to press on. She saw that they were now nearing the seething darkness in the centre.

The Achaean soldiers behind them were faltering, swallowed up by the horror of the Enemy. A distant shout told her that Orestes was sending in the second line. Helenus yelled, 'Onwards!'

His band charged forwards. Elissa and Silvius kept in step behind them.

The confusion of battle was all around. She jumped over bodies on the ground and could not tell if they were Achaeans or Enemy.

In front of them, Callias came to blows with two children; Tisamenos turned one of them into stone, but they were not quick enough to halt the other, and the Enemy child ran Callias through with his sword. 'Callias!' Silvius was distraught, Elissa could see. But they could not wait; they could not even stop to tend to him.

The hissing of the Enemy was filling the air from all around. It urged Elissa to put her weapon down. But she fixated on the light of Helenus, the light of Apollo, and on Silvius, and then on Tisamenos. He was pushing onwards. She had to push on too.

The Enemy ranks were dropping away from them, running to pick off the Achaean soldiers behind them. Elissa thought she heard the voice of Orestes. 'Keep fighting!'

Now Helenus paused, and the white light from his forehead shone bright. 'There he is,' said Helenus, awe and terror in his voice.

Ahead of them, spiralling, vast, was the great serpent Python.

A shiver of terror rushed through Elissa, and she felt small and vulnerable. How could they defeat this beast? It was impossible. In his scales, in his fangs, in his glowing red eyes, there was a power that would consume the world.

And what could she do to prevent that?

Her hand went to her neck. There was the little dolphin pendant her mother had given her. She hadn't known her own mother, but that didn't mean that others couldn't. If Python succeeded, there would be no more little girls playing with their mothers' hairbrushes, teasing their kittens, throwing pebbles into wells. She glanced at Silvius beside her, and saw that he too had been overcome with revulsion. Tisamenos was upright, the only one of them not trembling.

'It's time,' she said to Silvius. And he nodded, though his hands were shaking.

Tisamenos removed the cloth from the Last Gorgon's eyes.

Nothing happened. Then Elissa was horrified to see the snakes on her head begin to move and hiss.

A voice came from the head, calling, 'Father!'

'My own child cannot hurt me.' Python, voice distant and rumbling, laughed, and the Last Gorgon's head shivered and shattered into pieces. Tisamenos cried out in rage and fear.

Elissa had never felt more afraid.

The serpent's coils were so huge they looked like a range of small hills, their summits shrouded in mist, the sky behind them grey.

The Enemy soldiers were approaching from the rear. She could not hear Orestes. Perhaps they had all been destroyed. She saw Tisamenos throw a javelin that bounced off Python's scales uselessly. She saw Helenus fighting hand to hand with three Enemy soldiers. His little band of fighters was diminishing.

Silvius prepared the Arrow and passed it to her. It shone with white light, illuminating his desperate face. Then he was off, clashing with a towering foot soldier.

Elissa readied herself. The Bow was glowing golden. She had to shoot, and she had to shoot true. The light lit up the scales and fangs of the great Python.

All around her was the horror of battle. Helenus fell to the ground, defending himself against the thrusts of three swords. Tisamenos, wildly swinging, was hemmed in. Silvius was struggling. Desperate shouts came from every side, and more noise from the distance.

They were losing against the might of the Enemy.

She had to shut out the noise around her. She had to concentrate. Elissa, whole body trembling, sighted her target.

The Python's eye. Red and malevolent, it held her gaze, as if it was looking at her, and only her.

No. She would not give in to it. And, with the shouts and screams of those fighting around her, she shot the Arrow at Python's eye.

The sounds drained away.

Everything vanished.

She was no longer standing on a plain, and there were no armies battling to the death.

All that remained was the Arrow of Apollo, flying towards Python, but moving slowly now, as if it were being pushed back by some invisible force.

Silvius regarded Elissa in astonishment. Tisamenos also remained, with his sword, still fighting an opponent that was no longer there.

'What's happening?' He let his sword drop to his side. Both Silvius and Tisamenos were sweating with the heat of battle. 'Where are we?'

'It's Python,' answered Elissa. 'He's moved us here.'

She saw they were in an underground cavern.

It must be beneath the crater of the meteorite, where the star fell, she reasoned. Around them the rocks were smoking, and a stench of sulphur filled the air. Breathing in, she coughed.

The Arrow's flight paused. Everything was silent. The folds of the Python fell away as if they were nothing but air, and standing a few feet away from them now was a man.

His skin was scaly, his eyes were red, and his mouth opened to let out a forked tongue.

Python was walking ever more slowly, pace by pace, towards the Arrow, where it hung in the air. He paused at the edge of its aura, and held out a hand towards it. Then he sighed with displeasure. 'I cannot touch it, of course. I cannot touch the thing made by my enemy. But I can touch you.' Silvius was gazing at him, eyes glazing over.

Python flicked his head towards Silvius, and sent out a force that hurled him crashing into the smoking rocks, knocking him almost unconscious.

'You are not strong enough to shoot the Bow, Elissa,' hissed Python. 'Apollo is not often wrong. I will grant him that. But he was wrong to choose you.'

'You're wrong,' Tisamenos said. 'She has strength, and power.'

'The battle rages still,' said Python. 'Your father Orestes is not as good a fighter as he was, is he, Tisamenos?" he hissed, circling the boy. 'You could so easily have been like us. You and the Gorgon were alike in the end, were you not? How many people have you turned to stone?'

Tisamenos clutched his head.

'He is different!' Elissa spoke through her teeth. 'He has goodness in him. The Last Gorgon was a monster!'

'Silence, Elissa. The stones are talking to you now, Tisamenos, aren't they? And what are they saying to you?'

'I will not tell you!' answered Tisamenos.

Elissa rushed at Python, but he flicked her away, and she landed among the rocks. If only she could reach the Arrow. But Python was now between her and it.

She saw that Silvius was coming back to consciousness. Python was circling Tisamenos, whispering to him. Elissa was a few paces away from him, on her back.

She caught Silvius's eye. He looked dazed. She had to get him to help her. There was a meteoric rock just by his hand. A flicker of understanding passed over his eyes. Python's attention was distracted. Before Elissa could blink, Silvius had already grasped the rock, hefted it, aimed and flung it at Python's head.

Python stumbled, knocked flat onto his front. It was enough. The Arrow was still hanging suspended above him. She could get it if she jumped. She just needed him to stay down.

Tisamenos was now kneeling on the ground and touching the rock. And then he closed his eyes.

'You don't have to do it!' she called.

'I do.'

The noise was enough to make Python swing round. Elissa leapt upwards and grabbed the Arrow. Python went for her, and Elissa threw the Arrow to Silvius, who caught it, just. Now Elissa had the Bow, and Silvius the Arrow, and Python was between them.

The rocks were rumbling. Tisamenos's eyes were rolling into the back of his head, and he was trembling all over. There was a noise like a small landslide. The scree and rubble around them was quivering as if with its own life.

Elissa understood. The rocks were listening to him.

Tisamenos was commanding the stones. One by one they crept across the ground, until they began to pile up around Python's feet, building a prison of rock, trapping him.

'You're doing it! Tisamenos, you're doing it!' They could defeat him. The possibility was suddenly in front of her. Python's scaly body was disappearing under rubble, flints and stones surging, clambering over each other as if in a race to crush him.

But Python simply smiled.

And then he began to grow, the stones glancing off him like water.

'Quickly! The Arrow! Throw it to me!' Elissa cried, desperately trying to keep her self-possession.

Python's bulk was now larger than a horse, and though the stones were still rushing towards him, they were uselessly deflected. Elissa stretched out to Silvius. This was their only chance, now. But instead of passing the Arrow to Elissa, Silvius hurled it as hard as he could at Python. What was he doing?

It flew true.

And it stuck, quivering, into his neck.

Everything seemed to stop, and Elissa was suddenly aware of the steady drip of water from the cave roof. Silvius, caught in a stance, both arms outstretched, his sandals loose, his knees grazed. Tisamenos, shaking on the cold ground.

Breaking the stillness, Python screamed, a terrible scream that echoed round the cavern. And then he tore the Arrow from his wound, gushing black smoking blood in gouts. With a great roar he snapped it in two.

The energy expelled from the Arrow blasted Elissa and Silvius to the floor.

'It didn't work . . .' sobbed Silvius. 'He's still alive.'

Python's features were contorted in rage. 'You mortal fools . . .' He ran at them, half-man, half-snake, and Silvius clutched Elissa, about to pull her out of the way.

There was no way out. Elissa braced herself.

And then Python choked and halted, slipping a little in his own gore. His expression changed to one of confusion. His feet started to fuse together, into the shape of a snake's tail. He looked down in horror. His whole body began to shrink.

Soon he was the size and shape of a normal snake.

But it wasn't over yet. The snake reared and hissed, swaying alarmingly.

'Get him!' Silvius cried, and hurled another rock at him.

Uttering a hideous, inhuman shriek, the snake took the blow. Before Silvius or Elissa could do anything more, the remnant of Python had slithered away.

When they ran after him, they could not see any sign of him. Elissa collapsed, panting, Silvius next to her.

'Is Python dead?' he asked.

'I don't think so! I was meant to shoot him, Silvius! It was meant to be me! Dolphinlight, dolphin and light.'

'And one will die ... Tisamenos!' Silvius picked up the broken parts of the Arrow. He did not look at Elissa.

Tisamenos had collapsed. They went to him. He was limp. Elissa felt a sob of grief gathering in her stomach.

'He's just unconscious!' said Silvius.

'No,' answered Elissa, starkly. 'He's dead.'

Thirty-Eight

Out of the Spiral

'Look, there's light up there.' Silvius saw pale beams coming through a fissure. There must be a tunnel they could go through. Elissa was bloodied and dirtied and shaking. They took Tisamenos by the arms and legs, and half-carried, half-dragged him. The pool of light grew, and in a short while they saw a wide opening above them, at the end of a short incline. They scrambled up the stone ramp, struggling with Tisamenos. Silvius stumbled, sending rocks clattering down into the meteorite pit.

'Keep going . . . Almost there . . .' Elissa called.

Panting, they came out into daylight, and placed Tisamenos on the ground. He was heavy, like stone.

Silvius sank his head onto Tisamenos's chest. It was lifeless. His body was cold, his eyes shut.

Orestes's voice came from afar, and then he was groaning and wailing, pushing them aside. He threw himself onto his son's body and wept, his whole frame heaving with sobs. 'My son . . . my son . . .'

Silvius wept too, kneeling in the dirt around the boy's corpse.

He prayed and prayed, to Apollo, to Hermes, feeling that he had done wrong, that he had failed.

The sun's beams began to lighten the gloom, and the devastation of the army was revealed. Silvius, hardly knowing what he was doing, wandered through the battlefield. All around were corpses, many Achaeans; and many men, women and children too. The power of Python had left his army, and a huge group of confused Italians was clustered together, ragged and hungry, with no memory of what they had seen or what they had done. Among them were mothers and daughters, fathers and sons, brothers and sisters, husbands and wives, and those that remained found and clung to each other in the light.

Later, the sky was bright and clear. An ox was roasting for the soldiers, whilst the others were clearing up the battlefield, placing the bodies of the slain ready for the funeral pyres, picking up the weapons that they could salvage. Callias's long red hair was a bright gleam among the grime and greyness, covering his lifeless face. A comb was still attached to his hair.

Silvius returned to where Tisamenos lay. Elissa and Orestes were preparing him for burial, washing him carefully. In his white shift he looked young. 'He should not have died,' Orestes said, running a cloth over his son's face. 'I should have died instead of him. It is my fault. If I hadn't believed Erigone, he would not have left the kinghouse. I would not have allowed him to go. This was my duty.' He broke down in sobs once more. Orestes was a shadow. He had been wounded in the fighting, too, and he had lost a lot of blood, a bandage tight around his waist.

'He was brave,' said Silvius, touching Orestes's hand. 'He was braver than all of us. It was his destiny. We all had to do it.'

They sat for a moment in silence. Tisamenos was grey in death, but with the same determined expression that Silvius had last seen on his face. Once more he wept, and Orestes too. Elissa, wiping her eyes, went off on her own.

'I'm sorry,' said Silvius, watching her go. 'I'm sorry that you have lost your son.'

The old king grasped his hand. 'I said when I met you that he was about your age.' And then Silvius saw the expression on his face change, as he registered something happening behind him. Silvius turned around.

All of a sudden, Silvius was facing his father Aeneas.

He was pale, with enormous black bags under his eyes. His hair was much greyer than it had been. There was a deep gash on his cheek, which made his face look even more severe. And the wolf skin that was slung around his shoulders had lost none of its fierceness. Silvius's heart was thrumming in his chest, his nerves straining.

'You disobeyed me,' said Aeneas.

'Father, please . . .'

'You put yourself, and Elissa, into the greatest danger. You could have been killed.' His jaw clenched. 'Your mother is

339

beside herself, and your little brother calls for you every day.'

'I . . .' Silvius felt himself deflating. The tears now starting behind his eyes were not of grief, but of anger. Even his father did not understand.

Aeneas pulled his hand back, as if about to hit Silvius around the head. Silvius braced himself for the impact.

But it did not come.

Instead, those arms were around him, and he was lifted up in the air, his father embracing him, their tears mingled as his father whispered, 'You did well, my son. You did well, better than I could have done, and you have saved our family honour. And,' he placed Silvius back down on the ground again, 'you have given us new alliances.' He glanced at Orestes. 'Perhaps we can now seek to build a new world.'

It was true, thought Silvius. But he had lost his own ally, Tisamenos, and he had lost him through his own fault. Silvius could not say anything.

Elissa came running to him, and there was a familiar presence with her.

Now larger, Ruffler was bounding by her side and he almost knocked Silvius over. 'He came back! He came on a ship to Italia, and he found Aeneas!' Elissa then threw herself at Aeneas, and the old warrior's face creased into a joyful smile.

'There now, Elissa,' said Aeneas. 'You have done best of us all. The centaur knew, of course. He saw it in you.'

Elissa, affecting disdain, shook her hair from her eyes, but

Silvius could see that there was a deep sadness in them. The loss of Tisamenos was heavy on her.

'The funeral pyres are lit,' said a soldier, approaching gently.

Silvius, Elissa and Orestes bore the dead Tisamenos to the pyres on a bier. The body was heavy, but Silvius insisted on taking one end, whilst Elissa and Orestes shared the weight of the other. Aeneas was standing there gravely, head bowed.

Beside him, a fresh, long scar visible on his forearm, was Iulus. Iulus's face lit up when he saw his younger brother, and they clasped hands. There was no need for them to say anything. Silvius saw the humility in his brother's demeanour; the new tenderness.

Then Helenus, limping, appeared, and began to pray to Apollo. They were sombre once more as they watched the pyre, and Tisamenos, peaceful, ready to be placed on it, his father weeping by his side. Smoke billowed into the sky, and the fire crackled. All around them the sweat-stained soldiers paused in their work, and bowed their heads.

And as Helenus prayed, Silvius became aware of a presence by the pyre.

A curly-haired young man, handsome, dressed in white.

'This is the difference between you mortals and us,' he said quietly. 'Your bodies fall, and fade.' Then, turning to Silvius and Elissa, he said, 'You have done well, as Aeneas says. Apollo blesses you, and sends his thanks. But Python is not slain. The Arrow was not shot from the Bow, and it was not shot by Elissa. The prophecy was not fulfilled correctly. This is as it has always been – a prophecy is a mysterious thing, and mortals do with the knowledge of the gods what they will. Python will return. Not as he was, but in a different guise. There is much work ahead for you to do.'

Tears swelled up from deep within Silvius

'I cannot do this . . .' he said. 'I cannot.'

'I will help you,' said Elissa. Her face was drawn and pale, but her expression told Silvius what he already knew: that they had experienced terrors together already, and that this would only make them stronger. Silvius grasped her hand in thanks.

'You will have help from the Achaeans,' said Orestes. The men of Achaea roared their assent.

'And us too,' said Aeneas. 'The whole world will help you.'

'And Tisamenos,' said Elissa. She went to touch his cold cheek. 'We will always remember him.'

Hermes smiled.

He went to Tisamenos's body, and laid a hand on it.

There was a moment of stillness, and the rays of the sun seemed to play on the corpse. Even a god's touch could not bring back someone from the dead, thought Silvius.

Then the impossible happened.

At first, Silvius wasn't sure if he had seen correctly, thinking that his tears might have blurred his vision. But the others around him were looking puzzled too. And then he saw it again. It was true. Tisamenos had blinked. And now he coughed, and stretched, and sat bolt upright. He felt his head, his body, his fingers. He turned to Elissa, and a smile spread over his face. Orestes let out a gasp of astonishment and fell to his knees.

'His soul was flitting, lost in the Underworld,' said Hermes. 'His body is not entirely flesh, so he could be called back. The love for him here from Elissa, the despair that Silvius showed – these things helped to bring him back.'

'There's something odd about my body,' said Tisamenos. His voice was rasping. He kept prodding himself all over. The sheen on his skin was different, too, duller.

'A miracle!' Orestes sobbed. 'Hermes, I thank you . . . My son, my son . . .'

Elissa threw her arms around Tisamenos, and kissed him, and Orestes held him. They both pulled apart from him, looking at him strangely. 'I don't . . . I don't understand . . .' There was a note of confusion in Orestes's voice. He kept touching his son, then pulling away. 'What . . . what has happened?'

'Orestes – the Corinthian general wants you. Trouble with some of the men.'

Sighing, Orestes traced his finger down Tisamenos's cheek, then went off to do his duty.

Silvius, waiting by the side, stood quietly until Elissa had finished whispering to Tisamenos. She released him, brushing a tear away from her eye.

'Tisamenos,' he said, coming forwards shyly. 'It's good to see you again.'

'And you,' he answered. 'And you.' Something in his voice, something like an echo, made Silvius wonder.

'But what . . . what's happened to you?'

Tisamenos looked down, and his expression did not change. He rapped his knuckles on his head. 'I am stone,' he said. I am made of stone.'

Later, Silvius watched from the side as Tisamenos and Elissa held each other by the campfire, as the men feasted on roasted oxen and drank from bowls of dark wine. Silvius had had his fill of meat, but was eating his third apple.

Tisamenos was talking. 'I was in that terrible, empty place, and Hermes came down to me. He said that I could return, if I became like the rocks. My body would become a thing of hardness. But my soul would live still . . . Of course I came back. I could not stay down there. My mother said to me, before she went, "Don't make the same mistake as Achilleos." His soul was unhappy there, and I saw him, and he said to me he would rather be a farmer and live until he was a hundred than be Achilleos again . . . And, Elissa . . .' There was a tremor in his voice as he looked up at her. 'Do you still – do you still want me to go with you?'

Elissa looked right into Tisamenos's eyes, and said, 'Yes, always.'

Then the two of them noticed Silvius. They formed a triangle once more.

Above them rose the constellation of the Archer God, and to Silvius, it seemed that he drew his bow back and shot a flaming arrow into space.

The comet flared briefly above them, and vanished into the darkness between the stars.

Timeline of the Trojan Cycle

Greek and Roman myths consist of a series of fascinating connections. The following is the basic structure of the cycle around Troy. You will see that each moment is a direct cause of the next, and that each leads into many other possible ramifications. For some events there are different versions, but the essential arc is the same. In the text, Silvius refers to Achilles, whilst Tisamenos calls him Achilleos; though the latter is probably a more accurate representation of what the Greeks called him, I've chosen Achilles here, as well as the other usual spellings, such as Aegisthus.

The hero Peleus, who was one of the Argonauts, marries the sea goddess Thetis, against her will.

At their wedding, the gods attend. Eris, the goddess of strife, is not invited. She sends a golden apple, inscribed with the words 'To the most beautiful'.

The three goddesses Athene, Hera and Aphrodite argue amongst themselves. They appeal to Zeus.

Zeus, not wishing to show favour, chooses the mortal shepherd Paris to make the judgement.

Paris chooses Aphrodite, who offers him the most beautiful woman in the world: Helen, Queen of Sparta.

Paris, now accepted by his father Priam as a Trojan prince, sails to Sparta. Here, he either abducts Helen or she goes with him willingly back to Troy.

All the Greek princes swore an oath to protect Helen; Menelaus, her husband, assembles them under the leadership of Agamemnon.

They gather together, including an unwilling Odysseus, and try to sail for Troy. But there is no wind.

Agamemnon must then sacrifice his own daughter Iphigenia to the goddess Artemis. She is either killed or snatched away by the goddess at the last minute and placed in Tauris.

The Greek armies sail to Troy. Here, they fight, but do not succeed.

Achilles, the greatest warrior, withdraws from the war when his war prize, the maiden Briseis, is taken from him by Agamemnon.

The Greeks begin to be beaten back to their ships. Achilles's companion Patroclus puts on his armour, and fights in his place. He is killed.

Furious, Achilles enters the fray, slaughtering many Trojans, eventually killing Hector, their greatest prince.

Later in the war, Achilles is killed by Paris. The city eventually falls when Odysseus tricks the Trojans into pulling in a wooden horse, full of Greek fighters.

The Greeks are merciless in their destruction of the city, killing Priam, and taking his wife and daughters captive.

They return home. Agamemnon, when he reaches his

palace, is murdered by his wife Clytemnestra, in revenge for his killing of Iphigenia.

Orestes, who had been sent away, returns, and murders Clytemnestra along with her new husband Aegisthus, with the help of his sister Electra.

Appalled by the murder, the gods send the Furies to hound Orestes, chasing him through Greece, until he ends up in Athens.

He is absolved by Apollo. In some versions, the Furies continue to haunt him, so he is sent to retrieve a sacred statue of Artemis from Tauris.

Here Orestes eventually meets Iphigenia, recognises her, and the cycle is over.

Or is it?

Further Reading

I hope that you will want to read more about the wonderful stories that helped to inspire this novel.

For the tale of Aeneas, go to Virgil's epic poem, *The Aeneid*. Here you will find a passionate and vivid account of the fall of Troy, as well as the story of Dido, Queen of Carthage.

The cycle of Orestes is a dark one, and it is told best in Aeschylus's powerful trilogy, *The Oresteia*, which comprises three plays: *Agamemnon*, *The Libation Bearers* and *The Eumenides*. These relate how Agamemnon was killed, and Orestes took revenge on his mother and was then pursued by the Furies. Euripides's *Orestes* shows a less heroic side of the prince. We also have *Electra*, as told by both Euripides and Sophocles.

Homer's *The Iliad* concerns a few weeks in the long cycle of the Trojan War, in which the great fighter Achilles withdraws from battle.

If you are interested in Greek and Roman myth, a wealth of interpretations and retellings are available. My favourites as a boy were Roger Lancelyn Green's *Tales of the Greek Heroes*, and his charming *The Luck of Troy*.

Acknowledgements

Thank you to my family: my wife, Tatiana von Preussen, my parents, Richard and Marie Womack, and my parents-in-law, Andrew and Alexandra von Preussen, for helping to give me the space and time to write this book.

Thank you to Fiona Lensvelt, for taking on this project, and to Liz Garner, for her excellent, elegant editing skills, and to the rest of the team: Alexander Eccles, Hayley Shepherd, and everyone else at Unbound.

Thank you to Robert Christie for reading through the manuscript, and his always astute comments. And I would also like to thank those authors who have been so generous with their moral support, especially Katherine Rundell, Cressida Cowell and Philip Reeve.

Unbound is the world's first crowdfunding publisher, established in 2011.

We believe that wonderful things can happen when you clear a path for people who share a passion. That's why we've built a platform that brings together readers and authors to crowdfund books they believe in – and give fresh ideas that don't fit the traditional mould the chance they deserve.

This book is in your hands because readers made it possible. Everyone who pledged their support is listed below. Join them by visiting unbound.com and supporting a book today.

T C
Mina and Freya
    Caines
Cate Cannon
Ariadne Caroussis
Erietta Caroussis
Isidore Caroussis
Jim Carrington
Ellen Catherall
Esther Chadwick
David Chamberlain
Roland Chambers
Charlie Chappatte
Jessica Chiba
Jessie Childs
Robert Christie
Sandy Christie
Tomas Christie
Sarah Clapp
Sue Clark
Amabel Clarke
Margaret Clothier
Joanna Clough
Antonia Coad
Lucy Coats
Dom Conlon
James Cook
Jude Cook
Jenni Coombe
Katerina Costeletos
Sarah Courtauld

Cressida Cowell
Douglas Cowie
Karina Cox
Amanda Craig
Sophie Crocker -
    Tormead
Stephanie Cross
Charles Cumming
Mary Cundall
Keren David
Zanna Davidson
Michael Deacon
Alida Debenham
Octavia Dickinon
Antonia Donnelly
Jenny Doughty
Charlie Drury
Sophie Drysdale
Patrick Duncombe
Philip Eade
Fernanda Eberstadt
Lauren Elkin
Anna & James Elliot
Abi Elphinstone
Seb Emina
Mathilda Enderlein
Jessica Espey
Edward Evans
Hermione Eyre
Polly Faber
Ben Faccini

Francis Featherby
June Fellows
Oliver Fetiveau
Robert Finch
Noah, Otto & Lulu
    Fine
Tom Fleming
Paul Fletcher
Andrew Fogg
Peter Frankopan
John Fulton
Mike Gallagher
Sally Gardner
Rosie Garthwaite
Elizabeth Gatland
Beanie Geraedts-
    Espey
Adele Geras
Nayla Ghantous
Liz Gloyn
Benjamin Goldsmith
Edmund Gordon
Corinne Gotch
Sarah Govett
Luke Grant
Thomas Grant
Julia Gray
Kevin Gray
Caroline Green
Edward Greenhalgh
Gallia Grimston

Hector Grimston
Lorcan Grimston
Merlin Grimston
Ophelia Grimston
Karen Groos
Mafalda Groos
Alexis Guedroitz
Solina Guedroitz
Daniel Hahn
Gretel Hallett
Lucy Hallett
Susan Hallett
Leif-Erik Hannikainen
Frances Hardinge
Katherine Hardy
Sam Hare
Clare Harland
Horatia Harrod
A.F. Harrold
Lucy Hart
Selina Hastings
Maximilian Hawker
Robert Heaps
John Heaton-
    Armstrong
Bea Hemming
Henry Hemming
Patrick Hennessey
Kate Henson
Stuart Heritage
Cecilia Hewett

Rose Heyman
Fiona Higgins
Jacqueline Higgins
Isaac Apollo Hirst
Henry Hitchings
Ernestine Hocken
Mary Hoffman
The Hoffman Family
Ali Hollingshead
Iain Hollingshead
Ferelith Hordon
Chip Horne
Gabriel Hudson
Nell Hudson
Lizzie Huxley-Jones
Jasper Jackson
Cressida Jauncey
Ada Rae Jencks
Inigo Jencks
Lily Jencks
Simon Jerrome
Signe Johansen
Dylan John
Tristan John
Alfred Johnson
Marlene Johnson
Oliver Jones
Susanna Jones
Melissa Katsoulis
Judith Katz
Emmeline Kay

Rupert Kay
Lottie Kertesz
Dan Kieran
Mary Killen
Rebecca King
Katherine Kingsley
Josh Klarica
Hector Kociak
Dunstan Kornicki
Brian Lacy
Hugo Lacy
George Lamb
Paul Lay
Matisse Le Roch
    Platford
Jonathan Lee
Charlie Lee-Potter
Sam Leith
Mark Lennox-Boyd
Philippa Lennox-Boyd
Patricia Lennox-Boyd
    & Jamie Stevens
Fiona Lensvelt
Thomas Leonard
Mouse Lesser
Gill Lewis
Natacha Lippens
Adrian Lloyd
James Lonsdale
Soo-Lin Lui
Jack MacInnes

Alastair Mackeown

Anna Maconochie

Brigid Mahony

Lena Makda

Jessica Mann

Will Mann

Benjamin Markovits

Julia Marlow

Barty Martelli

Freddie Martelli

Conrad Mason

Taran Matharu

Melissa McAdden

Annabella McAughtry-
Hilliard

Geraldine
McCaughrean

Claire McCauley

Pandora McCormick

Magnus McCullagh

Gabriella McDonald

Edward McGovern

Joanne McGovern

Anthony McGowan

Lilou Melville

Charlie Mills

Sam Mills

John Mitchinson

Ivo Moncrieffe

Clare Monro

Ross Montgomery

Douglas Moody-
Stuart

Henry Moody-Stuart

Tom Moody-Stuart

Michael Mordue

Llewelyn Morgan

Sam Morgan

Rhel ná DecVandé

Sarah Naughton

Carlo Navato

Geordie Naylor-
Leyland

Erin Nelsen Parekh

Kalypso Nicolaidis

Charlotte Nourse

Adam O'Riordan

Fiona O'Rorke

Charlotte O'Sullivan

Cliodhna O'Sullivan

Deborah Orr

Olivier Henri Orteu

Samira Osman

Fox Parkin

Sarah Pennell

Nicholas Pierpan

Daniel Pimlott

Justin Pollard

Cressida Pollock

Potel Family

Alex Preston

Tatiana Preussen

Richard Price

Chris Priestley

T J Putnam

Sameer Rahim

Mahesh Rao

Shoo Rayner

Andrea Reece

Celia Rees

Philip Reeve

Helen Reid

Robert Riddell

Liam Riley

Adam Roberts

Laura Roberts

Suzy Robinson

Myrto Rochat

Alex Rooney

Tamsin Rosewell

Meg Rosoff

Lyra Rossetti-Wright

Katherine Rundell

Imogen Russell
Williams

Charles Rutter

SF Said

Francesca Sanders

Hugo Sanders

Nathalie Savić

Christoph Schmiedel

Beatrice Schutzer-
Weissmann

Jenny Schwarz

Rosemary Scott

James Scudamore

Marcus Sedgwick

Oliver Seyfried

Helen K. Shair

Andrew Shead

JA Sheppe

Luka Shields

Nicola Shulman

Max Silver

William Skidelsky

Nancy Sladek

H W Smee

Mark William Shigelu
Smith

Ava Celeste
Somerville

George Spalton

Francesca Spence

Josh Spero

Denise Spreag

Lauren St John

St Johns Primary
School

Alicia Stallings

Anna Stothard

Eliza Stothard

Michael Stothard

Stephanie Street

Arthur Stroud

Jonathan Stroud

Emma and Andrew
Sutcliffe

Camilla Swift

Elizabeth Swift

Lucy Taylor

Kathryn Tempest

Julia Thaxton

Edward Thomas

Agnes Thompson

Betsy Tobin

Sophie Tollemache

Piers Torday

Anna Tyzack

Iain Ure

Cara Usher

George Van den
Bergh

Gaby van Halteren

Sally Vince

Alex von Preussen

Andrew von Preussen

Beatrice von Preussen

Brigid von Preussen

Fritzi von Preussen

Rupert von Preussen

Florence Walker

Catriona Ward

Olivia Watchman

Holly Watt

Jonathan Weil

Venetia Welby

Mary Wellesley

Martin West

Ben Whately

Otto Wheeler

Piers Wheeler

Alan White

Thomas Wide

Willem

Matilda Willson

William Willson

Frances Wilson

Frederick Windsor

Robertus
Wiuhomarch

William Wolsey

Ashley William
Womack

Dr Marija Obradović
Womack

John Muir Womack

Richard Womack

Margaret Womack (in
loving memory)

George Woods

Isabella Woods

Tyler Woolcott

Janet Wright

Alex Wyndham

George Wyndham